AUDREY'S GONE AWOL

AUDREY'S GONE AWOL

Annie de Monchaux

ultimo
press

Published in 2024 by Ultimo Press,
an imprint of Hardie Grant Publishing

Ultimo Press
Gadigal Country
7, 45 Jones Street
Ultimo, NSW 2007
ultimopress.com.au

   ultimopress

A catalogue record for this work is available from the National Library of Australia

Audrey's Gone AWOL
ISBN 978 1 76115 305 1 (paperback)

Cover design Andy Warren Design
Cover illustrations Background texture by Unsplash; Woman by simplehappyart / iStock
Typesetting Kirby Jones | 11.5/18.5pt Sabon LT Std
Copyeditor Deonie Fiford
Proofreader Pamela Dunne

10 9 8 7 6 5 4 3 2 1

Printed in Australia by Opus Group Pty Ltd, an Accredited ISO AS/NZS 14001 Environmental Management System printer.

The paper this book is printed on is certified against the Forest Stewardship Council® Standards. Griffin Press – a member of the Opus Group – holds chain of custody certification SCS-COC-001185. FSC® promotes environmentally responsible, socially beneficial and economically viable management of the world's forests.

Ultimo Press acknowledges the Traditional Owners of the Country on which we work, the Gadigal People of the Eora Nation and the Wurundjeri People of the Kulin Nation, and recognises their continuing connection to the land, waters and culture. We pay our respects to their Elders past and present.

For Monty, Ellery, Ava & Christopher
(listed in order of appearance)

Rosalind
Happy birthday
and happy reading
I hope Bonny
x

1

I'd consider it a favour if lightning struck me now. But as another sheet cuts through the sky outside, the only thing striking me is *I wish I hadn't made this appointment.*

'How can I help you, Audrey?'

Like a pale grey nun, Naomi's expression is sombre, her voice is soft, and I'm mesmerised by her chin which is covered in a peach fuzz. I feel my own chin, then worry she may think I'm staring, so say, 'I got married, had children, and then became invisible. It suited all of us.'

'But it doesn't suit you now?'

Sister Naomi shifts back in her seat, pen still. I smile. Up near the ceiling, a draught catches the roller-blind and it ticks on the window frame. Why doesn't she say something else? She nods, unperturbed, and why would the silence worry her? This woman will get $210 whether I say another word or not.

'Suit me? I don't know. Something's going on …' Unable to name my mood, I ball my fist up and press it against my chest. 'It's like a rock has been moved and disturbed the slaters.'

She nods again and lowers her fountain pen towards her notepad.

If she isn't going to offer any insights, I could have stayed home and coloured myself in. The fact is I'm here. I will abandon garden analogies and continue.

'My pettiness is driving me mad. For example, I recently bought two hundred stainless-steel pegs, at huge expense, because I've become obsessed. T-shirts must have red pegs, white for sheets, underwear green, and so on. Now, the new pegs remind me of how ridiculous I am.'

A slight movement of her facial muscles indicates my therapist is still conscious.

'Tragic, no?' Nothing, her face says nothing.

'I can also tell you that the man who bought the house at the back of ours hasn't hung out one set of sheets in the nine months he's been living there. I shudder when I imagine what his bed must look like.'

'Have you considered he may have a tumble dryer?'

'No, I haven't. Maybe he does, in which case he shouldn't, not in our climate. Anyway, in the scale of things it's trivial. You see, I'm busybodying in other people's lives because I can't stand my own.'

Sister Naomi lifts her chin.

'It feels as if I have a hollow,' I continue, 'and within that hollow tiny things niggle away. Does that make sense?'

'I see.' She flips a page and writes something.

What does she see?

'Of course, it's entirely possible I'm simply on edge about many things. For example, my father died at sixty – cancer – and I'm nearly sixty.' I take a deep breath. 'My GP booked me in for a colonoscopy and the humiliation of strangers seeing my bottom is very disconcerting. That's probably it; my brain is on the run and silly things bother me, like pegs, a Japanese painting, diary entries. They're simply diversionary tactics from a generalised fear, don't you think?'

She tucks in her downy chin. 'It's a little early to tell. The colonoscopy must be a worry, but shall we start with,' she looks down at her notes, 'the Japanese painting? That's precise.'

I remove my handbag from the side of the chair and put it on the floor by my feet. 'Okay. It niggles me and has done for months. Simon says—'

'Who is Simon?'

'My husband. We've been together thirty-seven years and have three grown-up children.'

Head down, she writes. 'What are their names?'

'Gus, Thea and Orson. I love them. My reproductive years were glorious. The hormonal lurch to have children was like a narcotic yearning, and they're my sole achievement.' Clouds release another shower, and a sheet of water descends where a gutter must be broken. 'Simon says I've become preoccupied with the painting because the children have all moved out and left a yawning gap in my world. He may be right. To paraphrase, he says the oil painting is attractive, and I'm simply bored out of my brain.'

'Do you agree with him?'

I don't know the answer, and don't answer the question.

'Do you like the painting?'

Again, I don't know, and it feels as if Sister Naomi and I are on opposite sides of an abstraction, yet I must persist.

'It's been on the wall for years. I thought perhaps I was bored of it so I took it down recently, but Simon wanted it back up. He said we got *Stormy Sea at the Naruto Rapids* to commemorate our early days as a married couple. It seems sweet of him, but I don't remember getting it. I certainly recall watching the tide rush through the narrow strait and telling Simon I was pregnant with our first child. We went to Japan at least five times when we were first married and we'd always visit the rapids, watch the water, have a picnic. It was our place, our time away from Simon's conferences.'

'But it still bothers you?'

'It does. I even re-painted the sitting room in the hope it would bring some pleasure.'

'Did it?'

'No. However, I had an *Aha* moment while undercoating the architraves. Simon and I did not buy that Japanese artwork, I know it. I've replayed our visits to Tokyo, and I know we didn't buy it. Then again, I also accept the disturbing extent to which memory can be fictional.'

'So, Simon says you bought it, but you don't think you did?'

'Correct. On my way here, I found a large gilt-framed mirror, which I might buy to hang in its place.'

Sister Naomi leans back in her chair. 'Good for you.'

Not really. She clearly thinks the problem will be solved as soon as the mirror is up. I'll give up on the painting for now. I slide myself back in the chair and try to relax into the upholstery.

'Audrey, you mentioned your diaries?'

She was paying attention. 'I've kept them since I was a teen. My Aunt Pascale sent me my first. It was a French red leather beauty with all the wrong holidays for Australia.'

This appointment is like wading through treacle.

'I have a dual-pronged approach to diaries. I write down what's not to be forgotten: dog flea tablet, first Monday of every month; car registration due; make and bottle passata.'

'Very organised.'

I wait a moment in case she asks me which passata recipe I favour. No interruption. 'Organised maybe, enigmatic not.

Then at the end of a day I also write what happened: Orson's first word et cetera. Hundreds of moments chronologically ordered, a few are jumbled notes, and I'm not sure how to unpick them.'

'Are you looking for anything in particular?'

I nod, and then immediately shake my head. I'm not sure what she's asking and look at her face for clues. But Sister Naomi's features are perfectly formed to present stoic endurance when faced with a tedious client.

She takes pity and continues, 'These details are not what you're looking for?'

I shake my head.

Her upper body sways very slowly. 'So, perhaps you're looking for ...' Both her hands float, making small conductor's circles to draw out my deepest something or other. Then the dry scratch of her writing starts again. Finally, she looks up. 'May I ask you a question, Audrey?'

I splay my hands, arms wide.

'Okay. Let's say for a moment that you're looking for you?'

I'm not sure this is the case. I only know I'm irritated by something I haven't had time to articulate. However, she's the expert so I give her a little go-ahead nod.

'I've been doing some research with a colleague in the US, and I'd like to try this route.'

Being an experimental monkey is fine if we get to the bottom of all this. I smile my consent.

Sister Naomi takes a few deep breaths. 'Tell me, Audrey, did you buy your handbag?'

I check the black leather bag by my feet. It has three pockets and an over-the-shoulder strap.

'As a matter of fact, I did.'

She smiles. 'Did you know that the handbag a woman chooses is directly reflective of the way she perceives her vagina?'

The session didn't improve after that. She decided I was there for something like post-menopausal collapse. The remaining twenty minutes were terrifying. Perhaps she'd invite me to join a group where we'd sit around with hand mirrors and look at our fannies.

When it's over, she swipes my card and asks if I'd like her to put it straight through to Medicare. I would. Then she suggests another appointment.

There's no way I want to return and participate in vaginal steaming or a visual diary, but as always, I find I can't say no.

'Two weeks then.' She sends it through as a text. I smile and thank her.

What reason can I use to cancel said hour with Sister Naomi of the Holy Order of Handbags?

2

As I get ready to go to the school canteen, yesterday's hour with Sister Naomi slews around my head loosening rusty cogs. Why on earth couldn't I tell the therapist I didn't want another appointment? This leads me to all those times I've let shopkeepers down gently by saying, *I'll think about the shoes*, simply because I couldn't say, *Thank you but they are not for me*.

Howard bursts across the garden with a slimy, battered ball in his mouth. His tail thrashes and his rear end wiggles so hard it threatens to throw him off balance.

'Give.'

He drops the ball and scampers back in reverse. I throw it, he does a three-sixty, shoots off and soon the *squeak, squeak* of his prey can be heard.

'Bring it back, Howard.'

Without taking his eyes off the ball, he cocks his leg and releases a long stream on the grass.

'Howard, you've just had your walk. You know Victoria doesn't like you peeing on her lawn.'

Just the mention of Victoria and I feel gloomy, but my mother-in-law's opinion doesn't bother him; he is ball, not urine, obsessed. It's me who feels her hand at my throat.

It's me who throws buckets of water over his transgressions, so the yellow patches of grass don't give us away.

Looking around the garden, the weight of living here has never felt more oppressive. When Howard's stream eventually stops, I squeak the ball twice, throw it again, and force myself across the sweeping lawn. Mowing for hours wasn't an issue when it meant the kids had a massive playground, when it was the site of cricket games, picnics, pretend camping nights. Now, the lawn is a vast, green dog toilet, and hard work. Yet again, I note how the grassy tentacles have crept into the rose beds and started to writhe up around the thorns. I haven't made myself trim the borders for months and now I'll lose a lot of blood when I do.

Howard brings the ball, drops it at my feet.

'Good boy.' I ruffle his big head and throw his toy towards the house.

I add mowing the lawn and pruning the roses to my list, alongside *gutters*, *weed gravel*, *paint gate*. In the past this list of garden tasks has kept me busy, ticking off the items. Today it feels like an overwhelming, exhaustive shackle.

—

Unlock the door. Bring in the box of salad ingredients. Push the roller door up over the counter a smidge. Take the spreads out of the fridge, oven on. Having volunteered at the primary school canteen for far too long, this is a familiar routine. All the other volunteers, without exception, are Yummy Mummies whose kids are current students. The YMs come in, link their phones' playlists to the speaker and we do the shift bathed in Ventolin Blues: breathy, squeaking voices wailing about love.

Why didn't I move on after my kids left primary school? I've asked myself many times. Every school year I resolve that this will be my last, and at every Christmas party the headmistress seeks me out, says something flattering, begs me to stay. And I do. If she doesn't announce her retirement this year, I'll have to skip the party.

I'm the matriarch of volunteers and this year's crop of YMs have minds as sharp as cash registers. Their youthfulness creates a looming sense that a person my age will not understand what they're talking about. Never have I felt so obliged to maintain a coy silence.

Right now, though, my priority is to not pass wind. The pre-colonoscopy low-fibre diet has made my gut both unhappy and unpredictable. Years ago, I made sandwiches while diligently doing pelvic floor exercises; now I strangle potential farts.

I have a horrible suspicion the starting gun for my life went off some time ago, and I missed it.

'It's imbloodypossible to make sandwiches.' Olivia hurls a slice of ripped bread into the compost because the butter is too hard.

Amy lifts her head from rinsing tomatoes. 'Sorry, Audrey, we're both a little edgy. Synchronised biorhythms, you know.'

'Hormonal twins.'

I want to put a positive twist on their day. 'Would you like me to do the counter this morning?'

Amy slaps me on the shoulder. 'Thank god, would you? Oh, Audrey, you're a saint.'

I'm not. But the offer has freed them to vent at the back of the small kitchen. In order to fit in more grievances, they cut their sentences in half and rant about how their *husbands are dickheads*, *the kids are shits* and *the diet app doesn't effing work*. And I, at the counter, provide the smiling mask of motherhood.

9

I push the shutter all the way up.

Immediately there's the excited cacophony of recess: little faces flushed with the importance of discovering how to learn, wide-brimmed hats, grubby fingers. Many of their problems can be solved with a cuddle, a bandaid, or the first turn on the slide. As the *samiches* and boxes of *jooz* are passed across, I reclaim fleeting moments when my children were right there, barely able to peer over the counter.

A voucher for two dollars is slid across. 'Biscuit, Mrs Lamont.'

'Please, Amber.' I remind her as we trade.

'Please may I have a biscuit?'

'Thank you.' I remind them before they walk away into a game.

'Thanks, Mrs Lamont.'

Little Jakob jumps down the steps from his class and appears to one side of the canteen window. 'Morning, Mrs Lamont.'

I slide across the Harry Potter lunch box and tap the lid. 'There's a new thing in here this morning.'

Jakob wrestles the container open and his eyes swivel straight up to my face, his voice rising. 'Stringy cheese.'

'Indeed.'

He picks up one of the tubes to inspect it closely. 'Never had stringy cheese.'

'Me neither. I nearly took one, but then I thought, Jakob can tell me if it's nice or not.'

Jakob nods deeply, as though tasked with a very important matter.

On canteen duty days I pack one of the kids' old lunch boxes with lots of goodies for him. If squeezy tubes of yoghurt, or rice biscuits, are doing the playground fashionista rounds, then that's what he gets – alongside the sandwiches and fruit. Last week it was hummus dip; he wasn't keen but ate it all.

'I put two in, in case you want to share.'

His expression says that's never going to happen.

'But I think you're very hungry so you should probably eat them both.'

The other mothers say Jakob's parents are junkies; I've no idea if that's true. I do know the general rule seems to be: don't have him over for play dates. I also know Jakob comes to school alone, never has any food, and no one waits for him by the gate at the end of the day. Every time I collect the lunch box from a bench outside his class, there's a little drawing in it. He's a very fine artist.

Jakob carefully peels the first stringy cheese into strips and drops the pale pieces into his gaping mouth.

'You had better hurry up, young man, recess will be over soon.' I push the lunch box towards him.

He clicks the lid shut and lets the container dangle like a briefcase from his skinny arm. 'Do you want to know what the picture is today, Mrs Lamont?'

I lift both hands in mock horror. 'Goodness, no. That's my lovely surprise when I get home.'

'Do you want to guess?' His face says he wants me to guess.

'Let me see, um, it might be a picture of a velociraptor eating stringy cheese.'

The school siren weaves around the undercover area and the short people sprint, dawdle, shriek and file back into the classrooms. I shut the counter's roller door, pull the bolts across. Olivia and Amy are somewhat mollified and chatting about broadband providers and the distant memory of being able to stay up late to get pissed.

'Let me clean up here.' I flutter a hand to reinforce how easy this is for me.

'Thanks, you're a saint, Audrey.'

I'm not. The truth is the solitude of a closed canteen is preferable to anything else I've planned for today. I wipe down benches and listen to a class play sport noisily on the undercover court outside. I mop the floor and check my missed calls from this morning.

Should not have thought about her earlier because my mother-in-law has left a message.

'Audrey, won't be here June, July, to prune the roses, so I'll be over at the weekend to go through the process with you. Buy yourself a pair of Hidehisa Japanese secateurs. Expensive but worth it, and I'm sure Simon won't mind giving them to you as an early birthday present. The crepuscule climbing is going to need cutting right back – I'll show you what I mean.'

I add *secateurs* to today's uninspiring list alongside *charcoal shoe linings for Simon, oat milk for Orson,* and *bowel preparation from pharmacy.* I am not looking forward to drinking that tomorrow morning.

3

On the way home I pull into the hardware store carpark, then recall the vast amount of money I spent on therapy yesterday. Perhaps not buying secateurs, even cheap ones, might be a very good place to start making changes. Of course, Simon appreciates me keeping his mother happy, but no, not this time. A tingle of defiance starts up, which can only be described as pathetic. Never mind and thank you, Sister Naomi. Feeling like a rebel, I drive out the entrance then head for the antique store to pick up that gilt-framed mirror.

When I enter the kitchen at home, a gust of wind catches the back door. I put my foot out too late and it slams.

'Audrey.' My husband's voice chastises from the lounge room.

I knew it. 'Sorry, darling.'

This will not be a good time to hang the mirror. I tuck the beauty in the pantry, slip off my shoes, and pad quietly towards the lounge.

The room still bears the scent of new paint, lingering like a rumour. Cold autumn light ekes across the verandah and through the double-hung windows, making the reds in the Persian rug congeal. I'm tempted to flick on the overheads. But Simon is in his Eames chair, the one the kids and I gave him five years ago for his sixtieth, and a standard lamp casts a warm white puddle over his papers. His face is lit by the laptop. He's oblivious. I let my hand drop from the switch and walk over to the mantelpiece to retrieve my glasses. The little Japanese oil painting taunts me from above the fireplace.

'What?'

'I didn't say anything, honey. Just getting my specs.' I turn to show them in my hand. Simon lifts his eyes from the laptop. I take a step towards him. 'Are you excited about tonight?'

He makes as though to stand up, starts to collect his papers. 'I've got to finish this speech. I'm only asking for a few more hours, Audrey, and then it will be done.'

'Sit, sit.' I wave my glasses in the direction of the door. 'I'll leave you in peace.'

Simon leans back into the chair, as he almost certainly knew he would, then pulls his reading glasses off his forehead and onto his nose.

'Don't even think about me,' I say, 'I've got lots to do.'

I drop a kiss on his still-thick head of hair. He doesn't move a muscle – so busy, so focused. I've seen more of the top of my husband's head over the last three years than I have his face. It's the book, and now the launch; the grants, the research pressure, the fanfare he expects from the university, and the lectures he's already been invited to give.

'Audrey, if you're making tea …' a shaft of Simon's voice finds me in the kitchen.

'Sure.' I wasn't making tea, though. 'Cake?'

There's no reply. Either he hasn't heard me, or more likely he has and says nothing because he knows he should say no – another triathlon at the weekend. I'll take him a slice of banana cake, no added sugar, and he'll scowl at me because I'm supposed to remember he's not snacking, but the plate will be empty when I collect it later. It's comfortable to lean into these predictable moments.

I dunk the teabag and watch the water turn black. Outside heavy clouds threaten rain. Mustn't forget the washing. The pop of the cake-tin lid brings Howard into the kitchen with a purposeful lope.

'That's not your snack tin, old man.'

He sits, pretends he doesn't understand. I give him a chew stick, and he takes his trophy back out to the verandah.

I squeeze the teabag, add a slice of lemon then deliver it with the cake.

'Tea's there.'

'What? Oh yes, thanks.'

'Simon.'

He looks up, putting a finger on the spot where he's been forced to stop reading.

'After the launch, maybe we could go up north for a couple of days, go fishing, do some walks?'

'Audrey, now, really? If you want to go, go but—'

'Yep, I know, sorry, bad time.' Sometimes I hate the way I love my husband.

Out at the washing line, I take the pillowcases off, the shirts, underwear, towels, and sort them into piles for ironing. A few large drops fall from the sky to hit the verandah roof.

'Audrey had a knack with timing her laundry that many envied,' I tell the dog, visualising a thrilled TV crew, anxious to film the last of my stainless-steel pegs as they hit their basket. 'Will she, yet again, get everything in on time?'

The sound of the upstairs shower running shuts that fantasy down. Not long now and Simon's book will be launched, the speech will be done, and there'll be yet another notch on the academic bedpost of my husband's achievements.

I fly in and out of the kids' shower, slip on the bathmat, and catch my thigh on the towel rail; it is surprisingly painful. My green dress looks fine in the mirror, but the red shoes are a bit much. I swap them for a cream pair.

In our bedroom Simon finishes doing up the last two buttons on his shirt. 'What do you think?'

'You, my husband, look fabulous, you really do.'

He does. Tall, lithe, a striking man. He flicks a smile, but it doesn't ease the tension in his jaw. I know once he's on the podium, the nerves and all the work he has done will become subservient to his love of performing.

Simon reads his notes one last time as I drive us through the large sprawling university grounds. In the gloam of a wet night, and under fuzzy balls of light, the sharp-edged concrete architecture takes on a blurred softness. The older limestone monoliths are cut deep with shadows and the trees' bare autumn branches tangle with each other as the wind howls through.

We enter the dimly lit, over-catered soirée together. I know this moment will be the last I'll spend with Simon for the next few hours. He smiles and nods to comrades over my shoulder and then he leans in close. I straighten his collar, pop a kiss on his jaw, and inhale his familiar cedar and bergamot scent.

He hesitates a moment longer and whispers, 'If asked, perhaps it's best to say you work *at* the school. Simpler, don't you think?'

I nod and pat his arm. On the occasions when I have said I work *in* a school canteen, the responses have been savage. People's eyes glaze, then they turn away to scan between Simon, with his multiple degrees, Professor of Tribology and author of the definitive *Green Tribology – Reducing Friction and Wear in Renewable Energy Generation*, and Simon's wife, the canteen lady. They clearly expected someone much more interesting.

A student sails up on my right with a tray of red or white wine.

'Thanks.' White wine counts as clear fluids, doesn't it, and that's the pre-colonoscopy instruction for today.

I turn my back on the chancellor's wife, who looks poised to come over. Oh that I had the courage to change the course of this next conversation. When Sally arrives and says, *Audrey, remind me, what is it you do?* Tonight, I'll reply, *Evening Sally, I'm studying the effects of meat pies on the gastrointestinal tracts of Kookaburras.* She will salivate with enthusiasm and comment, *How fascinating. East or West Coast birds?* Or I could tell her I'm on a sabbatical. She'd like that too, and bob her head approvingly as thoughts like, *Fabulous woman, brilliant couple, must have them over for dinner*, scoot through her brain. *Perhaps it's best to say you work* at *the school.* Was my husband protecting me from them, or protecting himself from feeling ashamed? I've not considered this enough.

Simon wafts around the room amongst his adoring crowd. I remind myself not to eat one of the canapés, grab a second drink, and find somewhere inconspicuous to wait it all out. My lovely green dress fades into the plush green velvet of a couch against a side wall.

A trickle of academics and students pass by. I sit, smile glued to my face, and nod like the toy dog on a car's dashboard. It's about time I stop being tormented by the fact my husband's world finds me as interesting as a folded tea towel.

The burble of chat gives way to a few sonorous *ahem*s. These in turn dwindle until the whisper of hands being plunged deep into pockets are the last remnants of sound. Simon has taken to the podium and is introduced by the minister for something.

Even from the back of the room I can see everyone's approval for Simon. The way their necks strain out of their collars and the lightness with which members of the audience shift their weight between feet.

And then I see a thing. At first, I'm not sure if it's the play of light which catches his profile. But it builds, and when he moves his head left and down to look at a colleague by his side, the moment is intense. I peer hard, but other people's heads are in the way. There's something in his downcast face, the way his neck is purposefully arced. There's a sharpness along his jaw and I feel an electric frisson in the tilt of his head. I can't see his eyes, but I don't need to. It's a look I've never been offered.

Simon starts his speech and I feel impossibly alone.

Unable to witness any more – giddy, confused – I look along the empty green sofa towards the exit, then slip away. What did I just see?

4

This morning, I regret drinking those two wines. Pinot Grigio plus bowel preparation has resulted in me being very distracted. I barely understand the nurse when she asks me to change and take a seat in bay six. I need another moment and nip off to the bathroom. Just inside the door a woman stands back from the mirrors to observe herself, scrunching paper towels between her hands. She has the advantage of being fully dressed. I have the disadvantage of recognising her and not being able to slip past.

'Susie.'

She turns, looks vague, her hands come to a halt.

'It's Audrey,' I continue, 'Simon Lamont's wife.'

'Ah, Audrey, I didn't recognise you with your clothes off.'

I doubt she'd have recognised me dressed.

'Awful business this, isn't it?' She points to herself, 'Crohn's. Must have these dreadful things every couple of years. You?'

'Routine government screening thing.'

'Yes, everyone gets one of those kits in the post when they turn fifty, don't they? Or is it fifty-five?'

I shift a little to indicate I'd like to get past her. 'Would you excuse me please, Susie?'

She jerks forward. 'Silly me.'

I take the opportunity to nip into a cubicle.

'Good luck, Audrey, sure it will be nothing. See you at the chancellor's drinks.'

'Indeed.'

I don't know anything about the drinks – odd, Simon loves those events.

I don't need to use the bathroom, I had merely wanted to hide before they put me on a trolley and strangers look at my bottom, my wobbly thighs. And what happens if I … you know? The toilet bowl is cold on my thighs. I pull a sheet of loo paper out of its dispenser.

That look on Simon's face at the book launch swirls back. Then a memory emerges: I've seen the same intensity on the faces of tango dancers; their unflinching focus of mystery and seduction. Trouble is my husband's look was for another person.

If I'd caught that moment in a photo, and then used it for the opening shot of my biopic, the film's title might be *Everything Ends Last Night*. I rip another sheet out. I wonder what actors would play me, the children. Fold. But I don't want my biopic to be a romantic tragedy. I'd prefer a murder mystery, something edgy – me as a villain? That by-line would be tepid. *When Audrey finally tipped over the craggy brink, she took a hammer to a watermelon and fled; local police are uninterested.* Rip, fold.

The bathroom door opens, then there's the sound of feet shuffling on the hard polished floor. The door to the cubicle next door clicks. Someone else is avoiding the nurses, or perhaps she's simply voiding. Her arrival is my cue to leave this sanctuary. I concede defeat, lift the lid on the sanitary disposal bin, and drop the squares of paper inside, for old times' sake; it's been a while.

———

'Audrey?'

I blink, strain to focus. Two blue eyes and a mask hover.

'Audrey, how are you feeling?'

A black cuff on my left upper arm relaxes in short, pulsing bursts. There are curtains. My head lolls briefly right then left; piecing together snatches of information. Lower, a loose weave blanket emerges; it is white. I experiment with toes, move them and the blanket moves too. That's my body stretched out down there.

'It's over, Audrey. Have you any pain?' The nurse focuses on her writing, leaving only pale lids and a dark arc of eyelashes, like the swoop of a Japanese calligrapher.

Eventually I recall her question. 'I don't, thank you.' Despite my best efforts the words are slurred.

A flexible high-tech rod has been threaded through my body, and although the procedure is over, the remnant cold chill of the rod leaks into my cells. I pull the blanket up higher, for comfort.

An orderly arrives with a small tray bearing bitter brown tea and a packet of sandwiches. I thank him. Friends who're also in the over-fifty government poo club warned me the food and beverages are a test to be completed before the nurses will allow you to leave. I drag myself upright and skol the lukewarm liquid, then open the cellophane, tear at the bread, so it looks like something has been eaten. *Diet, Fluids* – tick.

There's the dry *swish–rattle* of a curtain being pulled and then my lower gastrointestinal surgeon, in blue scrubs, walks across mumbling, *Bay six*. His glance sweeps briefly over my face before he pulls out the clipboard at the end of the trolley. He looks about twelve.

Face composed in 'Things I must do this morning' furrows, he asks, 'Feeling all right?' But his eyes remain on the chart. There was the inflection of a question in those three words, but he doesn't wait for an answer. I nod and smile, unseen.

'We've removed a polyp.' He studies some photos in my file then drops the clipboard back in its holder. 'We'll have the results in about ten days. Make an appointment with your GP. The positive blood in your sample was probably from your haemorrhoids.' He squirts hand sanitiser into one palm, and his fingers fly through each other. It looks like they're signing to my feet.

I lower my voice, 'I don't have haemorrhoids.'

'Internal haemorrhoids, Mrs …' He looks down to the chart, but the exertion of adding my surname is clearly too much. 'Quite normal as you get older. Avoid getting constipated.'

My results are good, but the slump in his retreating back says otherwise. Nothing medically challenging in my bowel. Poor lad, talking to old ladies about piles all day. I want to call him back, tell him he just gave me good news, he should want the same for all patients. But that would be like telling an emergency department to be satisfied with ingrown toenails, and the occasional infected piercing.

Still woozy, gown tight so my bum isn't exposed, I get up, check for unseemly marks on the white sheets, and pull round the curtains; they offer a flimsy privacy.

Once dressed, I strip the trolley, fold the linen, and catch glimpses of myself in a small mirror above the oxygen nozzle. Matted red-blonde hair that a hand tries to shunt a little bounce back into. Pale eyebrows, green eyes, puffy flesh. The image is of miserable confusion, a faded old bint helpfully folding hospital linen, sorting things which don't need her attention. That woman in the mirror is a fossil clinging to domestic routines, fossicking in a world of pretence, for want of something better.

I lean in closer to the mirror and lift my chin to study it carefully, no peach fuzz – yet. But there is one, long, rogue eyebrow. Good lord, it's like the beginning of an antenna. I pinch it between two nails and pull. I wonder how long it's been there. Perhaps people think I use whiskers to estimate the width of doorways?

Phone up around my ear, I fake a call as I walk over to the nurses' desk. 'My husband can't find a parking spot.' I wave the phone vaguely in her direction. 'He's just out the front ...'

She understands and rattles off the standard post-procedure information.

Of course, Simon isn't downstairs. If asked, he wouldn't have a clue where I am. The family calendar lost meaning a long time ago, probably when the kids got driving licences.

I smile broadly until the nurse relents and lets me leave.

5

The metallic warmth of Simon's car bonnet tells me he's not long home. Under the verandah, the floorboards look parched, and spiders have built a web in one corner of the front-door glass.

'Look at the same things, Audrey, see the same things? And next time you see the therapist, do mention how you talk to yourself. If you see the therapist again.'

I stop talking out loud, step off the verandah and into the garden. The lawn is spongy underfoot, my shoes soak through in an instant. I feel suffocated and an urge to scream balls up under my diaphragm. The lawn begs to be clipped and curated when the whole place could be sumptuous, natural, filled with the song of clicking cicadas. I do a lap, imagining how this garden could look. I visualise a vegetable patch and homegrown produce for family meals, then I go indoors.

Inside the house, voices overlap. Flicking off wet shoes I listen for a moment and tuck my little hospital bag behind our hats on the hallstand, then head to the kitchen. Howard skids over the tiled floor, ecstatic; his dinner is imminent. I stroke his big golden head. Usually Wednesday night's family meal is a happy indulgence. Tonight, the edge of pleasure is dull, and when the kids file into the kitchen, I feel my expression fall into someone else's; lines they'll recognise: their mum.

Thea, the first to wander in, cradles her iPhone like a prayer book; its light bathes her face in an optimistic glow. Twenty-six, willowy, working for a judge, living with a friend in the city, and the only one to have inherited my strawberry-blonde hair.

'Mum, hey.'

'Hello, sweetie. You look lovely. I know, I know, I shouldn't say that, but don't tell me off tonight.'

She lifts her head from the screen to receive the compliment with a smile. 'It's fine and thank you.'

I hold her shoulders and kiss her forehead, noting an enviable fizz about her.

Thea puts the phone down and perches on the stool at the kitchen bench. 'Mum ...'

'Mother, when's dinner?' Gus breaks the moment with big strides, long arms, and a clang as he lifts and replaces the slow cooker's lid.

'Soon.'

He wraps his arms around me from behind and drops his head onto my shoulder. 'It's okay if it's not.'

'Well, how kind, thank you. It'll be ten minutes, your lordship.'

Gus is twenty-seven and avoids all the middle-class pathways our world has to offer. He lives in the attic of a large house which is being renovated and does odd jobs instead of paying rent. I doubt he's eaten all day, and if he has it will have been something high-sugar, low-nutritional value, that's easy to devour with a joint at smoko.

Thea presses her lips into a cute smile and leaves the bench with Gus deep in conversation. Whatever she was going to tell me remains unsaid. It's probably about who she's going to meet later, but I know better than to ask. Nor will I pry into what

Gus has eaten today. Although I want to know every detail of my children's lives, I've been told, in no uncertain terms, that I am not allowed to peer uninvited. Perhaps it's a good thing. Is knowing about each twitch and nuance of their worlds important? No, sit back, Audrey, be gracious and wait to see which gift of details you're offered. Oh, but it's so hard.

Orson, just turned twenty-nine, my textbook intellectual, sometimes vegan, quieter than the other two, arrives by my side. He reaches past my head to open a cupboard and grabs a handful of cashews. I push the curtain of hair from his eyes, he grins and shakes it back into place.

I make a show of scraping grated carrot into a beetroot chickpea salad. 'Cheese today or no cheese?'

'Cheese, cheers.'

Simon wanders in, eyes on his iPad. I could have scripted this moment. When the aromas of dinner seep through the house, a Pavlovian response kicks in and he emerges.

'Oh, beef bourguignon,' he murmurs. 'I had a late lunch, not sure I want to eat right now.'

The comment is delivered to the rich bubbling sauce, then he turns to join his children at the dinner table. He hasn't looked at me. My gut rolls uncomfortably. Howard is happy to be fed out on the back verandah.

Bread board, loaf, knife and butter to the table where Simon is recounting a funny story about a PhD student he interviewed. Bowls, side plates, cutlery. Back and forth to the table. No one asks if they can help. A bony finger prods at something like self-pity, but I blame myself. Over the years I batted away offers of help so often they've given up. They probably think their help would be a nuisance – in fact, I'm sure I've told them that.

Simon comes to the climax of a story about the new book and there's an explosion of laughter. He's a good raconteur and they're an appreciative audience. Another day I might have laughed with them. Finally, stew pot and haloumi salad on the table, they settle into the food. Even Simon's changed his mind and I serve him the bourguignon. The voices of my family rise and build into an impervious layer. This scene is all so normal, but I'm too bilious to eat and a cramp pins me against the kitchen bench. No one notices my chair is empty.

I scoop a couple of dropped cashews into the compost bin and pour a glass of water. A temptation to let it drop and smash on the tiled floor pulses just once, then the urge is gone. The rim feels heavy on my lip. I leave it there, feeling its weight. Simon's thin lips part to talk. I watch the up and down of his jaw, his rhythmic chew, gestures I know so well. What I don't know is the tango look I saw on his face at the book launch.

Do not overthink things, Audrey, I reprimand myself, pick up the calendar and rifle through the coming months – June, July, August. They're full of events: Simon's uni dates, exams, his trips, birthdays. December, my big six-oh is not written down.

'Mum, you all right?' Orson's voice breaks through the moment.

'Absolutely. I was miles away.'

They plop their plates and cutlery in the dishwasher then one by one, they offer hugs and reasons why they must go. I don't remember a single word they say. I give them a hug, smile, and thank them for coming. We all say, *See you soon*, which means texts will fly until next Wednesday when we do it all again.

Empty of family, the kitchen feels hollow.

The dog-flap clatters. Howard slopes in wet from the garden and leaves muddy prints across the floor. He sniffs around the dishwasher for anything which may have spilt. I look down too. It's badly stacked, but for once I have no urge to repack it.

'What am I doing, Howard?'

The old boy looks up as if to say, *I have no idea. My interest is purely food based.* This is the thing about labradors. I ladle a small spoon of stew onto the open dishwasher door thinking this would be a bad habit to get into. Howard clearly can't believe his luck and inhales the lot in one wet-tongued gulp before he saunters into the lounge room. I shut the door, turn the dishwasher on, and hover long enough to hear its diligent whirr.

The mirror is still behind the pantry door waiting to be hung, but not while Simon is here.

A few stray carrot shreds cling to the sink. I unleash a jet of cold water which captures most, but one or two climb the stainless walls elusively. I grab the dishcloth, and a few more orange rogues fall from between the fibres.

'Just leave them,' I tell myself.

The lure of a comfortable bed is irresistible. But Simon has had the power injection of interviewing, the aphrodisiac of making decisions about other people's lives followed by a self-congratulatory boozy lunch. During dinner his chest strained at its linen shirt with each fabulous witticism, all telltale signs he's on top of his game. Regrettably, history tells me he'll want to celebrate with sex. I do not.

If Simon knows I'm off to bed he'll close his iPad, leave it on the coffee table, and come upstairs. I'll hear him hum in the shower. He'll put on clean pyjama shorts then slide into bed with an anecdote, wafting cedar and bergamot oils. The years have reassured him that a gentle, witty overture makes him irresistible. The years have taught me to acquiesce because the gap between the glint in his eye and sleep is much shorter if I join in.

Tonight, I'll slink off quietly and feign sleep. This is a ruse seldom used and hence it remains effective. Tonight, he'll bring his iPad upstairs and shower in disappointed silence. This thought is curiously satisfying.

6

This morning clouds like dirty sheep frame little patches of turquoise, a good omen. Howard and I turn the last corner, I let him off his lead to bound ahead and greet the neighbour's dog. They do the daily anal sniff in circles, which reassures them both. Then they cavort on the verge until I open the gate and they both zoom across the lawn.

The lawn that is soon to go. Last night I put it up on the Facebook group 'Buy Nothing'. A lot of people commented they'd like to be considered and this morning I chose Tailor Swift, although I'm sure it's a pseudonym. She said, 'We'll be over at the end of next week to take the turf away.'

Having pretty much erased myself around here, this garden will be a good place to start carving out a niche.

'Yes, Audrey, the sun is trying to come out, more people pick up their dog poo than don't, and it's time to smell the roses.'

Howard and his friend stop their zoomies in case I mention the word bone.

Back to the roses: it's also time for them to go. Again 'Buy Nothing' is awash with people keen for the David Austins, the Abracadabras, the Albertine climbing, and the other forty-two varieties which I meticulously listed.

Tape measure in hand, I stride about the garden and make notes. The most important consideration is where the trees cast shade, and what areas are in full sun; that's it really.

In broad daylight it is blindingly obvious that the side of the shed will be perfect for vegetables. Should they be raised beds, easier on the back as I grow older?

Everything in the garden is coming out, except the trees, and it's all going to be waterwise natives. I will not be bullied by Victoria on this one. It's my garden after all, and, as Aunt Pascale has been known to say – *Better to ask for forgiveness after the event than grovel for permission before.*

Right now, a soil-testing kit, raised bed options, plus advice on what native flowers come out and when will be helpful. And on my way, I'll take Simon's signed copies of the book to the university.

I count out the twenty-two stairs to his office and wonder how many times I've done this climb. Up to help him, or one of his colleagues, type up a paper, to bring the kids for a visit when he works late, drop off a lunch.

Books on hip, I push open his office door and there, perched like a delicate bird on Simon's large leather chair, is a woman. An extraordinarily perfect Japanese work of art. Her porcelain skin is flawless, so it's impossible to determine her age. Blue-black hair hanging in a glossy, blunt cut shimmies over tiny shoulders. She uncoils her legs and stretches out dainty, bare feet, wiggles perfectly painted toes. On the floor, neatly placed to one side, are minuscule leather kitten-heel mules. I drag my eyes back across the grey carpet to my own enormous trainers, and then walk over to the desk. The room is suddenly oppressive. Despite her diminutive size she has sequestered all the air. I put the books down, careful not to disturb anything, and resist a ridiculous urge to apologise. In the absence of anything to say, I brush my hands together, wiping away imaginary grit from the bottom of the box.

'Audrey.'

She does not move to stand; she does not proffer a hand. She isn't asking if that's my name.

'Sorry to disturb, I've brought Simon's books, the signed copies.'

The woman stretches out a dainty hand and pats the cardboard. 'And now I can sign them too.'

My fingers slow their imaginary dusting.

'So, you are the co-author.' I read a book cover, Dr S. Lamont and Dr M. Crump. 'My delivery is good timing then.'

'Midori, Midori Crump.' She leans back.

I force a pleasant smile and assess her as she assesses me. I don't know what I'm looking for but see many things in the brief exchange. It is apparent she knows a great deal about me, whereas I am facing a stranger. The silence is not uncomfortable, it's necessary. When sufficient pieces fall into place and I'm ready, I step backwards, towards the door; understanding everything and nothing.

Her impassive face suggests she has never experienced a moment's doubt.

'The book is good timing, Audrey, yes.'

She lifts her chin a fraction, runs a finger along the gold chain that glistens at her neck.

I run my tongue along the back of my teeth and wonder if there's any more to be said, then turn and leave.

And now I'm in a garden centre, with no recollection of how I got here.

Where else should I be? What else can I do, when so unexpectedly confronted by someone who is almost certainly sleeping with my husband? The admission is terrifying, and yet I carry on with this morning's plan as though it might erase the truth.

A roly-poly person in uniform locates a soil-testing kit, then they direct me to the native plant section. I slip on the wet concrete and grab the trolley handle just in time. Rows of plants blur grey-green. The mist of sprinklers makes a cold morning colder. My fingers find the phone deep in my jacket pocket and dial.

There's the sound of metal being put down on metal. 'Laurence?'

'Hey, how're you doing?'

The sound of my brother's voice is soothing. 'Has my whole life been meaningless?'

'Audrey, what are you talking about? What's up?'

'I feel like I've spent a lot of time being fatuous.'

'I'm sorry, I don't know what you're getting at.'

'Laurence, Simon is having an affair.'

There's silence down the phone. Another soft whoosh of spray starts up over the perennials behind.

'He probably isn't, Audrey. You've been out of sorts for a while. This is you being oversensitive.'

'I just met the woman, by mistake.' I clutch my phone, too exhausted to pretend to study the bottlebrush or choose a grevillea.

'You could have read the meeting wrong. What is it Nick says at the start of *The Great Gatsby*?'

'*Reserving judgements is a matter of infinite hope.* I know, but something about this tells me my hope is no longer infinite, not today. Maybe it will be tomorrow. Anyway, I'm standing in a garden centre looking like a mad woman. I'm going home now to do an audit on my happiness. I'll call you tomorrow.'

'Audrey.'

'Dearest, I love you for just being there at the end of the phone. Thank you.' I put my phone on silent.

7

Planes in the crystal glass pop refracted light. A few mint leaves balance on one large ice cube until the shaft of gin disturbs them. The tonic sets everything moving. By contrast the house bulges with a rare stillness. Mesmerised by the liquid, I squeeze half a lemon between my fingers and let the juice run over the ball of my hand. Eventually, I lick the bitterness from my wrist and pluck pips from the clear liquid. And then I pull out the ironing.

Howard jabs his cold nose into my leg and jumps up onto the kitchen reading chair. It is best to pretend he's not there; the vacuum will get his hairs out tomorrow.

The iron hisses into life. The gin is aromatic, and I find a podcast about the Australian outback. A scientist with a sincere insect voice says, *In certain areas, cattle have stopped breeding due to droughts and rising temperatures*; and the bald facts keep coming. Glass empty, clothes smooth, the end of the world is nigh – none of these are helpful.

Still no text from Simon. Odd for a man so precise about his actions – or not, as I'm learning. Should I worry about a car accident? That would be too simple. My line of questioning should concentrate on more probing themes, but my upended head runs on with deeply unimportant questions like, what to do with the soil-testing kit?

At 11 pm pacing becomes an option. Kitchen: there are no solutions in the fridge, no consolations in the pantry. A desperate melody starts up behind my sternum. Devastation slithers over benchtops, glides across the floor. To put the ironed clothes away feels overwhelming. Upstairs: for what, a shower, bed? Back downstairs again: rehang coats in the hallway.

By eleven thirty the Japanese painting is intolerable. I take it down, stomp out of the house and put it on the garage bench. Then I hang the mirror over the mantelpiece, adjust the tilt so it is level, wipe the glass. Sister Naomi was wrong; this activity has done nothing to help.

At midnight a second gin and tonic, and because I know mess annoys Simon, I carry my diaries from the spare bedroom into the lounge. Sitting on the floor with them spread around me, I hover my hands over their covers like a Reiki therapist waiting for a vibe. This time my search focuses on the last three years: Simon's absences, opportunities he had to be with Dr Midori Crump. There were *three conferences* a year. I resist texting Simon.

At 2 am the security lights go on outside. I shoot into the kitchen, pour my third drink and saunter into the hallway exactly as Simon comes through the front door.

A pause strings out like a tightrope, and an acid creep starts along the back of my throat. There is something very wrong with this picture. I watch his mood plummet, his brow furrow, the lack of smile, the fact he doesn't look at me, except to glower. Usually I'd excuse that face, assume he is worried about work. Tonight, though, is different.

He shrugs off his coat. 'I believe you met Midori today.'

'Indeed. She seems well installed in your office. And I expect she was a much more appropriate companion at the chancellor's drinks this evening.'

His chin tucks into the back of his neck, and he swaps his

laptop bag from one hand to the other. The hallway lamp casts deep shadows across his rigid face. He swallows.

'We wrote the book together. Thought you'd be pleased I'd spared you another evening with my colleagues.'

'Rubbish.'

Time grows slack. He looks at me, the mother of his children, looks me in the eyes and defends her role in his life.

'How long has it been going on?'

'Audrey, you can be so stupid ...' He puts his bag down on the hallstand.

'Don't say another word to me if it's a lie.' I nod towards the lounge. 'I'll make you a drink.'

I squat by the kitchen chair and bury my head in Howard's flank. He rouses momentarily to lick my hand.

Simon stands to one side of the mess on the floor in the sitting room. He takes the glass and with his free hand waves dismissively towards the scattered diaries.

'Have you been looking back through your notes to find some dirt?'

'We're not here to talk about my journals, Simon.'

He rolls his neck. 'Audrey, it's late.'

'It appears I'm the one who's late to catch on. I won't sleep unless you explain what is going on with you and your colleague, Dr Crump.'

Suddenly I feel wary. His reply will either dismiss my suspicions further, shove me deeper into the ignorance corner, or it will upend my marriage.

Simon pulses his jaw for a few beats. 'We're talking about our options.'

I drop down into a chair, push myself into the upholstery, arms heavy, fingers clawed around the gin. 'We, *our* – meaning you and Midori?'

'Yes, Midori and me.' He looks towards the ceiling and then reluctantly back down again. 'Writing the book together has been intense, and we don't know if we've got anything on a personal level to move forward with. It's, uh, all unknown.'

That's one of the most incoherent sentences he's ever uttered. I pick through it slowly. 'You and Midori are *we*. As your wife I'll give you the tip, this is pretty painful to hear.'

He stiffens and fills the room.

'You don't understand. When you spend years with a person, working closely, sharing frustrations but always academically attuned, it's quite natural other emotions arise.'

Tall, broad, almost prancing, his muscled arms fly as he demonstrates his position in the world as a man caught in a difficult situation.

'You've no idea the intensity of such an endeavour, Audrey. There's a lot of pressure, it's a breakthrough in the field, a triumph for me personally and my profession.'

I get the impression I'm supposed to admire him, or perhaps feel sorry for him. But I feel as though I've just walked into a punch and am falling slowly to the ground.

'For god's sake, this isn't one of those passé scenarios where someone goes to work and falls for his secretary. Midori and I have something far more complicated than a trite office romance.'

I feel myself shrivel, yet I continue to watch The Great Simon on the horns of a dilemma. I know his body, every twist of his neck, the thrust of his hips and planted feet. Each of his movements feels as though it erases a little more of me, and I know the words he chooses are not the whole truth.

He takes the first sip of his drink. Stops moving. I'm torn between knowing this man so well and yet not knowing him at all. I feel nauseated and can't find anything to say.

'And here, Audrey, at home, what have we had?' He flicks a wrist, dismissing every domestic moment spent together. 'The chaos of the kids leaving home, moving back, shifting out again. Howard's vet bills. Should we get more solar panels put on the roof? Really. And you've been so bloody miserable, mooning about.'

I feel like I've been slapped. If he thought I was miserable why didn't he care enough to ask? When exactly did we arrive at this point?

He talks on and on. My scalp burns and shrinks, pulling upwards with the heat of humiliation. I feel pummelled under his invective – no wonder I've never dreamt of disputing him. The speed of his expressions doesn't allow for a subject to be discussed or analysed so much as exhausted.

At some point I stop trying to listen. I merely wait for a moment to speak. Breathe deeply to collect the remnants of me which he hasn't yet dispersed.

'Simon, you've not really told me anything. I'm going to bed, *alone*. In the morning I'd like you to try again. You're not *contemplating* an affair, Simon, you're having one. I'm not the fool you take me for. Tomorrow, perhaps you'll respect the mother of your children sufficiently to lay it out for me.'

'You're accusing me of lying?'

'I haven't read *The Etiquette of How to Approach a Splintered Marriage Without Upsetting the Narcissistic Ego of Your Husband*, but yes, I'm accusing you of lying.'

I feel so tired. I want to leave this disaster, but he starts ranting again. The initial icy distaste in his voice segues into shock, self-preservation, annoyance and finally he's back to arrogance as he tries to get on top of things once more.

'Simon, I need to go to bed. I can't hear a word you're saying.'

8

The morning is worse. The confrontation is still in my
bloodstream along with the gin, and Simon is ashen.

He stands from a kitchen stool. 'Coffee?'

'Simon, have you been having the affair these past three
years, the whole time you were writing the book?'

He leans his palms heavily on the bench and lets his head
drop.

Then I hear myself shout, but not one of my yelled protests
are registered. I've lost because of my volume. His calm, putrid
tone trumps my irrational shouting. I'm failing again, and I
can't stop screaming. His face says, *You don't live up to her*,
and I have the searing sensation of being an orphan.

His voice reaches me, civilised, chilly. 'We should keep this
away from the children, for now.'

'Which bit? The fact you're having an affair or that you're
going to move out with another woman?'

'Why would I move?' His top lip twitches.

'Oh yes, silly me. It was Mummy and Daddy's house wasn't
it, you couldn't possibly move out.'

Simon flicks his phone over, briefly, and turns it back face
down. He stretches out an irritation in his lower back.

'Do you have any idea how I'm feeling, Simon?'

'You, feeling? I'm the one who came home to be attacked, then was shunted off to the spare room.'

'Simon ...'

Full of despair I stop. What's the point of persisting? Listening to me is not one of Simon's strong points at the best of times. Any argument I try to put across will not make a dent in the mirrored barrier around my husband who believes himself to be staggeringly clever. This is why I never broach the tricky stuff. And I'm no better prepared this morning than I've ever been. My words all but dry up, and I realise I can't take any more.

'I'm going out.'

'Oh no you don't.' He turns around, puts his coffee mug down. 'That's what you always do, walk away when things get uncomfortable.' He moves to the sink, turns the tap off harder. 'You never hold a position, a— no.' He rests both hands on the sink and leans into his arms, puts on a squeaky voice to mimic me. '*If we get a dog, Simon, it won't go on the sofa.*' Sneering at this memory he drops his voice again, leaves the sink, and takes a step closer. 'How long did it take before Howard was allowed on the sofa next to you?'

I take the car key down off the pantry wall, feel its hard edges against my palm.

Simon's face is flushed. 'You're the one who wanted to clear this business up, so we're going to discuss it. Now.'

'This is a bit more serious than a dog on a sofa, Simon. I am going out because I can't stay and listen to you delete me for another second.'

My legs are weak, my arms tingle, but I shut the back door, quietly. I start the car, go to a servo, buy a packet of cigarettes – my first in thirty years. Then I drive out along the wharf road to the very end and park in the full face of the howling sea breeze.

Gusts of wind jolt the car. I pull a cigarette out of the packet and forage blindly in the door pocket for Gus's familiar, smooth Bic. He used to hide the fact he smoked pot, but we've gone beyond that now and for once I'm pleased.

The sea is the colour of wet denim, and the wind chops it into white breakers. A salt-heavy gale adds to my restlessness. Which way along the beach? What thought to hang on to? Is this the time when a wife of more than three decades takes to her corner and fights, tooth and nail, for her husband? Or do I go home and kill Simon? If I were American, I'd have a divorce lawyer on speed dial, but perhaps that's overly dramatic. What on earth will the kids think? Oh lord, what to do?

Fifty metres away, a lemon-yellow ute is parked along the beach, and a dog waits by its wheel. Its incessant barks urge the owner to hurry up. The person – a man, I think – is seated on the passenger side, bent over. Then he stands, and starts an irregular, jerking movement towards the ocean. The dog dances, twirls, happy.

Closer now I see a false leg leans up against the ute. There's a shoe, a grey sock pulled up over a pink plastic calf. At the top, leather straps hang unbuckled. The lurches make sense – he's hopping. One strong, wiry, leg – stump and arms balance the movement. When knee-deep in water, the man falls forward into a wave and looks like any other swimmer. I watch as he stretches out then amiably drifts, the dog by his side. Will they disappear into Tennyson's *stillness of the central sea*? Would it throw them up again?

It's time to go, but not home.

9

Like sane people everywhere who practise social distancing when there are bugs about, I resolve to keep my distance from Simon. After another hour I drive back to the house. His car has gone so it's time to make a move. I take only what's necessary: Howard, photographs, diaries, clothes, my computer. The rest can wait.

I plug my phone in and start the engine.

'Laurence?'

'Hey, how're you doing?'

'I was thinking Howard and I might stay with you for a while. I'm about to come over, if it's okay?'

'Of course, of course. Tell me—'

'We'll chat when I arrive. Thanks, Laurence.'

I hang up and see I've just missed a call from Tata.

My mother was French and her sister, our Aunt Pascale, our Tata, still lives in northern France. They were like chalk and cheese. My mother: dainty, rustling petticoats, cautious. Pascale by contrast has been a country lawyer for years and describes herself as having *a low centre of gravity*. Since Mum died, Tata and I speak every week, I adore her. She's a wonderfully pragmatic woman and part of me can't wait to tell her about Simon. I pull the car out of the driveway, happy not to need windscreen wipers. Howard farts noisily.

'Siri. Call Tata.'

A voice answers the call. '*Zero, six, vingt-sept, cinquante-neuf, vingt-deux, dix-huit.*'

The voice is French but not my aunt's. My core muscles tense.

'*Bonjour*, hello, this is Audrey, I missed a call.'

'Ah *oui*, Audrey, my name is Lilou. *Euh.*' The voice comes in staccato bursts.

'Where's Pascale? Where's my aunt?'

There's the sound of breathing, and then the voice tiptoes down the phone.

'Audrey, I'm sorry, I don't know how to put this. Your aunt clearly adores you and your brother, she talks about you often ...'

My head fills with the delicacy of the French language. Lilou starts gently with details about how she's lived next door to Pascale for three years, and what a delight this has been, and how very sad she is, and how my aunt doesn't want me to know. Then she stops talking.

'Doesn't want me to know what? Where is she?'

It's becoming difficult to get enough air in my lungs. I wonder if I should pull over.

The stranger's voice cracks with concern. 'I'm sorry. Look, yesterday, Pascale fell out of her cherry tree ...'

The call continues. I ask questions. This woman, Lilou, gives answers.

'Lilou, thank you. I'll tell my brother. Sorry, I must go.'

I clutch the steering wheel. My invincible Tata is all alone. I hate Simon. Howard slobbers out of a window, oblivious. I need to get this forty-minute drive out of the way.

Laurence lives up in the hills, on a block way back from the road. The colours of the native bushland on his property eddy and fade as they thin out towards the house.

Laurence is complex. He loves Ottolenghi and panelbeating in equal parts. Years ago, after Dad's funeral, my brother gave up being a dentist, and now he renovates Chevrolets. The ones from 1938 are his favourite.

I find my brother under a car and squat down to get his attention. He rolls out on the trolley, and we lean against a tyre while I tell him about our aunt.

Laurence wipes his fingers on a rag that is dirtier than his hands.

'You poor thing, Audrey. First Simon, who I'm guessing we'll talk about later, and now Tata. Do you think she's going to die?'

'All we know for sure is that when the neighbour found her Tata was still conscious. An ambulance took her to Saint Malo hospital. Lilou wasn't sure what was broken, and the doctors are doing tests. We don't even know why she fell. If it was a heart attack or stroke – maybe she will die. I'm trying to convince myself that surviving a fall from a cherry tree when you're eighty-seven is amazing.'

'Do you think one of us should go over to Brittany to see her?'

'I do, but then again no. Maybe. Right now, she doesn't know we know. She didn't want us to be told.'

Laurence takes my hand and leads me indoors, starts the tea ritual he's so fond of. It involves carefully measured scoops of dried herbs from glass jars, a great deal of boiling water, his cast iron teapot, the *tink* of fine bone china cups on saucers, transparent slivers of sliced lemon, and finally a display of bitter almond biscotti.

He picks up the laden tray. 'Sitting room.'

The china garden tinkles on the tray as we walk down the corridor, and Howard follows.

'She's got chickens, you know, and a cat. And her wonderful garden – it's spring over there, it'll be going wild. There are things we have to sort out.'

We sit next to each other on his sofa. He turns the pot three times, and waves silver sugar tongs towards me like a conductor. 'Doesn't she have paying guests during the summer?'

'She does. What will happen with them?'

'What are you thinking, Audrey?'

'It's just the worst timing. Thea has her book club lunch at our house every May. Orson has bought a flat and asked me to help him paint it. He said I have a knack. But I think it's because he doesn't want his relatively new girlfriend, Joolz, getting too enthusiastic about paint choices. And Simon's always so busy after a book launch with events, dinners, talks. I don't think I could leave him in the lurch.'

I stop myself; the porcelain cup is light on my lip. Those words run through my head again.

Laurence's head is cocked to one side. 'Audrey, do you hear yourself?'

'Bit tragic, isn't it, wearing "busy" as a badge of honour? But, in my defence, if I go away, all the threads of our lives get tangled like cables behind the printer; it's a nightmare.'

Laurence sips his tea, eyes ahead. 'Sister mine, you are very out of sorts. Have you seen the shrink I recommended?'

'Oh, Laurence, what would I tell her – I chipped a nail, Aldi is out of goat's cheese, and our lovely aunt just had an accident?'

Laurence's face tells me he's not buying any of it.

'I brought all my diaries – thirty-seven years soon to be spread over your spare bed. I've been in pursuit of god-knows-what, but they are fun when I am unable to sleep.'

44

Laurence gives my knee a squeeze. 'And the therapist?'

'Look, I have an appointment.' Which is true because I haven't cancelled, yet. 'But you know what, Laurence? I think I might go to Brittany.'

10

Metaphorically, Simon inserted a knife in my solar plexus, and it is pretty hard to live around that pain. However, the last few days with my brother have been a perfect respite. And, because I have not been home, Simon doesn't know about my plan to go to France. Some aspects of my departure he will be able to deal with, like shopping online instead of having to confront a supermarket. But there are things he will not be able to avoid, and I am happy to imagine him burdened by these. How do dirty clothes get from the laundry basket back into the wardrobe? Why isn't the shiraz already chilled for half an hour when he gets home? Why is there dog poo on the lawn?

More immediately, I have a list to tick off. I stop at a shop, gather travel essentials and join the queue. Although it is not a queue per se. We are five strangers, grouped in front of a counter, although we are all aware of the order in which we arrived. I'm number three. The young man serving has his head down and focuses on totals. When that customer is off, a dad with a child on his hip moves forward. I'm next.

Dad buys dried fruit. Cash is exchanged.

The shop assistant looks up, straightens. He recognises number four, a pretty young girl.

'Hey.'

'Hey.' Number four moves forward.

I bring my step to a halt and wait once more, roll my shoulders, lift my head. Number five gives me a wistful smile. Perhaps she saw what happened. Water starts to collect in my eyes, threatens to overflow. I turn away, embarrassed, feign interest in a packet of Dutch biscuits, casually press the end of my scarf against my eyes. I understand my age. I know my clothes make me transparent. It's the wardrobe of someone no longer fertile, not fuckable. But today pretending to be okay with it all is difficult.

Number four starts to pack her bag – no rush.

What if Simon had had an affair when the kids were young? When I was young? I'd probably have rolled with the punches.

At this stage of life, my reserves are depleted. Going away for a while will show him. He won't be able to have an affair if he hasn't got a wife. Midori may not look so attractive then.

Can Simon and I regain what I thought we had? Do I want the scraps after his affair implodes? Today the answer is probably yes, but I need more time to consider my options.

Now I'm getting irritated. Number Four has paid but she also has time for one more piece of gossip, and the man at the counter melts under her glow.

My next breath I allow to leave my nostrils in a noisy stream.

When I called Lilou, she was delighted to know I'd be there soon, but couldn't believe I didn't want her to cancel all the guests. She said there was nothing nice about cleaning, and people could be demanding. I said it would be no problem.

My turn. The young man doesn't look up. He swipes my three items, pushes the pay-and-wave box forward, and turns to replenish his stack of paper bags from a shelf behind him.

I swear I could have been an okapi in linen and he would not have noticed.

—

The school secretary appears more annoyed than sorry I won't be around. Brusque and glowering from under dark tattooed eyebrows she says, 'This is rather sudden, Audrey.'

They're her words, but she means: *Sensible, old volunteers shouldn't be so irresponsible.* I want to say, *I've been responsible for a very long time*, but I don't.

'I'd also like to pay for Jakob to have school lunches until the end of the year.' I pass across a carefully calculated pile of cash.

I untie Howard from the bench outside the headmaster's office and wait for Jakob by the gate. I watch him leave the schoolyard, matted hair, twisted clothes, knobbly-kneed; and yet again I'm struck by how children have a perpetual dawn-over-the-horizon gait, no matter what. When he realises we're waiting for him, he almost sprints, then skids across the verge on his knees to make a fuss of the dog. I hand him the lead and we walk on together.

'Jakob, if I ring your mum to check if it's okay, would you like to stop and get a hot chocolate?'

Jakob looks worried and clings to the lead.

I keep my voice light. 'We could get it in takeaway cups and drink it outside, with Howard.'

'Cool. But Mum probably won't answer.'

I can see his little knuckles are white as he clutches a handful of Howard's fur and tells me his mother's number. I smile and wait for her to answer, but he's right, she doesn't, and when I end the call, his face is shuttered off with resignation.

'You know, I think Howard really wants a marshmallow. I'm going to text your mum. I'll tell her what we're doing and where we'll be. She can always ring back if she's not happy.'

Jakob stays with Howard on the pavement while I order our drinks, ask for extra marshmallows and buy far too many organic human and dog snacks.

We settle on a bench at the edge of the park. I unhook Howard's lead so he can sniff and explore, but the marshmallows are more interesting. The dog sits to one side of Jakob's swinging feet, looking doe-eyed and adorable.

'I think he likes me.'

'Oh, he does, Jakob.' The boy looks so content I don't really want to go on. 'Jakob, I just want to tell you I won't be at school for two terms.'

Jakob's legs continue to swing, and he snaps another bone-shaped biscuit into little pieces.

'I've arranged for you to have lunches from the canteen, every day. You won't forget to go and get them, will you?'

Jakob's tongue comes out tentatively and he lets the tip of it touch the crumbling end of the dog biscuit. The assessment is slow and considered.

'But you won't be there?' Jakob holds the snack in his fist and Howard drools patiently.

'No, but there'll be yummy lunches for you every day.'

'Where will the Harry Potter lunch box be?' His legs stop swinging.

'How about Howard guards it for you?'

Jakob's eyes swivel to look at me for the first time. He opens his palm and Howard stretches his head in to delicately remove the biscuit and lick away the crumbs.

'I think Howard might lick all the pictures off my lunch box if he keeps it.'

'You're probably right. Tell you what, I'll drop it off to your teacher, and my email address will be under the lid.'

'I can't write properly.'

'Well not yet maybe, but you draw pictures, and Mrs Kay can email them.'

11

The sound of wheels on gravel and car doors slamming indicates everyone has arrived for the traditional Wednesday meal and it's nearly time to go. I take my suitcase out of the hallway cupboard.

Orson stops feeding Oreos into his mouth. 'Whose is that?'

'It's mine.' I concentrate unnecessarily hard on the handle.

'Wh-where are you going?' Gus looks up and runs a hand back and forth over his lips.

'France. Don't worry, sweetie.' I drop a kiss on his sawdusty head.

'But, Mum ... How come we didn't know?'

'Your mother, despite a long history of being horribly reliable, is capable of spontaneity.'

'I know you're worried about Aunt Pascale ...' Gus takes my wrist in his big paw and sits forward on the chair.

The front door rattles open and then slams shut. I know what that means: Simon, he's back from University, or wherever it is he's been. Howard doesn't get up. My back feels stiff.

Simon's eyes swivel between me and my suitcase in disbelief. 'Audrey!'

I have to say I enjoy his shock. 'I've called an Uber.'

'Mum, one of us can take you.' Thea's forehead furrows in plump little ridges, which will soon relax back, leaving no trace.

'Thank you, but no.' I hold up a hand. 'Let's leave it, please.'

Orson is stunned; I can tell he thinks I'm being rash. I briefly luxuriate in their spluttering objections. Until I realise they're rationalising my decision amongst themselves. I am apparently too old for a midlife crisis, so it can't be that. And menopause must be long gone, surely? Evidently my choice is baffling, and at no point does anyone ask me how I came to my decision, or why, or when. I'm grateful in some ways and note Simon doesn't offer any theories. He just flicks his eyes towards me occasionally, opening and shutting his mouth like a malfunctioning elevator door.

When everyone notices I haven't made a meal, the shock deepens. I could probably have cooked something, but that action would have come from a more generous time. Someone speaks to me, and I can hear my platitudes – everything's fine, I'm looking forward to seeing Tata – but they feel glacial, gnarled and alien on the inside.

The app says the car is close. I take my suitcase outside, look at the garden, think about my plans to change it. Foolish. What will happen out here while I'm away? What if I never come back?

The verandah lights cast black and yellow pools around the house. A few wet drops from another shower plop slowly from racing clouds. Should I remind Simon to wait for a couple of dry days before he cleans up the leaves? Ridiculous. He won't bother. The tipuana's elliptical leaves will float for a while then sink and crumble between the cracks.

The children burst out onto the verandah. Simon lurks behind in the hallway. Thea looks between her father's face and mine.

'What's going on here?'

The skein of my marriage has unspooled, but it's Simon's story so it's for him to reveal. It's cold. A ridiculous part of me wants my husband to tell me not to go. *Stay, Audrey. I'm sorry, we'll work it out together.* I wait in a vacuum, look towards the kids who are twitchy, then back over to my husband. The Uber swings in, stops and the boot pops open. Simon steps out onto the drive.

'Well, must be off. You'll need to make a start on dinner, Simon.' I give him a look, which he should understand, but he doesn't catch on and just glowers. I jerk my head slightly towards our progeny and drop my voice into a low hiss so they can't hear me. 'You need to tell them.'

He flicks the shortest of smiles then gives a curt nod. 'I'll sort it, yes.' But Simon's eyebrows nip into one straight line and there's a tremor along them. He's one wrong comment away from snapping.

Thea breaks the mood with a brainwave to set up a WhatsApp group so we can all share news while I'm away. She decides to call it Mumsgoneawol, which Gus and Orson think is *great* – forced enthusiasm. As she adds our names to the group, I place my hand over her typing fingers.

'Leave Dad off the list, please darling.'

'It's a family group chat, Mum,' she says, head down.

'I know, darling. And you know I'll love to hear all your news. Send me lots of photos, won't you?'

'So, Dad should be in here too.' She shrugs away my hand, fingers flying over the mobile phone.

'Sweetie.' I know that came out short. 'Please listen to me. Please. Do me this favour.' I fuss with the buttons on my coat. 'I'm serious.'

A drizzle wets the back of my neck as the Uber driver puts my suitcase in the boot. The children's shoulders hunch against the rain. I open the passenger door and kiss them all on their lovely cheeks.

Mr Uber checks which terminal we're going to. I thank him, the indicators flash into a deep puddle and we pull out into the rain. There's nothing but a sopping wet autumn evening beyond the windows. A downpour distorts the reds and blues of passing cars so they appear to be collapsing into the tarmac and the world is an ambiguous sludge.

The driver's spine is lithe, his head swivels right and left to check the traffic. For a few streets the silence is acceptable and then it yawns wide, filling the Hyundai.

'Have you been driving a cab for long?' My body tightens at the predictability of my question. 'I'm sorry, you must get asked that a lot. You don't look like this is *you* full time.'

'It isn't. I'm a musician.'

He leans forward in his seat and tells me about experimental music, how he's going to *expand and transcend the subgenre of surf rock*. Mr Uber navigates the wet journey all the while his mouth a geyser of *shattered chords* and *notes which hang like pearls*. *Oh*, I say, and *Gosh*, try to visualise the *synoptic reverb of drowsy distant guitars*. I don't want to stop the gallop of his speech. Our conversation condenses on the inside of the windows.

'There's a piece I'm working on, "Hope Dies Last". It offers a needed refuge from turmoil and anxiety.'

'Right.' Not convinced that's the most optimistic title.

The windscreen wipers metronome.

'This is my terminal thank you.'

Snapped out of his reverie he slows and pulls into the airport's drop-off zone. Headlights on other cars flare off the now driving rain.

'Would you like to hear something I composed?' he asks as I gather my handbag.

'Please.'

He plucks his phone down from its dashboard stand, and flicks through the screen. 'This is called "Priority Mail".'

There's a new tone in his voice – pride – and it drags my emotions closer to the surface. We sit in the Elantra and listen together, the rain drowned out by his music. There's something deeply satisfying about being bathed in someone's passion, and for a few moments after the song is finished the car is silent.

'Thank you.'

Pleasure cracks his voice. 'And you. What do you do?'

His look implies he means it, and for the first time today I feel seen. Seen in a way which doesn't make me uncomfortable but is warm and interested.

But then, this role I appear to have adopted, perhaps for years now, trips me up. Despite it not being his intent, his question pokes at all the self-doubts I've stored away for far too long. I can't stop what's become an automatic response.

'Oh nothing,' I hear myself say. 'I haven't got a creative bone in my body.'

I turn away, get out of the car, retrieve my suitcase, and bend to thank him again.

His neck cranes up. 'I bet it's not true.'

He drives away, fingers strumming the steering wheel.

12

Twenty-seven hours later the Charles de Gaulle airport railway station emerges at the base of many escalators. It is like being deep inside a rectangular pie dish; shiny walled and soulless. The decor is left for travellers to provide. Everyone is on the move, surging around the concourse in eddies.

From Perth to Singapore, I was bereft. From Singapore to Paris, I raged internally, drank steadily and slept fitfully. Now the alcohol has done cruel things. On a positive note, thank you suitcases on wheels and molten station coffee. My clever little phone has already switched over to French time. How long will it take my body to catch up? I find a chair directly in front of the departures board with twenty minutes to spare until my train to Brittany leaves.

The double pulse of a Mumsgoneawol WhatsApp call starts; it makes me smile and I press the blue dot. Briefly my face dominates the screen and then they appear, and our four heads make a chequerboard.

'Hey, Mum, where are you?' Orson tilts his head as though to see over my shoulder.

'Charles de Gaulle, at the *gare*.' I spin my phone around so they can see the crowds.

'You all right, Mum?'

'Fine, Thea. Tired, of course.'

Gus pulls a shocked face and holds it. 'You never let us say "fine", and I doubt you are. Dad's a dickhead.'

'Darling.' I let the word drag out, soft and cautionary.

Thea leans in close to her camera. 'No, he is. Your Uber hadn't even left the driveway when he jumps straight in and says, "I'll order pizza." Orson said, "I don't want to eat, I want to know what's going on." Then Dad says, "Well, suit yourself, I'm ordering," and he goes indoors. He had the body language he has when something is not up for discussion.' Thea sits up straight, furrows her brow, and presses her lips into a hard line. 'It was like we were seven again.'

Gus leans into his screen. 'I wanted pizza.'

He knows this will amuse me and it does. 'You think better with a full belly.'

'The man's a tool.'

'Orson, that's harsh.' Thea protests.

'It's true, Thea.' He looks at me. 'He tried to tell us you were having a difficult time and needed a break.' Orson is deep in a kitchen chair in his apartment.

'Orson was, actually, amazing,' Thea says. 'He eyeballed Dad and asked, slowly, calmly, "And what have you done to cause this?"' Thea claps her hands rapidly in front of her chin. 'Then Dad started to say something about you being stressed and Orson said we'd talk to you about how you felt, but what was his version.'

'So weird watching him squirm.' Gus shakes his head.

Orson cuts in. 'He was not squirming, the man has no compunction.'

'I think he was. He's not used to us being united.'

It's cute listening to my little ones all grown up. Little ones – hardly, they could all start having their own kids soon. That's a difficult reality, because try as I might I still think of them as my babies, which of course they're not. So, it's not cute, it's awful. They're conflicted – wondering if they should take sides or remain impartial. All this emotional clutter brought on by the foolishness of their parents.

'Mum.'

'Yes, honey.'

Thea nibbles at the corner of her thumb. 'You know Dad is thinking about starting a relationship with someone else?'

'I do know.'

Thinking about starting, that's an interesting way of putting it. Thinking of removing me from a picture which has been going on for three years, would be more to the point.

Gus leans forward, his face softened by confusion and wanting. 'He said you'd jumped the gun and gone to find this woman and then reacted irrationally because nothing is certain at all?'

Oh, that this were true, and I could ease this moment for them. But a fitful anger burns and it's hard not to scream *Jumped the gun*. The station tannoy continues announcing trains departing, trains arriving, as does the jostle of people with their bags.

'I love this group you've set up, thank you. I guess it must seem like I have gone AWOL. There is one thing I want to say before I head for my train. Two things, actually. I didn't set out to find Midori, it was an unpleasant coincidence. And Dad is still your dad. His relationship with you as a father is totally different from my relationship with him as a husband. He will be feeling bad – as your dad.' I stand and pull the handle of my suitcase up. 'Gotta go.' I turn the phone so they can see the departure board lit up with train details. 'Love you. Speak soon.'

'Love you, Mum.' Three voices plait themselves into one. I pull my earbuds out and head to my platform.

———

The train slides between massive retail outlets and the new brick, suburban outskirts of Saint Malo. Other passengers begin to shrug their jackets on, stand, hoick bags from overhead racks. The world outside slows: older brick houses, small shops, pedestrians, the station. And then the shriek of metal on metal and no movement at all.

Have I made a poor decision, walking away from Simon like this? The clatter of suitcase wheels chasing me along the pitted platform sounds like a refrain, *Audrey, you forgot to futureproof yourself.*

Outside the station, the sun is thin, the sky a watery blue and the moist air smells of ozone. Seagulls the size of chickens shriek from the steep town roofs, and a voice rises from my left.

'Audrey?'

Surprised to hear my name, I turn towards the voice. Approaching across the courtyard is a writhing froth of orange. It becomes apparent the roiling movement is a complex dress. Multi-layered skirts catch around, and between, the wearer's legs. But she strides on, batting away at the cloud of foam to ease her progress. And then the woman comes to a halt. Her ponytail continues to swing as the dress slowly subsides.

She thrusts out a hand. 'Lilou.'

I don't know why, but I'd assumed my aunt's neighbour would be less colourful, slower. Lilou is not as old as I pictured either, perhaps late twenties, maybe thirty?

'Oh goodness, I did not expect you.'

'I thought, given I had your travel details, I'd pick you up. Such a long journey. Shall we?'

She grabs my bag and strides off. The dress starts up again. I follow at a distance to avoid being caught in its layers.

'I'm so pleased you decided to come, Pascale will be delighted. Naturally she doesn't know anything about you being here.' Lilou slows her stride to put her finger up to her lips and wink at me. 'A very good secret.' She turns, drowning my case in a wave of orange organza. 'The *boulangère* says there's no evidence of a heart attack, nor stroke, which is good news. He also said she was discharged from hospital yesterday, or perhaps she'll be discharged tomorrow. It depends. She has a broken ankle you see, so can't go upstairs, and must stay with a friend.'

Interesting, the baker knows so much. Lilou pops the boot of her car and swings my twenty-two-kilogram suitcase in as though it were a box of tissues.

'But, can you believe it, the worst of her injuries is a broken ankle. Incredible. Lots of bruises, of course, the *boulangère* said.' She slams the boot closed and takes a deep breath. 'It is also unbelievably kind of you to come and help your aunt. Amazing.'

For the next twenty-five minutes we hurtle amongst surreal greens, pale tender fields, deep hedges, and under bold canopies of early summer trees. We do slow, occasionally, to pass through small, grey stone villages, or if something about Lilou's monologue requires her to remember a detail. In the last village I listen hard for a gap in Lilou's soliloquy to interject, before she slews violently under a tiny arch and pulls up at a Carrefour supermarket.

'You read my mind,' I say.

'I was going to buy a few things for you, but I don't have a clue about Australians. Perhaps you only eat marsupials, and drink lager and eucalyptus tea?'

I open the door. 'Is there anything I can pick up for you?'

Lilou turns in her seat to look me in the eye. One layer of her dress escapes to cover the gearstick.

'Oh, look at you all jetlagged and worried about your aunt, and yet you still have time to think about me. Are you adorable, or what?'

'Or what probably.'

The supermarket may have a lino floor and metal gondolas now, but I remember coming here with my mother and Tata when I was about eight. We'd walk in to the distinct, high-pitched smell of blue cheeses, and the base notes of fresh meat. The floorboards were wooden, oiled, and long benches sagged under baskets of artichokes, potatoes, apples. At one end there was a pile of metal, hexagonal weights, and big, brass scales which clanged and clunked.

My mother and Tata always gravitated to the back of the shop to chat with the butcher. Did a carrot have a role in cassoulet? Which flour was best for *crêpes paysannes*? Other women abandoned their shopping to join in, and the shop bulged with opinions.

This afternoon as I saunter around the two aisles, I can almost feel Laurence's little hand in mine as we waited for the debating to stop and I taught him how to count using tins of haricots from a shelf. I remember doing the same with my own children. I also remember that Lilou is waiting for me in the car and speed up.

But it's hard not to dawdle over the blissful price of goats' cheese, the variety of *lardons*, the butter: oh, the butter. These and other things with nostalgic value go into a basket. At the last second, I remember the obligatory kitchen paper towel every respectable French woman has and stroke the Sopalin four-pack, feeling at home.

By the time Lilou stops in the small potholed lane outside my aunt's cottage, I'm so rejuvenated I imagine I'll push open the gate and Tata won't have fallen out of a tree, she'll be there, wearing those boxy, utilitarian clothes which chop her body into unflattering sections.

Lilou insists on bringing my suitcase and plops it down inside the hayloft doorway.

'Well, I'm going to leave you in peace. I live in the house with blue shutters. If you want anything at all, walk in and help yourself, it's never locked. I'll see you tomorrow for the exercise. I'm going to Paris at the weekend, my partner, Pierre, lives there.' She drops her shoulders and lets out a dramatic exhalation. '*Mon dieu*, another lungful of smog, but I must catch up with friends, and I have a lot of meetings.'

'Exercise?'

Lilou laughs. 'You're so funny – we talked about it, after the supermarket. You said you thought it was a good idea. It is a good idea. See you tomorrow.'

I have no memory of any such conversation but, then again, she did say many, many things.

'Lilou, thank you for, you know, ringing and collecting me. Thank you.'

An awkward silence follows. Lilou steps towards me and rubs her hand up and down my upper arm. I'm surprised by her touch. I pat her hand defensively and press my lips together.

She takes a half-step back. 'Jet lag is *merde*.'

And with that she strides away like an exploded bottle of Fanta. For a few seconds there's the sound of her car driving down the lane, a door slams, and then everything is silent.

It strikes me I've lost my sense of ease with people. How long have I been dull and guarded?

I look around. What to do now?

13

My aunt used to live in the cottage, but these days it's reserved for holiday makers, visiting friends. She lives in the converted hayloft; or she did until her fall. Stretching between the two, grey stone dwellings is a terrace where the cherry tree grows, pushing through overhead wooden beams. Beyond this, the sprawling garden.

Tata's lawn is more of an orchard, dotted with ancient fruit trees, apple, pear, mirabelle and plum. Behind them the old stable, Tata's *remise*; what we'd call a shed. This is home for her work bench, tools, wood, bicycle, boxes and boxes filled with many things of uncertain origin. And the other side of the *remise* is the field, so overgrown it is hard to discern where the nettles end and the vegetable beds begin. Even the chickens look like a SWAT team on manoeuvres as they battle their way through the green chaos.

I head back to the terrace and the cherry tree to view the scene of Tata's rapid descent. The flagstones are irregular, ancient, and stained with her blood. The tree looks benign. If the *boulangère's* information is right, and she didn't have an episode of some sort up there, perhaps the only reason she fell is she shouldn't have been up there. And she shouldn't, not at her age. A shudder threads down my spine and I press both palms, hard, into the slabs as though I can somehow take away any pain she may have felt. If Tata were to walk in now, she'd scoff at the maudlin sight of me on my knees.

'Tata would clean, Audrey. Yes, she would. And while you're in France, you should give up talking out loud to yourself; the children might be used to you, but these neighbours are not.'

I fill a metal bucket with warm soapy water and drop a wooden brush amongst the bubbles. It sinks and lists for a moment then floats to the top and bobs. I can't bring myself to wash the blood away.

In the hayloft's tiny downstairs area, I rummage amongst the shopping for coffee and put the kettle on. I've arrived from a house where we have spare bedrooms, Persian rugs, a larder, laundry, vestibule. We own martini glasses, upstairs and downstairs cordless vacuums, and the hayloft is smaller than our triple garage. It is all so rudimentary. There are two and a half rooms, the walls are white, and the windows are double glazed, full stop.

The kettle screams. I fill the AeroPress, open the cream and enjoy the weight of the carton in my hand. All the milk at home is complicated: half-fat, skimmed, A2, almond, everyone has a preference. I use whatever is about to go out of date. My entire story is suddenly thrown into relief by dairy products. I'm not an equal in my marriage, I'm the keeper of other people's wants. No, I'm the pale wall which beautifully sets off the picture of Simon and his lover. Good god. I take a kitchen chair outside and place it carefully next to Tata's bloodstain. It's bizarrely comforting, and the coffee is perfection. The sun is the colour of margarine and I raise my mug to it. When the mug is empty, the habit of justifying my existence kicks in.

What should I do?

I'm not on a timetable. I should relax.

I don't win this battle.

Up the hayloft's spiral staircase, which is not anchored as soundly as I might have hoped, the bedroom emerges as a triangle under heavy beams where only half the floor space is accessible without stooping. The furniture up here is a bed, a bedside-table-chair, one rod suspended between two beams for the wardrobe and baskets for *other*. Electricity for the bedside lamp is provided via an extension lead that straggles up from a downstairs socket.

Making multiple trips I strip the bed, damp dust, and unpack my clothes. The only item of Tata's up here is a navy-blue cotton drill jacket on a coat hanger. She must have found it in a Chairman Mao second-hand shop, but the blue is beautiful. I don't know who moved the rest of her clothes. Nor do I know where she is. Tomorrow will reveal all this information.

Downstairs, Tata's washing machine behaves like a crazed jazz musician and sashays across the floor with the sheets on a spin cycle. On the deep windowsill an incredibly healthy chilli plant is going berserk. Its soil is damp, which tells me someone has been watering. The ancient fridge freezer has magnificent, large, seventies handles. Someone has emptied out all of Tata's perishables and there's only a jar of mustard and a small bicycle tyre repair kit in there. The socket sparks alarmingly when I plug it in. However, it splutters and burbles into life, so fingers crossed. And then my addled brain spots some cat food on a shelf which reminds me, Haricot should be somewhere.

'*Bonjour.*'

I swing around to see a short man at the doorway. '*Bonjour.*' He's familiar and my head clunks through the years to place him.

'Pascal,' he offers the prompt.

'Audrey.'

'Yes, I know, we've met many times.' His craggy face remains impassive.

Of course. The kids and I used to call him No-E because his is the male form of my aunt's name, and we thought it was funny.

'How are you, Pascal?'

'I am worried, naturally.' He brings his second foot up onto the threshold but moves no further.

'Naturally.' He would prefer my aunt to be in the kitchen.

'Will you feed the chickens tomorrow?'

'I will. Thanks, you've been—'

'I've eaten all the eggs.'

'Good.' He's really serious.

No-E turns a precise forty-five degrees and then turns back again.

'There will be more eggs tomorrow.' This time he completes his manoeuvre. 'I will tell your aunt you're here.'

'Where is she—'

Too late, he's gone. My French is good, so that's not what scared him off. I stare at the empty doorway to dig up images of No-E from previous visits. He was in Tata's garden a lot, and they often chatted away, but I don't think I ever had a real conversation with him. He was always kind to the kids. One morning we found he'd strung a swing from the oak tree. Another day he left them a discarded bird's nest to study. The children loved these mystery gifts, but when they tried to thank him, he'd simply shrug and say, *C'est normal*, it's normal. Our family mimicked his nonchalance for years.

Thanks for putting your clothes in the basket, Gus.

C'est normal.

Thanks for breakfast, Mum.

C'est normal.

I should get on with my list of things to do. The washbag is the last thing I put away in the bathroom. This is the back metre of the kitchen, separated off by a wood-panel wall and a sliding door. A long skinny window runs high under the eaves where a swallow has built her muddy nest. A central drainage hole in the floor tiles means cleaning with the shower hose will be easy.

'Audrey, you're not here to focus on domestic conveniences.'

I put my toothbrush out on a little side shelf.

'Right. This distilled world feels nice, secure, and if I can get over the feeling of being filled with wet sand, it could be full of potential. And you're doing it again: answering yourself, out loud.'

My smartwatch buzzes. 'Where's my phone?'

It takes a while to find it out on the terrace and, with glasses on, I see the message alert is an email from Simon. Knees buckling, I sit down heavily on a step. This is it. Already. I push the phone hard into my thigh and feel a booming under my ribs. A robin lands on the bird table. This could go one of two ways. The marriage is over. Or he's sorry and wants me back home. My fingers stick on the screen. I notice the bucket of water I was planning to clean the bloodstained tiles with is cold now, and the brush languishes towards the bottom. I don't want to open the email, but I do.

> Audrey,
> I'm at a loss for words. I didn't have you down as a vindictive person, but I'm flabbergasted. Please explain. Where is the lawn?
> Simon

I jerk upright, pulled by a much higher force.

'That's it? What about, *Are you all right?* No, of course not – you want your turf back.'

Pacing, I reply.

Simon,
Join Facebook. Sign up to the 'Buy Nothing' group in our area. Contact Tailor Swift (who may be back on tour, check out her dates), and arrange to be reunited with your buffalo grass.
    Audrey

I make myself stand still, press send, and then kick the bucket with all I've got.

14

A low rumble emanates from the basket I've placed my knickers in. Then I realise my aunt's cat sleeps in there. Haricot stands, stretches dramatically, and leaps onto the foot of the bed. He absently cleans a paw with his pale pink tongue and needles me with violet eyes – the original cat scan. I'm grateful for his company. We've been a dog family, so I don't know much about felines, but I suspect he's driven by the same ulterior motives as Howard: he wants to be fed.

I stroke his silky head. 'Soon. I'll feed you and the chickens, make coffee, message the children.' The things tethering me to the earth.

Looking up through the Velux window I see an uncertain sky, so I snuggle back into the soft sheets, which drape in luxuriant folds wherever I move over the mattress. *I*, being the operative word. Simon doesn't have a side here. Oh, and the pillows are perfection; each one cradles my head like a midwife.

Outside there's the sound of crunching gravel, and then it stops. I lie still. No more noise. But I've gone blind in one eye. Through my left eye is the bedside-table-chair, and on it a solitary hair grip. In the tiny metal arch is a dry flake of dead skin. Then more useful information seeps in. The cat is perched on the highest point in the bed, which is my left shoulder, and therefore my right eye is simply buried in a marshmallow pillow.

'Jesus, I was worried for a minute.' I turn to lie on my back.

'*Coucou, cherie*. Audrey, are you up there? Is Simon with you?' Tata's distinctive voice pierces through the filigree of the spiral staircase.

'Tata, yes, I'm here. One minute. No, I'm alone. Hang on. Gosh.'

Pulling clothes on, I fly downstairs to see my lovely aunt.

She is not as I remember. A bent, battered version stands in her place.

'If I'd wanted help, I'd have told you about my little mishap,' she says. 'Ridiculous spending all that money on flights, what are you doing here?' Tata attempts to straighten a little.

'Well, hello, Tata, it's lovely to see you too. I'm here to help, obviously.'

'Who were you talking to?'

'Myself, thought I'd gone blind.'

'Your mother used to talk to herself all the time, you know. It drove me mad, drove your father to distraction. He never knew whether he was supposed to reply or not.'

'I reply to me. In fact, some of the longest conversations I've had are with me, and the radio.'

Tata heaves herself further into the kitchen and slumps down onto one of the kitchen chairs. There's a moon boot on one leg and her arms are covered in Fixomull dressings. Worst of all, the right side of her face is black, and a row of stitches up near her hairline is raw, clotted.

She lets me study her for a minute and then lifts a hand. 'Do not, under any circumstances, ask me how I am. Instead tell me, how are you?'

I fill the kettle, light the stove.

'We're all well, but then again none of us has recently base-jumped out of a fruit tree.'

Tata roams her eyes over me. 'Your family might be well, but you … I'm sorry, dear girl, only your skin appears to hold you together.' Tata's bony fingers wrap around my wrist. 'Sit down.'

I obey, with a beautifully composed and cheery grin. My aunt has strong opinions about the human condition, which I love her for, and have no doubt she'd be very helpful to my situation. However, this is not the time to snivel.

'Audrey?'

'I'm fine, just jet lag, and I misplaced my reading glasses last night about seven o'clock. There's a ton of gardening to be done, I see, and some rat activity around the chicken food. I'm busy, busy. It's great being here.'

Haricot trots down the stairs and sneers at the biscuits in his bowl. I could go through the if-you're-hungry-you'll-eat-them routine, but the cat probably has more stamina than me.

'Ignore the cat. The scene here is,' she waves a bony hand around my face, 'dishevelled cat lady.'

'Tata, can't we talk about you? What do you need immediately, and long term? And where are you staying, and what happened, exactly?'

'I'm staying somewhere without stairs.'

She leans back and glowers. I suspect this is another battle I'm not going to win. Our silent stalemate is broken by the cat mewling around Tata's ankles.

'Audrey, I've done nothing but tell people how I am, how I'm feeling, how the pain is, for days and days. I don't want to talk about it anymore, not today. Come along, tell me what's going on, and I don't want a property update.'

Haricot lets me stroke him, although affection is not what he wants.

'I'm embarrassed to admit, Tata, but I've ignored a few things over the years. The result is my life has become adrift with banalities. If I'd spent my child-rearing years painting, studying, learning the piano, *anything* – I might have become quite good. But it's as though other people were leading my life during those years. Here I am, my children are off doing their thing, and I'm not about to win any prizes for anything. So, if you ask me what's my most tricky conundrum, my answer is – does a nest of tables trump one coffee table?'

'Of course it does, very space efficient.'

She shifts uncomfortably on the chair, looks at her watch.

'If you were a client, sitting in my *notaire's* office, and I was trying to get the truth out of you, I would say you've concocted a reductive version of what's really going on. But you're not a client, you're my niece, and you'll tell me in your own good time.'

Tata heaves herself up and spends some moments aligning her spine. 'Coffee next time. I have physio in town now, and I just dropped in because I heard you were here, and to tell you I was cross. But I've changed my mind. I'm pleased to see you. Now help me.'

Tata takes my arm to negotiate the step. Outside, on the gravel, is a large red, electric mobility scooter. She backs up to the seat and lets me lift her legs onto the footplate, then she tucks her walking cane under a buttock, and turns the ignition.

'The *garagiste* got this beast for me, on trial. I'm not sure. They're only ever up for sale when the owner has died. Plus, it's already bogged itself in the gravel. Give me a push, *s'il te plaît.*'

After a great deal of shunting and flying stones, Tata makes it back out onto the lane. She pulls out sunglasses from the front wicker basket, and gingerly puts them over her bruised nose.

'Audrey.' She beckons for me to come closer, puts a wounded

hand on my cheek. '*Cherie,* some might say it's putting the cart before the horse to think about winning a significant prize when you haven't prepared for it. But fantasy is probably more palatable than some of the facts in your life. This I understand.'

Tata turns the vehicle so she's facing across the lane, then she stops again.

'I've read you should visualise what you want, and it will manifest. Jury's out on that one, but I suppose it's harmless.'

She continues to complete her formula-one, three-point turn with no regard for the hydrangeas lining the lane.

'I assume you've got a French sim card, text me your number. You look a mess.'

'As do you.'

Her black and blue, grazed and gored face softens for the first time. 'There's my girl.'

There are many things wrong with the vision of Tata bouncing along the lane on her red scooter. It's the first time I've seen her wear a skirt, which now blooms above the wheels as she gets up speed. And the way her blouse flopped over razor-sharp bones, caught in the deep crevasses of her collarbones – so much weight loss. I cannot believe it's all since the fall.

To compound these anomalies, it is most un-Tata to mention manifestation. Her mantra has always been, *Better to state how things are rather than how they should be.* Has she become sentimental? Did the fall do a great deal of damage?

Haricot wants food – now – and walks his front legs up my shins, spine arced. Then he leans deeper into his stretch and curls his claws into the flesh above my knees.

'Ow, Haricot.'

I shake my leg to get him off, which releases a random niggle – did Lilou and I make a plan, or was it a vague idea left open?

'So, cat, if I were to manifest a future where I get my act together and become famous, Graham Norton might interview me. He'd open with, *Audrey, you first came to the public's attention as an influencer.* Or perhaps, *Audrey, is it true the same day you discovered Simon was a wanker, you discovered you could sing like an angel and won* The Voice? I'll blush. Jason Momoa and Javier Bardem – both on the same program, on the same couch – will beam, charmed by my modesty.'

I roll my tracksuit pant legs up, a few dots of blood ooze where Haricot's claws punctured the skin. I stare into his violet eyes. He stares back.

'I will admit my mind has a certain ability when it comes to fanciful tangents. So, if you stop attacking me, I'll stop daydreaming – after all it's a delay tactic and, regrettably, I can't run away from myself.'

I squeeze the sardine sachet into his bowl and mix it with the biscuits. 'There.'

His needs, at least, have been met.

15

About to go out and start on my aunt's garden, I hear the gate squeak and Lilou bounds across the gravel looking like a seal. Neck to ankle, she's clad in a skin-tight grey fabric that slides around her body so snugly I doubt there is any peripheral circulation. Her hair is drawn up into a savage bun. Any strands which may have contemplated escaping won't, because they're clamped under a rubberised, sequined band.

She scans me dubiously. 'Are you ready?'

I glance down at my pink t-shirt and black tracksuit pants and think perhaps I'm not.

'I'm not sure I agreed to come with you.'

'We had an in-depth conversation in the car, you can't back out now. Exercise is a miracle cure for fatigue, and it'll loosen up all those cabin-stiff joints. There's a lot of evidence to support this.'

'I don't disagree, but no study or study of studies is ever perfect. And what happens if I'm not built for group classes? I may be more of a solitary-confinement type of girl?'

The drive into Dinan is as manic as the drive from the railway station. Many of the country lanes are single-car narrow, and the grassy banks higher than the wing mirrors. It is like being in a luge team. But we survive. Lilou parks, which is a euphemism for stopping the car wherever it takes her fancy.

The building is a renovated hodgepodge of stone and brick, nestled up against a break in the old city wall. Looking out from the rampart, ancient buildings line a steep, cobbled street, which twists its way down the hill. At the bottom is the old port, encrusted with tiny pedestrians, and seesawing pleasure boats. The middle of the river pops with shards of erratic sunlight as it flows under a humped-back bridge, towards Tata's village, and then the sea. I feel encouraged.

Inside there's a little café, and a noticeboard offers salsa, charity meetings, wool spinning, yoga, children's tuition. I'm further reassured as we come alongside a dimly lit room with large plate-glass windows overlooking the river. The people who arrived early lie on their backs in two semi-circles. A herby fragrance oozes out of the room, and schmaltzy music is audible in the way fungi chat with tree roots.

'Come on.' Lilou strides past that sanctuary and descends a flight of stairs. At the bottom is THE WELLNESS ROOM. This is written in bold letters on a sandwich board, which is placed across the corridor so we can go no further. The board promises the earth, including a trim, taut bum, and to prove the point is a photo of the fittest woman in the world.

Lilou undoes her bun and releases a ponytail which drops heavily and swishes below her shoulders. 'This woman is incredible. She's an ex-Parisian like me. She was in the armed forces, and she knows about fitness.'

Lilou pulls two little towels out of her bag, hands me one and pushes open the door. The odour clinging to the damp basement walls is something else. It's the smell that results from when too many people have sweated in here for decades.

Lilou squeezes my arm. 'Go at your own pace, Audrey. Ready?'

'Not at all.'

Lilou weaves to the front of the room and I find a spot towards the back.

———

Forty minutes later, I'm fading. The cycling and swimming I do several times a week are no preparation for this. The trainer is a sort of Joan of Arc on methamphetamine, and I wish she'd stayed in Paris. *Go at your own pace*, Lilou said. *Huh.* On Joan's watch no one is allowed to stop moving unless a doctor pronounces you dead.

We complete a particularly unpleasant circuit using weights and trampolines and I would prefer to die than endure another minute.

Joan's voice comes at us from a group of speakers hung high against the old basement ceiling. She bellows, 'You can take a thirty-second rest.' There's a silence while she wipes the hint of sweat from her chest. 'On your back, lift those legs, cross your ankles and swing them over your head.'

That is not my definition of rest. I'm beginning to be irritated by Joan, but I also refuse to give into this crazed dictator. I scan the room, claw back a little hope from the other bright red faces which are rigid with terror.

'Hup, hup, hup. Hook station,' Joan shrieks in a pitch that implies everyone must be thrilled.

I heave myself off the ground and lean on my knees for a moment. Lilou arrives at my side, looking relaxed. Now that I can study her more closely, I see how long lean cyclists' thighs merge into perfect knees then slender calves. Her shoulders are sharp, and the clearly defined muscles in her arms swoop around their bones like an infinity curve.

Joan prowls through the room handing out pads and gloves, shooing everyone into pairs.

Lilou winks at me. 'I'll be your partner.'

She nods for me to put the gloves on and straps a red vinyl pad to one of her wrought-iron forearms. I cannot think of a time when I've wanted to hit someone, and the urge isn't coming now.

With no regard for local noise abatement legislation, Methamphetamine Joan instructs everyone at one hundred and twenty decibels. 'Swing the dominant hand out to one side, and then bring it across your body and punch your partner's pad.'

That's the theory. I recall Hilary Swank in *Million Dollar Baby*, I'll never be coordinated like that. Plus, the mirrors taunt me with a realistic image of unruly hair, apple cheeks and an oversized pink t-shirt.

By contrast Lilou is yet to break a sweat. She shifts her weight between left and right foot, and her ponytail swishes menacingly. I suspect it will take a front-end loader to bring her down.

A combination of fatigue, delirium and pride leads me to swing out, but I go far too wide, gaining more momentum than is necessary. My right fist skims the red pad and keeps moving. My arm hooks all the way round, and back into my cheek. For a second, everything stops.

Lilou leaps forward. '*Mon dieu*, you okay?'

Then the shock lifts and I realise I've punched myself in the face. Startled, I remove the gloves to gingerly walk my fingers over the side of my face, wonder if the orbital arch of my eye might be broken. Probably not. Then I look around the room and start to laugh.

'You know what? Yes. But, um, maybe … let's swap.'

By comparison, Lilou's aim is true. Her gaze does not flinch from the square red target, and I wonder who she imagines it to be. Who has upset this woman, what on earth has she set out to purge? I do not let on that my wrist is being disassembled with every one of her accurate blows.

During those very painful minutes, Joan must have snuck out the back and topped up her drug levels because she's now screaming, 'Die, you bastards. Die!'

Or perhaps that's just the effect of her words, and I'm too tired to translate properly. Then Joan tells us she wants us to pick up tractor tyres and hula-hoop with them. I don't think she said that either. I wasn't really listening because this wellness class is killing me.

The stairs feel much steeper going up. Someone poured lead in both of my legs. My arms are several inches longer than they used to be. And coordinating various body parts, which I've had for a long time, is difficult. I buy a coffee and find a table to one side of the café. A tinkle of achievement starts up inside me, but that could be pins and needles from neurological damage, or an abnormal euphoria brought on by concussion.

The café owner brings ice over and indicates for me to put it on my cheek.

To think I've been worried about my sixtieth birthday. Sixty. Six-oh. A number that shouted at me back in Australia. It loomed tall and wide in my head and blocked access to potentially remarkable thoughts. Sixty refused to sit down quietly with its hands folded, it had no composure. But now it can shut up. Now, thanks to lessons learnt in that Abattoir of Hope at the bottom of the stairs, where I felt certain I would die, I will be honoured to turn sixty.

Lilou comes over to sit with me. 'Audrey, I'm so sorry. Let me see your face.'

I lift the ice away for a moment and both her hands shoot up to her mouth. '*Oula*. Your eye is going to be very colourful. What can I do? I have some excellent concealer.'

'Honestly, it's fine, just a flesh wound. The only thing I need is to never do that class again. But you're right, I've forgotten about jet lag.'

16

Lilou drops me off by her house and, crossing the lane, I see the diminutive No-E's back disappear into the hayloft kitchen. Before I've had time to shut the squeaking gate, he's out again.

'*Bonjour*, Audrey, you weren't here. I have the radio.' He holds it high above his head.

'Of course.'

'If you want it back, you'll be doing me a favour. I'll only listen to a program about my team – foot. They are very bad. But I am a fool. I listen to the program week after week, hopeful of a miracle. When they're relegated – grief. When they climb to the top – this is a temporary bliss. Now it is the off season, and I am worried about what will happen in August. I am a rational man, and this is irrational. Foot makes my hair go grey.'

I think it's age and genetics, but I say, 'Take the radio, Pascal.'

'Oh, I wish you wanted it.'

No-E's hangdog jowls droop further as he turns and shuffles off, the radio a terrible weight in his hand. He mutters all the way across the lawn, up the step, and into Tata's *remise*.

Both my legs are filled with jellied eels and the spiral staircase is sixteen steps too far. I really want to snooze, but a short siesta could so easily slip into a protracted coma.

'Do I care? I will tonight when I'm wide awake. Prune the holly hedge, the willow, do something. Check your emails, Audrey.'

The hayloft walls are a metre deep so I curl up on the windowsill in a puddle of sun and open the computer.

Mrs Lamont,
Mrs Kay is writing this.
I will write the next letter.
Guess what the picture is before you look.
Jakob at Primary School

Bless him. I let the mouse hover over the attachment. I think it will be an aeroplane. But the image is of a person with wild hair and a large coat or tunic. The feet are oversized, the hands last-minute additions, and there's a bubble coming out of a shouting mouth with the words *Helo i m franz*.

Jakob,
Thank you for the interesting drawing.
Does Franz live in France? France is a country, like
Australia, but smaller.
I will look out for him.
Please thank Mrs Kay for being our special post office.
Mrs Lamont

The second email is from my GP asking me to make an appointment. The silly thing is I gave them my email address when I told them I'd be away and unable to make an appointment. I reply, reiterating I'm in Brittany. They reply almost immediately saying they'll happily send the results to a French GP. Fighting an impressive battle with the desire to sleep, I google a local GP, explain my situation to them, and they agree to see me. I'm sure I can hear the pillows whispering my name as I set the alarm for thirty minutes. A little nap won't hurt. But the phone rings and it is the French GP.

'Madame Lamont are you able to go and have a blood test? It's something we do with all our new patients. The nurses' office is open until six o'clock. If you can go this afternoon, I will send them a form immediately.'

Immediately – right then. I head off along a back road to the bureau located behind the church. Two inquisitive goats perched on top of a garage cock their heads. A tractor purrs along the edge of a field cleaning ditches. Butterflies flick and skim over verge grasses. The images come piecemeal. It may only be a fifteen-minute walk, but on weak legs, with no sleep, the remnants of an aeroplane hangover and facial bruising, it feels like trudging the Kokoda track.

The receptionist has not got my form and asks me to please take a seat in the waiting room.

I read the make of the water cooler, the security sign on the double-glazed window, fiddle with my cuticles. I take note of two women's handbags. One is minute, red and glossy, the other is more function over fashion. I know someone who'd be interested in them; I should probably make a Zoom appointment with Sister Naomi.

They still do not have my form.

A young man wearing far too much aftershave, one child, one baby and two elderly people come into the waiting room and have their blood taken while I sit here. Everyone, except the baby, gives me a sympathetic, knowing glance. Eventually I realise their sympathy is not about my wait, but because my cheek and eye are developing quite the bruise.

I wonder if No-E is listening to the radio, driving himself mad with the ups and downs, little wins (one–nil), unfortunate losses (two–one). And afterwards the dissection of the game – if so-and-so had passed earlier, if that player hadn't been subbed. Indeed, if Simon hadn't written the book, would the outcomes be different? Football, like life, is a low-scoring game.

I shouldn't be passive and wait for Simon to come to his senses. I need to be ready. The book is done, the dust will settle, and he'll realise it was a fleeting, regrettable fling. I'll set parameters, for the first time. No more liaising with Midori. No more burying himself in a book for a couple of years. We'll take a long trip together and start to repair the damage. I can see a way past all this. It seems that, despite this crushing fatigue, Lilou's exercise class has me thinking very clearly.

'Madame Lamont, I have your form.'

The nurse blocks my way. She holds my chin in her hand and turns my face first this way, then that.

'Excuse me, but I must ask, what happened to your eye socket?'

'Exercise class, self-inflicted.' I mimic the action from this morning.

Head tilted; she drums her fingers on her chin. She thinks I'm lying.

'It was an accident, in an exercise class.' I realise I'm Hilary Swanking from foot to foot and stop.

The nurse keeps her eyes on me as she ticks off paperwork, collects an assortment of tubes and prepares her tray before cutting off the blood supply between my hand and my shoulder with an instrument of torture.

Tapping my veins with her fingers she says, 'Little scratch.'

Like hell. More like, *Hold still, I'm just going to impale you on a spear.* But I will not flinch. Nursey definitely thinks I lied.

The dark red disappears into little purple, green and yellow tubes. She grumbles about not being able to open the window;

and her gel shoe inserts are uncomfortable. I am not prepared to antagonise a woman who's put a twelve-foot needle in my arm so I let her vent about her ventilation and feet and coo every now and then in a way I hope will be soothing. She releases the tourniquet. Blood returns to my fingers, and we're done.

Walking home I hammer Mumsgoneawol with texts. *If you're hungry there's lots of pasta sauce in the freezer. I think I forgot to give Howard his flea tablet, would you check please? Wondering if your car registration is due, Orson?* I send a photo of the bridge, which they'll remember from our holidays. Gus sends me a picture of the surf. Thea asks if she can have my gravy recipe because she's doing a roast for book club lunch. I hope I've got something more illuminating to pass on than recipes and vehicle service schedules. I hope I've said some smart, memorable stuff over the years, shared wisdom with my children, which they'll quote back to their children.

I'm so awash with maternal hormones, I wonder about changing my ticket and going back home. I could find a cleaner to help Tata with the guests. But I know I should wait for Simon to say the affair is a non-starter. After that admission, and when he's finished grieving the lawn, he'll really start to miss me.

'I should be loved.'

'*Oui, bonjour.*' A woman walking two Irish wolfhounds waves enthusiastically.

I don't know what she thinks I said, but I wave back and point to the blue sky.

Rounding the hedge, I see Tata's electric beast parked in the drive, but no one is around. Someone, however, has opened the gate to the field and the chickens are soft-shoe shuffling in the cottage garden. My watch says it's five thirty, a perfectly respectable time to go to bed. But I should shut the chickens in their coop first.

'Shoo, shoo.' I flap my arms and make fatuous scooping gestures with my hands.

'*Coucou, cherie*. What do you think you're doing?' Tata hobbles forward at the cottage doorway. 'Calisthenics? *Mais non*, you don't have the free-flowing movement of ribbon so, *euh* ... I know, you are demonstrating the interpersonal relationship between woman and chicken.' She chuckles at her own wry wit, descends gingerly from the step.

'Chickens plural; they're all out.'

'Forget the chickens, the cock will put them to bed. What's this about you needing a blood test?'

I wonder if her speech isn't a little slurred, or perhaps the bruising to her face is more painful than she admits.

'The jungle drums are effective.' I walk with Tata over to the terrace and help her ease onto a chair. 'Is there anywhere which doesn't hurt, where I might kiss you?'

'Left elbow, right earlobe.' Tata squeezes my hand and gives the cherry tree a disdainful glance.

'Tell me, Tata, did you have a heart attack up there, is that why you fell?'

'*Non*. And why do you keep sitting me down, I'm not crippled.'

'Gravel and uneven slabs are not your friends right now. And, you're not being very candid about your accident, so I think caution is reasonable. I don't even know where you're staying. I'm guessing—'

Tata lifts a bony hand and looks around the terrace. 'Laurence emailed. Have you come here to leave Simon permanently?'

I feel that question in my belly and have to take a moment. 'Permanently has not been on my radar. He's been working closely with a woman, but now that's over so ... perhaps things are redeemable.'

Tata lays a bruised hand on my arm. 'Has he apologised?'

'Nope, no grand apology; no tiny one either. It's early days.'

We watch a pigeon crash-land on the bird table and skid through the seed, which sprays onto the gravel below.

'I put the radio back. No-E gets so worked up about his foot.' Tata picks at a loose corner of a dressing. 'Audrey, I'd like to tell you something and then perhaps tomorrow we can talk about it.'

'Not sure how much I'm going to take in, Tata. I feel as though I have a mild concussion, all my joints have been prised open with a kitchen knife, and somebody has crushed me under several tons of gravel.'

'Not too bad then.' She grins and waves for me to sit down.

'I used to spend a lot of time in Australia, when my sister was alive, and I remember the day you found out you were pregnant with Orson. It changed something fundamental in you. I never had children so I expect this is a gross understatement. But I watched you through all your pregnancies. It was like you were being forced to live slowly, inside yourself, and at the same time it seemed you had a spectacularly large view to consider. There was no room for anything else in your world – you were pregnant, that's what you were doing.

'One by one, the babies came home, and you put most of your energy into them. They expanded your world. You supported Simon and grew your babies.

'Equally I observed Simon. His life didn't change so much with the arrival of children, or so it seemed. I don't think he understood the commotion. He confided in me one day. I have an excellent memory, and I'm certain I can relate what he said accurately. He said, *She tortures me with her endless theories and about-turns. I know it's hormones, but it's like she's been colonised, and if I'm to survive I'm going to have to recede.* Orson was three, Gus two, Thea maybe one.

'If you decide to persist with him, you might need to go back to the time before children. There was a mutuality in those years. Since the children, it's been Simon for Simon and you for everyone.'

Go back. Those words chafe horribly. No one, ever, in the history of man has been able to go back in time. Except ayahuasca users, or in films. I haven't been distilling strange leaves and this isn't a film. *Go back* seems such a waste having got this far surely … I don't know. I feel delirious.

17

Tata insists we set off early to a particular field near the lock keeper's cottage, where she says they never use chemicals. She also says it's where they put François, the village horse, when his pasture is low. Tata doesn't want François beheading her precious dandelions, nor does she want the yellow heads to explode into seed. The field is a loud green, heavily populated with jolly yellow suns, and my aunt's contented expression says she's timed our foray perfectly.

Thankfully Tata agrees to stay on her scooter and bounces over the rough terrain, imparting her extensive knowledge in the art of beheading dandelions. Only when we've filled five Carrefour bags, and my spine is bent like a pretzel, does she say we can stop.

She peers at the little clock on the buggy's handlebars. 'Seven o'clock, very good. We've beaten the crowds.' Then she winks, nods towards an approaching car, and accelerates away through the damp grass.

The vehicle slows, crawls along one side of the field, and then stops. The *crowd* is two miffed matriarchs who decant themselves awkwardly and scowl at our haul.

'Is it their field, Tata?'

'It's nobody's field. Trust me, more people will be along soon and tomorrow the dandelions will all be gone. I watch the plants, see when they're ready, and harvest early; the Benoist sisters know it too. They beat me, once, fifteen years ago, and this year, because of my fall, they would have expected to win again.'

In the kitchen Tata demonstrates how to remove anything green from the yellow heads, then pushes the tiny nail scissors across the table to me. Haricot hops onto her lap.

'Every bit of green, Audrey, or the jelly will be bitter.'

The process is exacting, absorbing. 'What if I start a *confiture* enterprise? We could give samples of homemade produce to the guests, who'll then want to buy jars of the stuff, at London prices.'

'Only one lot come from London – every year, unfortunately. And you're already a domestic goddess. It's time to spread your wings.'

'I could put up rails on the bird table to stop the pigeons stealing all the seed. I could make a proper bedside table.'

Tata's bottom lip pokes out as she considers these ideas. 'If you fail at fine furniture making, you may need other options. It doesn't have to be a practical skill.'

'Horseriding has always appealed, or journalism, floristry. Tap dancing – there's something I've never considered and now I can. I could make noises with my feet as I cook and clean. Imagine me at parties.'

'Do you go to parties?'

'Not often, rarely, not if I can help it. But that is even better because I'd be dancing for me, and it wouldn't matter a fig if I wasn't any good. Perfectionism is the voice of the oppressor.'

'Good girl. Perfect is unreal and boring. Word of warning, Audrey: it's all very well taking up or giving up something – it's remembering to keep up the taking or giving up that's the difficult part.'

'Pascale, Audrey, *bonjour.*'

No-E is at the hayloft doorway holding a large TV, which is much wider than him.

'*Bonjour,* Pascal.' I get up and walk towards him. 'I must ask, why are you holding that enormous thing?'

'Your aunt told me to take this out of the cottage,' he says to me, giving Tata a look. 'She says if the guests use their phones or computers to watch rubbish, that's their choice.'

Tata leans forward, disturbing the cat, and waves a hand towards No-E. 'For god's sake put it in the wheelbarrow before you break something.'

No-E's bullet black eyes are just visible over the top of the box. 'Your aunt also made me get rid of mine.'

I look between the two of them, then squeeze past No-E to bring the wheelbarrow across to him.

He deposits the TV onto the tray and heaves the barrow handles up. 'She says it's not good to sit on oversized sofas and let our bodies get bigger.' Leaning into the task, he and the TV move across the gravel, then out the back gate into the lane.

There is absolutely nothing big about No-E, except his nose. You could call him gaunt.

'Do you think he has a sofa, Tata?' Somehow, I can't imagine wiry, functional No-E having such a squishy item of furniture. I return to boiling dandelion heads.

'He does. Add the juice of three lemons now.'

'I don't think he's warmed to me; his visits are like ram raids. Does he even do warm? He must have once, if he has a sofa he probably shared it with someone.'

Apart from Howard, I certainly don't want to share an overstuffed piece of furniture with anyone. A few days ago I didn't want Simon in the same suburb. Simon. His name has reminded me.

'Some friends – or rather, some people Simon and I have socialised with for years – are in Saint Malo. They've invited me to join them for lunch. I'm not sure whether to go. I think the only reason I might want to is—'

'Because you might hear some useful gossip about your husband.'

'Perhaps. But that is a bad reason to go. And what if they start prying?'

'I'm having my dressings changed tomorrow morning. Lilou is taking me, so why don't you get a lift with us and have lunch with your friends. You love Saint Malo.' Tata leans her head on the back of the chair.

I decant clear, lava-hot liquid into small glass jars. Because I've spoken his name *that* niggle starts again – the Japanese painting, my diaries. Did I have suspicions all along about Simon's loyalty, yet chose to overlook the signs? My journals are full of his extended conferences and research trips, which I never questioned. Perhaps I should have risked feeling neurotic and asked him why he had to stay longer. But *what-if* is an impossibly thin, fragile line to tread. Although it appears I should have been more inquisitive during the writing of his latest book.

The next time I look across, the cat and my aunt are both asleep. Tata's chin has dropped onto her chest and her mouth gapes open, little strangled gurgles escaping between grazed lips. Haricot, by comparison, is comfortably strewn, and rumbles with satisfaction.

18

As we cross the causeway, the impressive walls of Saint Malo are less ominous than the meal I'm due to attend. The Brittany ferry honks its departure. Lilou stops the car within the prescribed white lines near the water's edge, and we all get out. Herring gull cries pierce the air, and the low hush of groaning boat fenders rolls up from the moorings. Tata puts her hand in the crook of my elbow. Lilou untangles her impossibly big trouser flares and says she's going to nip ahead to buy papers.

'Audrey.' Tata pulls on my arm. 'These friends, who you've known for many years, are on holiday, and they want to see you. It's natural. I'm sure they won't be gauche enough to mention anything about your husband. They'll be far more interested in telling you about themselves, the cheeses they've discovered, the wine.'

Lilou leaves the *tabac* in a flurry of billowing sleeves, the papers swaddled in fabric. 'What are you two talking about?'

'Audrey's lunch with her friends.' Tata pats my hand.

Lilou swirls in next to my aunt and takes her arm. 'We're all going to be late.'

The cobblestones create a challenge for Tata in her moon boot, and their departure is slow. I wish I was the one taking my aunt to get her dressings off.

I contemplate climbing up onto the walls and going right around the little city. But hundreds of tourists have already claimed that route, so I stick to the narrow streets below. The Maison du Beurre window is full of pale pats of butter, a basket of speckled quails' eggs, and wooden artefacts from the store's ancient origins.

Inside the blue and white tiled *poissonnerie* plump-eyed fish look up from beds of ice. Oysters lurk in thin wooden punnets. The floor, the surfaces – everything is damp and salty. A fishmonger deftly fillets a pink-skinned beauty and I wonder how many times she's done that. I wonder if she's married to the man who shucks oysters at her side. Am I watching the narrowness of unvaried routines in a long-married couple? Is what I see as skilful, poetic movements experienced by them as the crush of daily details? To shop or work here may be aesthetically pleasing, but at the end of the day, work is work, grocery shopping is grocery shopping.

I circle past Charly's Bar, which is, strictly speaking, off my route but the temptation to sit under the red awning and drink coffee by myself beckons. It won't do. I speed up and make it to the Place Chateaubriand on time.

And there they are.

A waiter in a long black apron stands alongside Susie as she waves her arms and issues instructions. 'Angle the parasol this way, not that way, no – like this.'

All the while her husband, James, drags chairs around, their metal legs shrieking over the stone ground.

'Audrey, Audrey, Audrey, Audrey!' Susie flaps an arm for me to come across. Then her voice goes up an octave as she nips at the waiter's implacable heels: 'Water now, and *du pain.*'

His face says nothing.

There are five empty chairs which means more people than I expected. My heart doesn't know whether to be relieved or to simply stop beating.

'Audrey.' Susie clutches my arm and shoos her husband with her free hand. 'James, do go and see if you can find the others. Audrey, James is going to find Pamela, David and Jeffrey – you know, history faculty. Bit of a late addition, I'm afraid. We were supposed to catch up with them next week in Paris, but.' With this statement she tightens her grip and levers me into the seat next to her. 'We're so sorry about you and Simon. Did it come as a shock? How are the children? I suppose they're not children anymore so it won't upset them too much, will it?'

I ignore her, feign adjusting my chair. James returns from the direction of the hotel, head bobbing as he circles back and forth to herd his flock of three.

'Ah, Pamela, David, Jeffrey, you remember Simon's wife, don't you? Audrey. Audrey and I were just saying we're not going to talk about Simon.' Susie leers at me with a horrible wink and whispers wet and low, 'We'll have our own little tête-à-tête after lunch, all right, dear?' Then she waves for the others to sit.

'Hello, Audrey.' Pamela squeezes my shoulder a bit too long, transmitting her deepest condolences through the palm of her podgy hand.

The men dip their heads – Team Simon – undoubtedly relieved that the subject of their friend's marriage has been closed.

Susie's face turns from red to puce as she waits for them all to sit, adjust clothing, shift chairs, remove jackets. Then James says something, and her colour deepens further until she explodes.

'I think we'll all simply agree that Simon and Audrey are facing a sticky situation. There, the subject is closed. I'll tell you something funny instead. Audrey and I never manage to catch up outside those dreadful uni things. However, we did run into each other a few weeks ago when we had our colonoscopies on the same day. How about that?'

Everyone but Susie looks down at their laminated menus, and I follow suit. I had hoped to hear something soothing like, *Midori isn't a patch on you, Audrey,* or *Midori has gone back to her university on the other side of the world.* I'd hoped Susie would tell me that the last time she saw Simon he looked shocking. But it appears any news of Simon will remain sequestered behind closed doors. I suspect my invitation to this lunch is so she can find out what I know, or don't know. I believe this is called a stalemate.

James is the first to look up. 'I think I'll have the sole meunière.'

Susie's jaw is clenched, the sinews in her neck taut. She wrings the poor unsuspecting linen napkin on her lap.

Jeffrey lifts his head and stares into the middle distance.

Pamela is the one to rescue the silence. 'David, if you have the beef, I'll have the pork and we can share?'

David protests about having such a heavy lunch and Jeffrey then reads the entire menu out.

A sadness, like a snake, slides neatly into my belly.

Susie lets go her murderous grip and smooths the cloth across her knees. 'I must say one thing, Audrey, you've lost weight. It looks good on you. Don't you agree, Pamela? Don't you think Audrey is looking lovely? That's—'

'Did you know,' Jeffrey's baritone cuts in neatly, 'when Chateaubriand sailed to America, he had the crew tie him to the mast. Extraordinary to—'

I don't listen to the rest of his thundering rumble, but I'm grateful to him for saving everyone from whatever it was Susie was about to say. His motive is almost certainly loyalty to Simon, and I know I should have fended Susie off myself.

It's my turn to squeeze Susie's arm and whisper in her ear. 'Excuse me, one moment.'

'Toilet's that way, through the bar. Shall we order an aperitif for you?' She waves at the waiter. 'Six kir royales, *s'il vous plaît.*'

As I weave between the tables, she starts up again. I can hear her words prod into my unhealed wounds. Then her voice eventually fades, and the conversations of other diners replace her piercing tone, but I feel weakened.

The bar is all dark wood, plush chairs and low-slung boat detritus. In one corner, wiping glasses in the gloom, a shadowy French waiter nods towards my destination. The bathroom is as white as an operating theatre and smells of cinnamon. And here I stay in the full force of one million lumens. I wash my hands, twice, while one woman, then another, leave their cubicles. When a third woman enters my sanctuary, I change it up and peer into the mirror as though something were buried deep under an eyelid. This is ridiculous.

Leaving my reflection, and the bathroom, it appears my body understands my needs better than me. As if by magic I push through swing doors and enter a bustling kitchen. The staff do not look perturbed. We smile and nod as I wander through. Someone slides past with two plates. There's the clang of pots and aromatic steam rises from a bank of ovens. I weave past fridges, boxes of vegetables and leave the hotel by a small back door. In the narrow alley, I cling tenuously to efforts not to cry. I look at my watch. There's an hour and a half before I'm due to meet Tata and Lilou back at the car.

The only thing I want is to talk with my children about what they're up to. But the times between us are wrong. I could walk along the beach to Paramé, if it wasn't for the sand yachts.

They zip about with poky little sails which tells me the tide is going out.

Exhausted, I head down to the main beach and sit on a rock to watch seagulls launch themselves off the medieval walls above. Their flight is caught in shadows as they swoop on long wings, and I can see what Richard Bach was on about. If I were a gull? I'd probably haunt the harbour, steal chips, peck at dropped ice-cream cones, and poo on people's cars. Perhaps I'd eat a poisoned clam and participate, more fully than planned, in the food cycle. I'd fall out of the sky and die in the oily slick of a ship. The sea would suck all my flesh off and a few feathers would tangle in mooring ropes. That'd be it. But then, if reincarnation is a thing, I might evolve into a spiritually enlightened possum. Simon? He'd be reborn as something glossy with a pedigree. Our differences are hard to reconcile.

The tide gallops out, umbrellas at the Bar du Soleil flap, and people stroll.

What will I tell my aunt about lunch? I was childish. What will Simon's colleagues think when it becomes apparent I'm not returning for the aperitif nor the meal?

I take a deep, salt-filled breath and relax. I can't control what the lunching professors will say, but I'll tell Lilou and Tata that lunch was fine. I won't spit it out through gritted teeth – the way fine is so often said. I'll say, 'Lunch was fine,' and walk away, stiff backed, to keep further questions at bay.

Tata knows that fine is a complicated word. She will read my tone, the context, take them into account and understand.

19

After a very bumpy, sleep-deprived first week, where I set alarms, counted steps, ate three times a day, and related everything back to Simon – this cheese is his favourite; that man's wearing a blue shirt, Simon has a blue shirt – I finally stopped. Not entirely sure why but no one around me was behaving so anally, and my actions were causing friction in the hedge rows.

The second week I watched plants triple in size and weeds multiply. Where one afternoon there had been a stinging nettle, the next morning its entire family, even cousins and second cousins, had appeared.

Now I get up when the sky changes colour through the Velux window, or the cat sits on my chest. If the lawn is not too damp – I mow it, weaving between the fruit trees like a drunken linesman. If it drizzles, I make jam, prepare the cottage for the guests, spy on pigeons.

Tata may appear once, three times or no times a day. I've given up asking, where are you staying, are the doctors happy with your progress, do you feel much better? Lilou is either here or not. No-E is ever the conundrum.

In other village news, and in no particular order: on Wednesdays, François the horse pulls a cart with a tank on the back and two council workers water the communal flowerpots. Sundays, François takes tourists in the same cart down to the renovated mill. Thursdays, I walk the towpath into Dinan for their market. Saturdays, a stall is set up in front of the *Marie*, selling crepes and oysters – who can resist.

All in all, the garden birds are happier with the way I'm living and nest undisturbed now the manic Australian has stopped scuttling over gravel.

Letting day upon day accumulate between Simon and me is rejuvenating. And sometimes I giggle at my newfound luxury, reading a book in the middle of the afternoon because I feel like it. Indeed, I begin to feel quite in control of the future.

AUDREY'S HOROSCOPE
by Audrey

If you recall what you were doing last June, your life for the foreseeable future is nothing like that. Simon finds his mind and body are ravaged by syphilis, and he is carted off campus by security.

Take pride in your bold and winning combination of cherry and rose-petal jam. Initial reservations are quashed when reviews from Madame Potdevin, your neighbour-but-one, come in.

Lucky savoury nibble: Radish and sea salt.

Monthly tip: Don't waste anymore sriracha on Lilou.

Favourite birdsong: Blackbird.

I've also stopped checking my inbox every few hours to see if *he's* written. Occasionally there are lovely long epistles from the children who've extended their communication beyond the text. Laurence is taking some of his cars to a film shoot and sends progress photos of their trip: a Nullarbor roadhouse, Tim eating ice cream in a motel, the Sydney Opera House. And of course, there are Jakob's notes.

Last week I thought his art was a meticulously drawn picket fence. He corrected me: *mi claz on a scurshun*. Having interpreted children for years, I realised my mistake. Mrs Kay organised a school outing; the pickets were his classmates. Today's drawing looks like boats becalmed either side of a mountain.

> Jakob,
> Did you draw this great picture after your excursion?
> Perhaps one day you can draw my chickens. I'll attach a photo so you can see them.
> Mrs Lamont

I brace myself to read the other epistle that has whooshed in. I imagine Susie is livid. To abandon lunch is unspeakable but not to apologise later; yes, this is going to be one helluva reprimand.

> Audrey,
> I'm going to remind you of how we met. James and I were both lecturing, none of us had kids then, but Simon volunteered you to look after my brother's children once a week. My brother was the chancellor if you recall, and Simon undoubtedly thought it would help his own trajectory.
> On the first day, determined to impress everyone, you blew the door off their microwave attempting to cook boiled eggs. What a mess – remember? You were in such a tizz.
> My brother and his wife said it didn't matter because they needed to redecorate. The kitchen had, until that point, been painted Tuscan Hush. A colour which may have looked

good on the little sample card from Bunnings, but when plastered all over the kitchen walls – even before the addition of egg – was more like Tuscan-permanently-hushed-by-exsanguination. It was high time they got rid of the horrible colour, but you insisted on doing the work as penance.

My brother didn't want to shatter your confidence further, and agreed, apprehensively.

The point is, your project of contrition revealed that lurking within the newlywed, domestic ingenue was a genius. You had such a way with colour and intuitively understood the way light changes tones in shadows. You approached the kitchen window walls and alcoves with an intelligent delicacy; frames and trims with the finesse of someone applying eyeliner.

My brother and his wife have never redecorated, not in all these years.

I remind you of this now, Audrey, because I think you need a little bolstering. I certainly did when James had his affair with a student. Rotten on so many levels.

I had hoped to talk with you about this in St Malo.

Not to be.

But you can always email if it would help.

And bravo for leaving us like that.

Susie

Well, well, well. How nice that I was so wrong about her. She didn't want to dangle my misery like raw meat, then feast on it. I close my emails feeling light as a feather.

I had completely forgotten about the exploding eggs, and I have done an awful lot of decorating since then, our whole house over the years, and Laurence's various homes. Decorating as a career option? It holds no appeal – good to know.

Therefore, this will be a good time to start tap dancing. As Tata said, it's been easy to forget that I said I'd take it up.

'Audrey, you must come, now.' No-E stands at the hayloft doorway.

I jerk up from the table. 'Has something happened to Tata?'

'*Non.* Here, take this, we must go.' He thrusts a small bag into my hand and marches off.

I follow obediently, peer in the bag for clues. There's a small bottle of liquid, an old tin, a box of matches, my gardening gloves, and various other items. In the lane, No-E graciously opens the door to a small white van, I get in, and then follows some of the most appalling driving I've ever endured. He bounces over kerbs, goes over rather than around the roundabouts, and uses whichever side of the road takes his fancy, all in first gear. I'm preposterously grateful when No-E pulls into the council recycling yard.

The *déchetterie* is busy with cars and vans being unloaded of green waste, wine bottles, old batteries, dead furniture, metal sheets. Each bin is carefully labelled, and no one cheats.

'Come, come.' No-E scuttles towards a mountain of tree branches. 'When I was young, I ran over a hedgehog with my bicycle. *Traumatisme.* I cannot touch them.'

He instructs me to put on my gloves, lifts a few now-crispy pine needle fronds, and there indeed is a hedgehog. The poor little thing puts up no resistance as I examine him, and his whole body is covered in glossy, black ticks. No-E produces an old oil drum for me to sit on, and like a surgical nurse he hands over assorted tick removers.

'Couldn't we do this back at the cottage, Pascal?'

'*Oula, non*, this is his home. His family will be in there somewhere.' He flings his arms towards the expanse of rotting vegetation.

I have negotiated school headlice plagues, twice, in the privacy of a bathroom; open-air tick removal and all the interest it generates is something else. Other *déchetterie* users peer and grunt, offer technical advice about the twist or the flick as the approved wrist action. No-E watches on. And, as instructed, I drop each tick into the tin which is now filled with the unknown liquid.

'I think they're all out.' I check the hedgehog once more.

No-E informs the little crowd, 'Fifty-two, no wonder he was weak.' Then he lifts pine branches to make a nest. Next, he produces a sachet of Haricot's cat food and squeezes out little piles for the patient, and a bystander lights the liquid in the tin.

As I finish installing the hedgehog amongst the branches, the ticks start to explode behind me like popcorn. The sound is so vulgar I want to run away, hands up to my ears.

'You monitor the fire, Pascal, I'll walk home.'

Back at the cottage with a creamy coffee, recovering from the *traumatisme* of being Nurse Exploding Tick Dolittle, I recall my original plan for today: learn tap dancing.

—

In the *remise*, under a bench is an enormous box which once housed a washing machine. I remove the staples and spread it out in one big sheet over the compacted earth floor. Then I open my laptop and scroll through YouTube tap-dancing tutorials.

Haricot enters the *remise* at speed. His soft coat moves like a wheat field in whorls of air. And then he leaves again – a dog is much easier to read.

'The Shim Sham Shimmy' appeals. It starts with the Shim Sham and we add the Shimmy later, apparently.

Stamp, brush, step. Step, brush, ball change.

The YouTube man expects me to clap in there.

Start on the eight.

Why?

Five, six, seven, eight.

I forgot to start. Step, no stamp. I'm going to have to rewind. The glittering landscape of my imagination is more tarnished than I'd realised. Is there really any point trying to acquire a talent?

Stamp, brush, step. Stamp, brush, step.

Do not give up. Remember how you nurtured the kids to do piano practice until they were sixteen, sitting with them day after day, listening to the same pieces being played by three people again and again over many years?

'Persist Audrey. This is the time to discover a genius. Dance will liberate your mind–body coordination. You will come alive.'

Dot the toe. Hop. Step back.

When did he introduce the *dot*? I slide the YouTube red line back to the start of the tutorial, back to the jaunty dance hall music.

Hop out, slide in, and end with a clap.

Sneakers do not slide.

Heel, step, step. And now we're positioned for our break.

The tap-dance *break* is a misnomer, not a break at all. The *break* is a bunch of different steps like a chorus. I stop for a proper break. The tutor moves on to the 'Tack Annie'. I watch his feet. Then my eyes wander beyond him, through windows, which could do with a clean. Out beyond the smears is the field, filled with the cheek of summer. Raspberry canes bulge with growth, weeds have started to creep up my aunt's huge pile of rocks, the compost bins are an eyesore. Peony heads loll on robust stalks and the madness of a rose clambers the entire length of one fence. I should be in the garden.

On the screen the instructor has put all his steps together and looks smug. I mute his tip-tapping. Even then he looks so utterly in control of his faculties, I shut the lid, fold the cardboard, and slide it back under the bench.

He's given me an idea though. I can break my situation down into elementary steps.

Who's the enemy?

There's more than one enemy: Simon, Midori and my mediocrity.

The battle? I gave him thirty-seven years of my life, and it appears he didn't want them.

Sub-clause: twenty-nine of those years were mothering, and I don't regret one, which brings it down to eight years.

Summation: I am at war with three adversaries, and I am going to need a freedom song, with themes of well-earned victory laps.

And when will be the right time to debut this opus? Ah, that is a tricky question. When I'm back home? When Simon apologises? When Midori explodes like a tick and leaves my world alone? Here's hoping I know when I've triumphed.

The phone buzzes with a Mumsgoneawol call – my twenty-nine good years on the phone. I jog across the gravel, to the bench on the terrace, where I sit and watch their lovely faces.

Thea's in the passenger seat of what looks like Gus's car. He's reversing, and through the windows are the distinct Moreton Bay fig trees of the university grounds. She swirls the phone around to reveal Orson in the back seat. He raises a hand and clicks his seatbelt in.

'What a gorgeous surprise. You all going somewhere?'

Orson leans over. 'Just had breakfast with Dad.'

'Nice.'

Thea positions the phone high in front of her face. 'Mum, Dad says you moved everything.'

'Darling, don't start your day worrying.'

'Mum, listen, he says you packed up your diaries, photo albums, clothes, and took them to Laurence's. He says you have no plan to move back home.'

My head falls back heavily. I open my eyes and stare into the cherry tree, then bring my head back slowly.

'I did move a lot of things … I have not made a decision about my future. At the time I simply reacted.'

'I get that.' Gus turns to grin into the phone.

Thea positions herself again. 'Dad says you won't talk to him.'

'It's not true, honey. I told your dad I'd like him to contact me when he is ready to tell me the whole story. He has some gaps to fill in and he's also got decisions to make.'

'He says when a party moves out of the family home in such a final way it sends a strong personal statement, and legally it weakens your position.'

I'm just a tenant who outstayed her lease. The cords around my throat pull tight yet I keep the strangulation from shattering my composure. That's motherhood for you, the great teacher of keeping silent about what I feel or might know. Motherhood and the art of pretence – I am an exemplary student, with my wistful smile spread across bleached lips, keeping up appearances.

I drag a hand through my hair. 'Honey, all I can say is I'm so sorry you're worried, and I understand why. I was, and I am, upset your dad is interested in another person. However, it happens, I'm not naïve. I understand people change their minds; everything changes all the time. But I do need your father to tell me the truth about what's gone on.'

'What do you mean?' Orson takes the phone from his sister.

'I meant what's going on.'

'I don't think you did, Mum. How long has it been going on?'

'I don't know for sure. I do know it's his story, and he should be the one to tell it. Anything I say will be speculation.'

Orson sits back, chews his bottom lip. 'Do you really want the gory details?'

Gory details. A great question. Is the truth gory? But I feel paralysed, snared in my 'marriage', and I think I need to hear Simon say, 'I don't love you.' But, given he has brought up the legal implications of separation, it seems I can wait as long as I like to hear the truth, he's already moved forward.

'I know you're not children anymore and I'm truly sorry, but there's nothing I can say to soothe you. For the time being I'm fine and in the best place for me.'

It's true, I couldn't face being a spectator on the sidelines as my marriage accelerates into disaster. Simon will undoubtedly fill in some details later. I expect he'll say, *You walked away and that means you get nothing, Audrey. And I get everything else because it was my career, and my money. Oh, you can have the dog, and your novels.*

'If you were here, maybe you'd be able to influence Dad to come to his senses?' Gus wobbles his head as if to weigh up his own suggestion.

Thea twists the phone. 'I think Mum's right, she's better off away from here while Dad sorts things out.'

Orson leans in. 'While Dad shoots himself in the foot, you mean. You have a good time, Mum – chill, drink wine and don't worry about us.'

'And don't any of you worry about me. Gus, concentrate on the road. The traffic looks bad.'

The city's concrete and glass buildings are in the background as their car snaggles in an early morning traffic jam.

'I'll jump out here, Gus,' Thea says. 'Bye, Mum.' She waves into the camera.

'Thanks for calling.'

That victory march I was planning just turned into *Music for Violin Alone*. I sit on the terrace flagstones and let the naked simplicity of sadness creep into my lungs. How could staying with my brother for a breather be the death knell to reconciliation? What happens if I never sleep in my home again? All I want to do is pull my legs and head in like a turtle and hide.

20

The gate squeaks. This is followed by the sound of Lilou's distinctive stride. Oh goodness, not now.

Today she wears a harlequin catsuit with matching headscarf. Her pale skin is almost translucent, and there's no softness around her wide mouth. Can I ask her to come back when I feel more resilient? No. I heave myself up and walk across to the kitchen.

Lilou leans against the doorframe. 'Do you wish ...?' The words trail off.

Wish I could curl up in bed and howl? Yes, I do. 'Wish what?'

Lilou rolls her head. 'Audrey, would you think badly of me if I had an emotional vomit?'

I shake my head. It'll be good to focus on something other than the sound of legal doors being slammed shut in Australia. 'Go ahead.' I haul myself over to the kettle, bang out old coffee grounds into the compost bin, and hold the pot up as a question.

She smiles and nods. 'Please.' Then she unloads. 'Before the pandemic I ran my advertising agency from Paris, but once we were all locked in, I looked at the city and saw it was hideous. So now I work from here and go to Paris maybe once a month.'

'Good for you. And your lovely Pierre, does he like it this way?'

I haven't met Lilou's fiancé, partner, boyfriend – I'm not sure of their status – but he sounds like such a solid, lovely man.

'Pierre understands completely, but he works as a paramedic and there is more work for him in Paris. But Pierre is what I want to discuss and why I feel exhausted.'

Lilou scans my face. Dark grey hoops underscore her eyes, and while I'm also exhausted, I can't tell a high-octane advertising executive that a two-stroke housewife understands. I put two mugs on a tray, alongside a jug of cream, and rattle the cutlery draw for a spoon.

'When his body stirs with early morning ardour …'

I did not expect to hear about Pierre's erection. I know his 'early morning ardour' is only a reflex to being alive at that hour, or a full bladder. But I don't say any of this because her face suggests she hasn't finished.

'In Paris, yesterday morning, I woke up next to Pierre and looked down into his still unconscious face. But his penis was awake, nudging my thigh. I felt disappointment, Audrey. A part of me was saying – *Oh no, not again.*' She turns to lean on the other door post. 'I didn't want to feel his erection, I didn't want to see his face. I wished there was a new body lying next to me.'

I hope I didn't flinch. 'Gosh, tricky.'

'In the past, if he brought me a coffee, or the papers …' her voice tapers away. 'A long time ago that might have worked, but feeling cherished is not enough now. Nothing seduces me anymore.'

We take our coffees outside to the table.

'These days,' she continues, 'I don't like to walk around the flat naked. When I finish a shower, I get dressed like a high-speed ninja.'

'Why? Because naked means sex?'

'Yes, and I can't be affectionate either because a kiss means sex.'

'Beige curtains mean sex to men, my darling girl.' I can't believe I just said that, but it is true.

'You're right, everything means sex to Pierre, and I can't remember the last time I felt any desire.'

I understand. Perhaps I can discuss this with Sister Naomi when I get back. She'd not cringe at the thought of old people having sex: saggy breasts, balls swinging in loose, hairy sacks. She'd read my handbag choice and understand that, while I haven't been excited for years, it doesn't mean I don't miss good sex.

I splash cream into the black liquid. A pale swirl writhes until it envelops the coffee completely and the alchemy is forever altered.

'You miss yearning for him, a drowning-in-love mood, which will only be satisfied by orgasm.'

Lilou looks stunned. I should have kept that for Sister Naomi.

'Yes, thirty years old and I've lost my mojo. Of course, we've been having sex, but I haven't *wanted* it. But with a permanently erect partner, what can I do? What happens if I never feel aroused again?'

I can't help wondering about Simon, and whether he ever came to bed thinking about Midori. Were the times I read his passion for us really anger I wasn't someone else?

Lilou cocks her head. 'Have I upset you with talk of erections?'

'Not at all.'

She pokes a leaf into the table cracks. 'We're supposed to be getting married. But how can I marry someone I don't want to have sex with? And that's not all. If Pierre had his way, we'd drink beer out of plastic cups and get married at a Paris Saint-Germain football match.'

'If football makes you happy then ...'

'It doesn't. Audrey, what do you think?'

'Dear me, I don't know if you want to get married or not, Lilou, but I am not the person to consult. What you need is a marriage native, if there is such a person. Someone who finds marriage and weddings simple, easy, stages in our lives. Someone who doesn't over-analyse the situation. Perhaps someone like that will help you get to the altar, if that's what you want.'

'Or perhaps it's too late.' Lilou adjusts her headscarf. 'Naturally, we did not have sex yesterday. We got up and Pierre looked at me. He was worried I might snap at him – which made me want to snap at him. The poor man, naked, flaccid, and then he said, "You don't want to marry me, do you, Lilou?"'

'Damn.'

'*Zut*, indeed. And I said, "No. I'm sorry, I don't want to change anything." I realised he'd understood the problem, even solved it, and for a split second I felt a surge of romantic love for him, but I think it was probably gratitude.'

We both take a sip of coffee. Mine is cold now.

'I always thought that I would get married one day, Audrey, but maybe I won't.'

'It used to be a benchmark women aspired to when our options were limited. But in these days of enlightenment and pronouns?'

'Yes. It would prove I was loveable, and not some hard-nosed, career-driven monster.'

Although Thea is a few years younger than Lilou, I wonder if it's the same for her. Do her friends believe in marriage? Is it still a thing?

'Is that it then? The end of your relationship?'

Lilou's hands fly up in horror. 'Oh no. He's the sweetest person. I'd be lost without him, and he knows it. No more marriage, that's all. I feel bad that I've hurt him. And if Pierre said he didn't fancy sex with me anymore, I'd be devastated. Hypocrisy and confusion are my *métier*.'

In the circumstances it would be a natural segue for Lilou to ask me about my marriage, but I can't enter that vortex of unknowns. She needs to go.

'I got some things ready to repair the bird table.' I point to the garden trug filled with narrow bits of wood, a hammer and nails. 'Would you mind if I carried on? Even though I have never done any carpentry in my life, I am planning to put up little railings so the pigeons can't fit onto the bird table anymore. If a nuthatch happens to spray a few seeds onto the gravel, the pigeons can eat them.'

Lilou shakes a leg, fluffing the bell bottom trim on her catsuit. 'Audrey, have I ruined your morning with my vomit about not wanting to marry the nicest man in the world?'

'Not at all. I'm sorry, for both of you.'

'Is your husband the nicest man in the world?'

Pretending I haven't heard, I carry the bird table over to the terrace, hold up the new strips, measure the gaps between the uprights, and mark the wood with a fingernail.

'How big do you think a blackbird is? I don't mind if they eat up here.'

She sashays over to consider the matter. We move the bars up and down the assessing options.

'Maybe a blackbird is twenty-five centimetres, and a pigeon thirty-two.'

'That's very precise, thank you.'

Lilou holds the crosspieces in place, I hammer nails. The wood splits, and when we step back the newly installed horizontals are not level.

'Oh, these things don't matter, Audrey. The pigeon will only know he does not fit on your table anymore.'

I like her confidence and return the table to the gravel. Lilou and I sit back to see if the revolutionary design works. Two collared doves shunt the gravel below looking for seeds. Good sign. A blue tit steals bits of broken peanut off the table above. Lilou and I turn to each other and silently share the moment. There's a pigeon on the woodpile, head twitching as he eyes up the new situation. We keep very, very still.

Eventually I gawp at my phone in soap-opera horror. 'Is that the time?' I push the chair back. 'I have beds to make up in the cottage.'

'I can help you.' She stands and stretches out one harlequin-clad leg then the other.

'No need, but thanks. One thing before you go.' I flick through some of Jakob's emails. 'Look, here's a recent picture from that little boy I told you about.'

I open the image Jakob has sent me of my dog; he's canary yellow on a background of peach and periwinkle swirls. Underneath is written, *thi iz a picsha f Howod incays you mis he.*

Lilou peers into the image, studies it closely. 'Do you miss your life over there?'

'I miss the dog.'

After the gate squeaks shut behind her, I turn to check the pigeon. He's asleep, head tucked under a wing. It's nice to think that the complicated spatial calculations of how to squeeze onto the table exhausted him. I also like to think his being asleep is an avian nod to the renovation's success. Audrey – one, pigeon – nil.

21

'I've been thinking about the pigeons all week. Have they been on the table?' Lilou is back and making a beeline for the terrace. Her suit is so luminescent she must be visible from space. When she does a twirl, the jacket tails flare out and startle the cat. 'Do you like it? Citrine, a lovely colour.'

'I don't think you'll see a pigeon, or any village bird, until they acclimatise to your outfit,' I respond. 'But I do like it, very up-tempo.' My phone vibrates deep in my pocket. 'Excuse me a moment.'

'We have a cancellation, Madame Lamont.' It's the GP surgery. 'Can you come at eleven thirty?'

When they first contacted me, it was *très* important I get my blood taken that same day, and I assumed I'd see the GP shortly after. However, it has been weeks and now is not a particularly convenient time.

But I say, 'Of course, thank you.' I wave the phone at Lilou. 'I have an appointment in the village.'

'I'll walk with you. You see, I'm wondering if I've made a terrible mistake, about Pierre.'

'Oh, okay.' This is about the third time she's doubted her decision. 'Look at this,' I hand her my phone, open at one of Jakob's pictures, 'while I change.'

I dash into the hayloft; I only have twenty minutes. In my rush I forget I moved the table to mop the floor and cork my thigh on the dresser. Then I slip on the over-soaped tiles in the shower and bring the curtain rail down on my head. Alarmingly a warm trickle of blood descends from my hairline. I'm going to need an emergency department not a GP.

When I finally head outside, Lilou gasps and slams the phone down. 'What have you done, Audrey? Should we drive?'

'Goodness, no. It's almost a way of life for me now – crashing into things, things crashing into me.'

She grimaces at the bloody tissue. 'If you're sure ...'

I nod and flap a hand, trying to display complacent disregard for the throb near my hairline.

'So, Jakob's drawing ... what are they, dragon fruit?'

'I thought they were boats either side of a mountain. He says they're human eyes. And he wants to know if there are children in France, and do they eat chocolate.'

'But of course.' Lilou twirls ahead. 'Audrey, we must do something fun for him. I will think of a wonderful plan.' Both her hands cup the air around her face again and again until her arms shoot out straight so she looks like a radioactive tree. 'I have it! We will film something. Don't worry, leave everything to me.'

———

There's only one other person in the doctor's waiting room, an elderly gentleman on a corner chair.

'*Bonjour.*'

'*Bonjour.*'

Spine straight, he resumes his low whistling. His bright, rheumy eyes gaze at some memory in his wispy-haired skull. It seems to please him. His reedy, Celtic tune weaves around the room. He must be eighty and I wonder why he's here. He's not yellow, not sweaty, there are no bandages evident, no missing limbs. Perhaps he's diabetic or getting routine heart medications. Maybe he is going to alter his end-of-life care plan? Mind you, it doesn't look like he's clawing his way over harsh ground. No, I get the impression he's still got plenty of time for cider and witty comments.

Somewhere down a hallway there's the sound of a door opening, followed by muffled voices. The old man straightens and cocks his head like a dog. Silence follows. His spine relaxes.

Perhaps ten minutes pass before we hear another door. This time a slow mishmash of footsteps can be heard along the corridor. A bent woman in a housecoat and slippers appears outside the glass waiting room. Another woman, presumably a doctor, is holding her elbow. The old woman and Monsieur Whistler exchange the faintest upward turn of their lips. He stands, needing a few seconds to let the stiffness in his body ease away. The doctor waits for him to come alongside and take Madame Whistler's arm, then the doctor stretches her neck to look over the old lady's head and gives a small shake. The old man purses his lips in acknowledgement and turns to his wife with a smile.

Monsieur and Madame Whistler shuffle in a slow semi-circular dance to face the exit. They look directly at me before going. He says, 'Bon journée.' His wife, sultana eyes in a squished-up face, follows suit. I bon journée them both with a little dip of my head, and they leave.

Another few minutes pass where I look through the window, watch a tractor rumble by, and count the variously sized white vans parked around the bar. This means it's after twelve and all the workers everywhere in Brittany are at lunch. Including the doctor, I suspect.

A voice wafts into the waiting room. 'Madame Lamont, I am Dr Catherine H …' Then she glides away, turning at the last minute as though she's just remembered something. 'Follow me please.'

We enter her vast consulting room. I wait for an invitation to sit. Across the room Dr H slowly replaces the paper towel on an examination couch. There's a wooden bookshelf stuffed with medical journals, sample tablet packages, tomes of heavy-duty anatomy books, pamphlets, and the ceramic imprint of a child's foot. Organ music from the church next door plays as clearly as if I were in the back pew.

After a few more apparently aimless movements the doctor appears behind the large desk looking surprised to see me there.

'*Bonjour.*'

'*Bonjour.*' I feel confident the consult will begin.

Nothing.

I wonder if this is a normal French medical assessment. Is she observing me for obvious haemorrhage, gross tremor? She's so vague it's hard to tell.

Dr H gestures towards the examination couch, but in such a floppy way I'm not sure whether she means I need to go over there, or she's telling me she's exhausted and going for a nap. I take a punt and move over to the couch. She flips my wrist and presses three fingertips against my pulse. Satisfied, she looks in my mouth, down my throat, then depresses my tongue with a dry wooden spatula. It makes me retch then cough. She moves both hands down my neck and gently palpates for glands with her delicate pianist fingers. She takes my blood pressure from my right arm and then left arm. She bobs down into a squat and lets her fingertips push the skin over my feet and ankles. Then, with precisely landed chops of a rubber hammer, she checks my reflexes. Finally, she puts a plastic tip over a thermometer and sticks it in my left ear, then right. Dr H asks me to lie down and takes her stethoscope and taps its round plate. This crawls over my chest, front and back, while she listens to every bronchiole. I obediently breathe deeply through my mouth. She moves all my joints this way and that. Finally, she parts my hair in segments and peers at my scalp. I am unfamiliar with this; perhaps she's worried about ticks. I did remove a lot from that hedgehog.

As her fingers move across my right temple she exclaims, quite literally, 'Oo *la la!*'

I laugh.

'You have bruises on your shins, cuts on your hands, the remnants of a black eye, and a gash here on your head. There will be a little scar.'

'I don't think it will ruin my beauty.'

Dr H raises her eyebrows and insists on cleaning the area before she stretches a couple of Steri-Strips across the broken skin. 'I think it's too late, but it will be better. All your little wounds, do you hurry all the time?'

'I don't think so.'

'So why are you covered in injuries?'

'A foggy mind. There's been a lot going on.'

She says nothing. Her eyes hold a bracing clarity which indicates she reads the mental state of all her patients.

I'm invited back to the desk. She sits across from me and takes the file I've brought with all my Australian health records. She peers, shuffles the papers then apologises her English isn't good anymore. I explain again I've just come to get some colonoscopy results. Next, she turns to the computer screen. There's keyboard tapping and hmms as she scrolls up and down. Dr H leans in close to the screen, leans back, then turns it towards me.

Tilted forward, I hold the screen with one hand, so she can't turn it away too soon, and read my results, slowly.

'Madame Lamont, you have haemorrhoids and the polyps were benign.'

Then Dr H bends over an A4 letterheaded pad and picks up an elegant ink pen. She appears to derive enormous pleasure from her broad cursive. I'm hypnotised by her hand and gentle reassurances. At last, the longest prescription known to woman emerges from the penmanship of her looping black ink. If initially there was a lack of precision about this appointment, it doesn't matter now.

Dr H rotates her pad so I can read the pharmacist's tome. She runs an elegant finger alongside each item and explains how these things will help me relax, focus, sleep, boost my immune system and give me wings. I take the paper and fold it in two.

'Thank you. All I need is the delicacy of homeopathy?'

She leans in, smiles, demands I look her in the eye. 'No. You need to avoid sitting, sitting is as bad as smoking, and you need to take more care of yourself. These bumps and bruises are not good. Where are your family?'

'In Australia.'

'*Oo la la*. You are here because of your aunt. Pascale is a wonderful woman, she was my *notaire*.' Dr H puts both her hands on my knees. 'Who do you talk with? Something is causing you much anxiety.'

'I write in my diary every evening.'

'Good. But you don't know if what you write is the truth.'

She's absolutely right.

'So, what else do you do for yourself, Audrey? Tell me.'

I freeze, but her face is so open I could fall into it.

'I'm learning to tap dance. I think about things, which I've never really had time to do before.'

'What do you think about?'

'Life is funny, and sometimes it is not, but everything is relative. In balance my life has worked out to be positive, because otherwise I'd have changed things, *non*? Or is it possible to watch something happen, and not see it at all?'

Dr H clasps one of my hands between both of hers, puts her head back and laughs. 'This is a discussion to be had with wine.'

'You're prescribing wine?'

'Oh yes indeed. Wine and conversation, Audrey. But not with yourself, with good people.'

22

Wine and conversation. I know she didn't say with a horse, but I stop to pat François and pick him handfuls of the long grass that grows out of his reach. His rubbery, prehensile lips slobber over my palm and his teeth grind.

'You know, François, here's the thing. If I take the doctor's advice, and share some truths, tell people at home, *I used to be invisible, and I didn't need a magic cloak to achieve it* they'd think I was mad. Is this perhaps something I shouldn't mention, except to people who've felt the same?'

François' response is to rub his nose up and down my blouse.

Through the *remise* window I see Tata and No-E fossicking about, heads bobbing, and then as I approach the door, I hear No-E proclaim, 'The road to hell is paved with good people.'

I keep walking.

So, the gateleg table is as far back as I can move it in the hayloft's tiny kitchen. The chairs are on the draining board, and I'm ready, raring to do fifteen minutes of tap from yet another beginners YouTube tutorial. This instructor, Bill, is lean, taut, and he's an optimist. He says I'll get the two essential tools of tap dance easily, in no time at all. Bill has never met me.

Shoulders in line with your toes. No straight legs in tap. Shake out your calf, let the foot flop. The relaxed ankle is a key principle. Ball heel. Ball dig, heel drop.

Rewind, replay.

Lift heel, drop it. One foot then the other, side to side, knees bent. Faster side to side.

Rewind, replay.

Ball dig, weight goes onto the front foot. Put the two beats together.

There are no beats. Everything is quiet. Bare feet on terracotta tiles do not *tap*. But Bill is very lithe. I glimpse his chest where a shirt button gapes. His easy smile. The fluid way he twists at the waist.

Now would be a good time to go back to the start of the lesson and get these ankles moving, loosen my knees. I say goodbye to Bill, who's putting all his moves together, and start the video again.

'Let's not gallop ahead, Audrey. The paradiddle, the single buffalo, chop suey – these and many more steps, will all be yours ... by the time you're eighty.'

Back to basics – right foot up, drop the ball of the foot, now the heel. Other foot, ball, heel, left, right, marching rhythm, again and again. Shake out the ankle tension. Repeat. Brush step – forward, back in a J, repeat. It's going well. Another twenty minutes and I can do them both without checking the screen. Hooray. I twirl around the kitchen in a celebratory routine of my own choreography, which Bill would shudder at, but I think has potential.

Tomorrow is 'shuffle' day. Lovely Bill says this is crucial.

Before then I need to buy drawing pins. If I have enough in the soles of my sneakers, it'll help tap out the rhythms, which is the whole point.

But for the moment my soles are black, leathery, like a perfectly preserved Viking Wallet. I fill a bucket with cold water, sit on the hayloft step, and immerse both my sore feet to soak the angry skin.

The chickens are out again. These days I observe them to be a loosely knit aggregate, whose members are bound by their fascination with the philosophical weight and dramaturgical potential of silence. Rubbish. I know the chickens' existence, like the cat's, is the pursuit of sun-drenched sand baths to snooze in, and food. Frank, the cock, changes it up sometimes; right now he's sitting on La Follette. This appears to be for comfort, rather than a clumsy sexual move. Poor old La Follette doesn't have the brains to shake him off her white fluffy back. Mid dance routine, I had to shoo Frieda off the laptop. She was trying to roost and momentarily blocked my view of Bill. No-E tells me I should keep the gate to the field closed, and he's horrified I've named my stock. He says it will make eating the chickens difficult. I will not be eating them.

Tata leaves the *remise* and crosses the garden. Her shoulders are back, she's not peering at the ground, and she's got the hang of her cane.

I blow her a kiss and wave towards the bucket to justify not getting up. 'You look almost comfortable, are you?'

'I am, and you – a pedicure in the middle of the day? Very relaxed.'

'My feet are a mess.'

Tata comes across the gravel, stops, and leans on her cane, both hands clasped over its knob. 'The water butts are nearly empty, remind me to show you the pump, if you don't mind.'

I nod, massage a foot.

'Audrey, I'm not sure reflexology is going to be sufficient. My recommendation is you work on restoring your sense of humour. Seeing things in a humorous light is an essential tool. And, having peeked at you tap dancing, I think you need to rekindle your capacity to laugh at yourself.'

'If I didn't know you better, I'd be offended.'

Tata lifts her cane and taps my knee with its rubber stopper. 'What did the doctor say about your results?' She prods me again with her cane, harder this time.

'All my results are perfectly normal. The doctor's only worry were my scrapes and bruises, and for them she recommends wine and good conversation. My turn – what were you doing in the *remise*?'

'We were looking for things.'

'I wish you'd stop being all French Revolution, knitting secrets which only you and No-E understand.'

Tata shifts her weight across both feet.

'All right, is No-E renovating? There's a lot going on at his cottage. Is he selling? I could buy it and live next door to you.'

'Or you could live here.' Tata turns slightly and waves her cane towards the cottage. 'Why have you saved those pieces from the hedge?'

'The willow is for another idea.'

'*Bien*. You have done a wonderful job with the garden, Audrey, thank you. I've rather let it get away from me.' Tata appears to have frozen on the spot. 'And the vegetable seedlings, I appreciate it. Mind you, Pascal says you'll regret putting in so many courgettes.' She shuffles, stiff hipped, to look around.

'Ironically when I worked full time this whole property was pristine. I had rabbits and many more chickens. I killed them all myself – plucked, skinned, the whole thing. The supermarket was only for coffee, baking paper, that sort of thing. Everything else we swapped. The natural world was the most effective antidepressant a person could ask for. Now, when I could do with cheering up, I shuffle from one indoors to another, taking a long time to accomplish very little. Don't get old, Audrey.'

'I want to grow old,' I say, 'have another chance at a different phase of life, I want to be wonderful like you. The kids and I remember you providing for our meals. No waste, no plastic wrapping; life and death, no mystery. They thought you were an Amazon. Well, Orson didn't, he went vegetarian at fifteen, which was the last time we were all here together.'

I take my prune-like feet out of the bucket, stand, and give her a bear hug from behind. Strangely she doesn't brush me off with a clever quip.

'Has Simon made contact?'

'Not since the email about his lawn, no, and quite frankly I'm telling myself perhaps it's a good thing.'

I cross my fingers on both hands and hold them up in front of her.

'When I started studying history at uni, they said looking at the past requires more than fact-checking. You must consider the mood of the time, the tone, the feelings lived; they are the things which resonate. The fact Simon has been with another woman while he wrote this last book is just that: a previously omitted detail. I had a good time being a mother, having a home, a dog. I'm not going to let one horrid little *fact* from the recent past put me off everything. You shouldn't let your accident put you off either.'

Tata turns and I drop my hands.

'The fact your husband is having sex with another woman is nothing more than a tiny bug in the ointment of life?'

'Unlike you I've not had a career. What I see as my strengths are derived from being a mother. I am resourceful and resilient.'

'*Oui.* You are that and much more. I've always thought you were too good for Simon. Indeed, I've always thought he was a selfish bastard.' Tata smiles. 'Do you remember what I said when you got engaged?'

'Never marry a man who wears slip-on shoes. And what did Simon wear the first day I met him? White t-shirt, blue shorts, leather boat shoes.'

'I get no pleasure from being right.'

Her skin ruches over her cheeks as she beams, letting me know this isn't true; Tata is very proud of herself. I dip my head, splay my palms in exaggerated deference to her wisdom.

'Audrey, if we are controlled by forces we do not understand, and conditions we don't understand, the term for that state is ignorance. I think you may find there are a few more questions to be answered between you and Simon.'

Not only has Tata's gait improved, but her acuity is back in full force. 'You are right.'

She sighs deeply. 'Pascal is making lunch, god help me. Do you want to join us?'

'Thank you but I have willow to weave.'

—

Should, should, should – that word has got to go. I *should* be gardening, yes, but as gardening is a pleasure is it a *should*?

It's hard to tell what Tata has been up to out here. There are bald patches where things have not thrived, and other beds are crowded like a Tokyo train. One of the complications is I don't know European plants, nor am I familiar with the soil. Does this something-or-other plant need to be split, pruned or left well alone? I could ask Tata, but I'm scared she'll try to help. I take cuttings and write labels on lollipop sticks, but the writing becomes illegible because the indelible ink runs. Does that mean its delible ink?

So yes, I *could* prioritise more weeding, in readiness for guests, but I'm not. Today's creation is experimental wicker panels, which might become gazebos, for chicken enrichment.

I tug at a green piece of willow. It springs free from the pile and whips me across the cheek. My skin smarts like the devil.

Haricot climbs onto the osier pile and bats at a butterfly until he understands to pursue this action will require energy.

As I work, the wicker panels grow wonky with protruding twigs. I twist the fronds in tighter, snip recalcitrant pieces, push another length between the writhing plaits. If I look at the cat, his violet glare penetrates my thoughts and exposes the painfully slow, evolving relationship I have with my marriage. But if I let myself simply be out here, in chicken land, where my feathery friends and I foster a cross-cultural exchange, weaving willow, breaking nails, and even slashing my face – it feels like progress.

'Indeed, Haricot, I have been a pushover, but no more.'

I hurl the blade of a spade into the brown earth, and dig out multiple deep slits, then I bury both ends of my willow sheets. The result? Enormous, irregular croquet hoops. The chickens are inquisitive. The cat leaps from crest to crest with unusual athleticism. Viewed from a distance, my creation could be likened to the classical arches seen in dusky photos of the mythical Loch Ness monster, but without a head.

23

Having slept with the cat for over a month now I've become attuned to his purrs. They are syrupy, his rumbling flows slippery, and when he's on a roll his beat sections are irresistible. He sounds as though he's having more fun than all of humanity. He probably is. But I can't lie around with him today; it's *Vide Grenier* day. 'Empty your attic' day is the literal translation, and many stalls look as though the seller has done precisely this. The Australian equivalent is a car boot sale, but less orderly. A *Vide Grenier* includes alcohol, family picnics, trip hazards, and food stalls run by people with little experience.

The only clean t-shirt I have is heavy white cotton with neat black print, *I thought growing old would take longer*. It was a present for my mother's eightieth. She was amused, but never wore it, and after she died, I rescued it from her drawer. Simon said he hoped I was going to keep it for gardening.

I'm about to leave the hayloft when I see No-E doing something at the side gate. It's difficult to make out what. As always, the man is a mystery.

His stone cottage is at the south end of the lane, and last night I noticed, as I do every Saturday, his week's wardrobe has been washed and hung over the woodpile. I think he only has one pair of brown leather boots, which start every day polished to a chestnut gleam. I've also seen him cutting his own hair with an ancient pair of orange secateurs. And I've noted he doesn't appear to visit anyone else in our little hamlet.

Tata comes bowling down the lane on her red Harley. As I join her it becomes apparent that No-E is lubricating the gate's hinges with butter. My aunt's face doesn't flinch at his culinary remedy. He opens and shuts the gate a few times to work the butter into the crannies. No more squeak. Then he folds the paper around the dirty remnant pat and beams, holding it out towards me.

'Do you have enough indoors? It will be fine for cooking, I think.'

'Thank you, Pascal, but I've plenty.' Mossy, rust-soaked, paint-flaked butter is quite possibly a delicacy somewhere, but it's not one I hanker for.

Tata scoots on past us both. '*Vite, vite*, Audrey.'

Scurrying to keep up, I wave my hand back down towards No-E's activities at the gate.

'Tata, don't you think—'

She cuts me off. 'I have thought about Pascal a great deal over the years, and now I think it's best to simply accept him the way he is.' Then she accelerates a little.

At the start of the village three men are mid Cassavetes screaming match. Despite the fact it's only nine thirty, wine is involved, as well as a trailer, a horse float, and the mangled remains of a chest of drawers. Who did what in which order is the gist of the volume.

Along from them, and dozing in her camp chair, is our neighbour, Madame Potdevin, whose favourite jam so far is the cherry and rose petal combo. She returns the empty jars every four days, which is my cue to replenish her stocks. I'm flattered and nearly out of jam. Madame Potdevin's jam jar deliveries are also an opportunity for her to tell me about various unsuccessful surgeries she has endured. So far, I've heard about a dismal cataract removal and an unsatisfactory left hip replacement. Tata says I can look forward to a failed Dupuytren's contracture repair and a near-death experience with a grizzly appendix. Then, apparently, she'll go back to the cataract and stroll through the litany of disasters again. Strangely, when I deliver a fresh jar of jam to her house, I'm invited in and shown photos of her daughter, who lives in Marseille and never visits. Or she'll show me plastic tablemats she bought during a holiday in Belgium. Sometimes she brings out the intricate lacework her husband made during the war. No mention of ailments. Today she's dozing behind a card table with nothing on it.

Everyone we pass says hello to Tata.

The village's main street starts at a bar by the roundabout. Next the *Marie* with its imposing brickwork and fluttering flags. Then there's the village playing field and church. On the opposite side is a *boulangèrie*. They have recently installed a two-euro, automatic baguette dispensing machine outside for after-hour emergencies. Next door to this is a florist, a school, a rusted cider press, two old wells and the field where they keep François. The far end of the street dips down to the bridge and lock keeper's house. The gaps between these focal points of village life are filled with narrow houses, twenty per cent of which are rented out during the summer. Then to top it all off the whole street, the whole village, is dotted with randomly placed concrete council pots full of either red geraniums or red roses. While many councils go in for lush flower beds and hanging baskets, this one doesn't.

Today the street is alive with haphazardly balanced umbrellas, draped carpets, higgledy-piggledy displays. Tiny dogs pull on thin leads, always at forty-five degrees to the direction of their owner. Children clamber over the roundabout. The woman from the *tabac* points with pride to her second-hand breadmaker. No, thank you. A foot spa perhaps? I smile and shake my head. I don't want or need anything, but these events hold all the promise of the unknown. Like staring at the sea, unable to blink in case you miss a whale breach or a giant wave build. On a rickety table behind the Dubrovnik souvenir plate and the old cider bottle, I might find a treasure so precious it's outstanding.

We move past the stalls in a sea of hands. Fists grip phones, lacquered nails and bitten cuticles. Fingers curl around bag straps and splay out protectively against a child's body.

The vendors price their items using a bizarre algorithm based on optimism. Of course, someone will pay fifteen euros for the rusty oilcan. Or maybe a hangover determined the empty bottle of holy water is available for ten euros. Those three strings of hanging ceramic chillies are one euro each, two for all three. Compared to the empty plastic Mary they seem cheap.

Tata is in deep discussion with the *garagiste*. I dawdle too long, and a woman thinks I'm interested in the ceramic chillies; I feel obliged to buy them. She's pleased. I'm pleased she's pleased. The chillies tinkle as Madame wraps them in a sheet of old local paper, the *Petit Bleu*. About to move along when Madame points to three ornate, gold-framed mirrors, and holds up five fingers. She clearly thinks I need to spend more time grooming; her smile seems to say, *being chic is only a few euros away*. I don't say no, so she thinks I've said yes, and starts to wrap these in more newspaper. Then she beckons for me to give her back the ceramics. 'They are heavy,' she says dramatically, turning her mouth down. She will keep my bargains behind her table, and I can collect them later. I hand over the five euros. I'll put the mirrors on the terrace wall. Madame then lifts a chipped butter dish in a grand gesture. This, apparently, is a gift because I'm such a lovely customer. It is hideous, but I smile. She's delighted, or she thinks I'm a fool.

Tata is delayed by a group of people who want advice on a collapsed fence.

For the next few stalls, I am careful to keep a distance which says, *Having a lovely time, but just looking.*

A few stallholders sit deep in camp chairs and conversation, happy not to be disturbed. One woman arranges clothes, possibly out of her laundry basket, onto a professional rack. *Vide Panier à Linge* day – Empty Laundry Basket day – that would save on doing the washing.

There are incomplete Lego sets, jars, one small mechanical lawnmower (ideal for apartment living), and a mug with a penis for a handle. I'm tempted to buy the latter for Lilou.

A Mitchell fishing reel takes my attention. Its black, alien lines are familiar. Simon started collecting them when he was a boy, when he used to fish with his dad. Then his university studies got in the way. For a long time, he would say, 'I'll fish for hours one day. For now, though, the romance of fishing with these beautiful things is something which will have to wait.' I'd like to buy this one for Simon, take it home, watch him clip it up with the other six or seven on the rod above his desk. But that time has passed. It is surprisingly hard to walk past the reel. I pick it up from the nest of old fishing line and try to recall if Simon has this model. I flick the silver handle over and it makes a soft clunk. Chills swarm over my skin like unwanted midges.

It's not the reel, but the last time I was in his office. Midori installed on his chair. How that moment bowled over my marriage. The way she didn't stand to greet me or apologise,

although she would have known our meeting had the potential
to cause a great deal of pain.

I am so angry I stop in between two stalls and send a text.

I'd appreciate some information about you and Midori. I have
plans to make.

Tata's scooter bumps the back of my legs.

'You look like you've seen a ghost. Perhaps a *sausage frites*
will help? The football club do the best catering, but today it's
the *pompiers*.'

We head towards three well-worn refreshment tents being
run by the firefighters, and Tata steers me to buy tickets from
a woman sitting under a minuscule sign: TICKETS FOR BEER,
WINE, WATER, SAUSAGE, CREPE, FRITES.

Money and food should be kept apart, but apparently flies,
which buzz over bags of raw sausages, are okay. Wielding
boiling fat in ancient chip fryers like a demented banshee
near your colleagues is okay. You certainly never read reports
in the Monday papers that *forty people died of salmonella
poisoning following a* Vide Grenier. Nor are there gruesome
stories along the lines of: *Frites Man spontaneously combusts
over record crowds*. No. There's simply a delicious, delirious,
use-your-common-sense culinary anarchy. Back home it
would be all hi-vis, safety glasses and antibacterial sprays.

When it is our turn, we exchange tickets for sausages and
are asked to wait because the *frites* have not been synchronised
to come out at the same time. Then we exchange drinks
tickets for two rosés, and once again a little crowd gathers
around Tata.

I must delete the text to Simon.

Tata looks at her watch and beckons me over.

'Audrey, I think you'll have to skip the *frites* and head back. Your guests will be here soon.'

'Guests, today?'

'*Oui, cherie.* I warn you; this lot are overbearing.'

She slides around on her scooter seat and holds her rosé up in a toast.

'I feel bad leaving you to deal with not only your first guests, but these ones in particular. I can't face them because they'll fawn and gawp at my bruises.' She waves a hand towards the moon boot on her foot and then around the fading bruises along the side of her face. 'You don't mind, do you?'

'Not at all. I don't want you to help anyway. It'll be fine.'

'My old colleague, Monsieur Lugand, and his family have invited me to spend a week with them by the coast.'

'Perfect.'

'Your week might not be so perfect.'

24

Shit. When I open the now smooth-as-silk gate and enter the yard, three people sit on the lawn, and one squats behind the trio. It's *Le Déjeuner sur l'herbe*. Except of course in Manet's actual painting, the women are naked whereas the ones on my lawn are fully clothed. I put the mirrors and ceramic chillies down. Thank god I made up the cottage a few days ago. I try to generate host-like enthusiasm.

Tata has told me these people have been here before and I know she usually has lunch with her guests on the first day. So they expect to be fed, but I've just eaten, and I don't want to eat again. But it would be rude to say, *I've just had a sausage because I forgot you were coming,* so I will have to join them. Perhaps I can pretend I have a squiffy tummy. Why am I making a fuss? This is not a difficult situation to navigate.

I stride out to the guests, beaming. 'Hello, welcome. I'm Audrey, Pascale's niece.'

'Oh, where's our wonderful Tante Pascale? We simply adore her.'

I'd forgotten outsiders wouldn't have heard about Tata's fall. 'I'm sorry to say she had a nasty accident in May.'

'How dreadful! What accident if you don't mind us asking?'

Everyone tuts and swivels their heads like owls.

I glance across to the cherry tree, the bloodstain on the terrace below it and choose my words carefully. 'She was in the garden at the time.'

The tall, sandy-haired man speaks again. 'Awful, and yet brilliant. How very wonderful to be doing what you love. I'd like my accident to be in the middle of a court case. I'll announce a recess and then stumble off the podium.'

'This is exactly what will happen if you continue to drink like a fish when you're sixty.' The sharp-edged woman in linen trousers looks around to enjoy the rippling coo from the others.

A man with a cauliflower ear and a dimpled chin clears his throat. 'I will be in my Manhattan office, seeing off a coup somewhere.' He waves a beefy hand vaguely towards the field. 'I'll probably inhale an artichoke heart and my secretary will rush in to save me.'

I rather hope his secretary is at lunch and misses the opportunity to be a heroine.

Then a girl, who looks far too sweet to be with this lot, turns her face towards the sun, stretches languidly and says softly, 'I'll fall down a cave while spelunking.'

The others do not approve at all. I give them names as their own aren't offered. Big chin – Jaws – leers lasciviously at Rose – the blue-jean caver. It seems he plans on bedding her this weekend. My guess is he won't be successful.

'Egg salad?'

Ms Lud – the pointy woman – remembers I'm there and swings around.

'Oh yes, great idea. Did you know the current thinking is that four eggs a week can reduce your chance of developing type two diabetes by thirty-seven per cent?'

I think this advice will be updated by doctors before we've finished our meal, but I keep my tone light. 'Oh?'

I cross the terrace and wipe the table, pull out two more chairs. Then make multiple trips in and out of the hayloft to lay mismatched plates, cloth napkins, cutlery, bread, butter, glasses, salad, and three small vases of flowers. What's missing? Water.

They meander down from the lawn to sit in the green cool of the terrace and tell me how clever my aunt was to have made a dining area out here and how marvellous that she built the terrace around the cherry tree.

I'm pretty sure the tree grew despite the beams, and I certainly don't mention Pascale was up amongst those branches when she plummeted. They rip a baguette into pieces and hand around the salad. There's a lot of chatter about how one should never cut a roll, nor a baguette.

I go back to the kitchen to steel myself. I've catered so many times, I can do it again. I decant red and white *cardbordeaux* into carafes and take a deep breath.

'Haricot, I'm going outside and may be some time.'

His response is to twitch the last centimetre of his tail.

Mr Lud takes a chunk of baguette. 'You know your aunt used to advise me if I had EU property clients, or cross-channel settlements in a divorce, that sort of thing. Our woman on the ground, so to speak. I hope she recovers quickly.'

I produce a wistful smile and wish I had not put a plate out for me. The four of them would be quite happy. Plus, the conversation has turned to the scales of justice being a metaphor for weighing the merit of arguments. Do I think so? I note a hint of condescension in the question – they feel obliged to engage me. It is not as if they really want the opinion of an old sheila from Australia. I take a sip of the white and contemplate my answer. Play dumb? Have an opinion? They wait. I have to say something.

'I once did jury duty and have doubts that justice is always served. I suppose I think the truth doesn't always emerge.'

Jaws, mouth full of food, corrects me. 'The adversarial system is designed to resolve disputes rather than discover the truth.'

The baguette and salad mix, which rolls between his gaping fleshy lips, disturbs me, but not as much as his statement. If what he says is true, it's a sad fact. 'Sorry, I'm lost.'

There's a bit more owl head-swivelling as they decide who will help me out. Ms Lud is tasked and puts her knife and fork down.

'The results of a trial regularly favour the party whose argument is most persuasive. You'll often find zealous, competitive behaviour tends to trump the fair administration of justice.'

Ms Lud actually slows her speech down to tell me this. Rose notices and glances over to me, clearly embarrassed by her friend. Somewhat encouraged, I tell the group, 'I think this is unfair.'

Jaws, mouth full of egg, taps the table a few times with agitated fingers. 'Unfair, because someone is more eloquent and better researched than his or her adversary?'

I shouldn't have tried to join in and scramble for an analogy. 'Unfair in the same way universities give academic slots to superb athletes who run up mountains and swim in the Olympics. Or wealthy football clubs buy their talent so competition then becomes about precision and show ponies, money, and no longer two locally sourced teams having a go, with the best man winning.'

There is silence. Three of them lean back in their chairs. I don't think I will maintain my aunt's Super Host status this summer. Their pillowcases may well be beautifully ironed, but this is where the positives will end.

Rose winks at me and pours more wine for everyone. The Luds and Jaws bring up something which happened on the ferry. Their body language shifts to exclude me. Their banter isn't that of comfortable chums, it is rampant individualism amidst flimsy connections. This week will be about shared experiences to tighten bonds, while keeping them loose at the same time. I recall many such holidays with my husband and his friends. I would sit at exactly such a meal, desperate not to be abandoned, feeling easily disposable.

The gate clicks shut then there's the distinctive, and very welcome, crunching footfall of Lilou on gravel. She storms towards us looking like an inverted mermaid. The tightest green dress clings from her knees to her collarbones. From there up is a vast, convoluted burst of fabric which defies gravity and stands boldly around her head.

'*Bon retour.*' She leaps onto the terrace and kisses the seated Luds, and Jaws, then her pace slows.

Rose stands and extends a hand.

Lilou pushes it to one side and kisses her too. 'Pff, formality. Lilou, pleased to meet you.'

Lilou swims across and lays a hand on my shoulder. 'So, you've met Pascale's talented niece then?' With her other hand she takes up a glass.

A twinge of intrigue splutters across their faces.

'Yes, we have an artist in our midst. Aren't we lucky?' Lilou sits and sips her wine.

There are rumbles around the table and a general readjusting of postures and opinions. I slide my foot out and kick Lilou's ankle, gently, while I prepare a correction to this massive porky pie.

Lilou squeezes my shoulder a little too hard. 'Not only is she working on a few fine sculptures, I've hijacked some of Audrey's time to consult on the odd tricky portfolio. She came up with

141

a blinding album title for a band I'm doing the marketing for: *Velcro'd to a Monkey*. They're so impressed they're going to call their post Edinburgh Fringe tour the same.' Lilou beams at me beatifically.

Since she removed marriage from the equation, Lilou has changed her mind many times. She loves Pierre, he's such a good person. She loathes penises, never liked them. Isn't cooperation and contentment a good basis for marriage? Oh, how she longs for a blinding orgasm. Back and forth she's goes, and one day I suggested having a mind that swerved so violently must be like being velcro'd to a chimpanzee.

Lilou slides along the bench now, animated by her story. 'They're an anti-establishment group and you can imagine the associated images will be *magnifique*.'

Ms Lud leans forward and delicately places her elbows on the table. She clasps her hands together under her pointy chin. 'Audrey, do tell us more.'

'Hah!' Lilou's palms fly up. 'You want my reclusive genius to reveal her secrets? There's no chance, she's so modest. I literally bully Audrey to give me some of her time.'

With great pleasure I excuse myself and leave them to it. Jaws brings out bottles of wine from their car, Rose lights a joint, but I'm the one who is free as a bird.

In the hayloft I turn on the transistor radio. Spontini's *La Vestale* oozes out of the little round speaker sounding tinny. I lean on the sink and breathe. Haricot wheedles for food, which I'm delighted to provide. The sink fills with warm soapy water.

Lilou comes into the hayloft with both hands full of table debris.

'Oh thanks, you're sweet.'

She stands alongside me and puts her fingers over my sudsy hand. 'You know, Audrey, what I said was kind of true.

You of all people know how messy I've been recently, and during a particularly tedious back-and-forth Zoom meeting with those clients, who are legit, I threw out your words. They fell on them like I'd struck gold. I suppose you'll want to be paid now?'

'Payment is rescuing me from … out there.'

'Arrogance is the word you're looking for. How about a t-shirt as a souvenir of your genius?'

'Three t-shirts, one for each child?'

'Deal. Dear old Mum writes for cult bands; your street credibility will soar.'

'Where do you want these?' Rose arrives with plates stacked along one arm. Her past clearly includes waiting tables.

'Anywhere you can find a spot, thanks.'

Lilou stands straighter, flicks her mane of hair back and together they make two more journeys with things from the table. I note a poetry in their movements: the way they cooperate to top up the water jug, return the butter to the fridge. When the last item has been delivered, they stand, squished together in the doorway, and pass the joint back and forth. There's a sweetness in those gestures, a delicacy as their fingers swap the precious drug from one hand to another in the cocoon of Lilou's ludicrous collar.

My instincts tell me I am a witness to something.

Simon would say I wasn't witnessing anything at all. He'd say, *Instinct is a physical response emanating from the amygdala. Lilou and Rose, like all animals, have merely noted help was appropriate, and are demonstrating a fixed pattern of behaviour in such a situation.*

I'd then say something like, *Well, my intuition tells me there's something between those two.*

He'd snort back, *Intuition has pernicious flaws.*

And that would be the end of that.

Bugger him. I trust my gut on this one. I should have trusted it in the past and been less easily shunted off course. The soft laughter from the doorway makes me smile. Rose's lips part in laughter and a twist of smoke rises around Lilou's cheek. Poor Pierre, alone in Paris. Would he want to be a fly on the wall? I wash the crockery until the low pulse of a WhatsApp call rescues me.

'Mum.' Thea grins, and behind her the surging winter sea throws spray into a grizzly sky.

'Hello, darling. Why are you whispering?'

'You don't have to whisper, Thea; they can't hear you.' Gus sticks his face into the screen. 'Hey, Mum.'

'Hello.' I blow them both a kiss. 'Who's they?'

'Dad and Midori. He invited us to meet her over dinner, but none of us wanted to, so we're having brunch with them.'

Them – the word degrades me; and it sounds so final, but Gus and Thea are watching for my reaction.

'I suppose it had to happen sooner or later. Where's Orson?'

'He's giving them a hard time.' Gus leans back in.

'That part, Orson being staunch, is great.' Thea nibbles a cuticle. 'Gus and I said we'd buy the Sunday papers before they sold out, but really it was so we could call you.'

'I'll say it again: you three must not alter your relationship with your father because of our marital issues.'

'Yeah, you say that, and it's recommended in the psychotherapy books, but, in real life family members murder each other. Or the unit splits apart only to regroup when it's time to witness someone's last gasp – if you're lucky.'

'I'm glad to see you haven't lost your sense of humour, Gus.'

'Midori is dreadful.' Thea pulls an eating lemons face.

'Darling, she's beautiful and terribly clever, she may also be nice.'

'No chance. When Orson asked her where they'd met, and Dad tried to reply, Orson kept his eyes directed at Midori and said, "I think Midori remembers." Then she kind of rose in her seat a little, squared her scrawny shoulders and eyeballed him back. She thought she was taking on a kid, but she was so wrong.'

Gus nods deeply, fully appreciating the memory of his brother taking on the enemy.

'Midori said she was Dad's professor when he was at university, and Orson was straight in there to fact check when that was. She turned to Dad, smiled,' Thea grimaces, 'and turned back to say, "Forty-one long years."' Thea shakes out a theatrical shudder, but her face is drawn. 'The way she said it, Mum, I wanted to punch her.'

I know Thea probably does want to punch her, but I can see she's also alive with indignation. This scenario will fill her chat groups, and that's fine if it helps her process things. Keeping a Mona Lisa smile over the mounting ache in my chest is difficult.

Gus starts to cavort along the footpath. 'The fact we're loud, and Orson is relentless, makes her wince. It's like a cat lover has been put in a pen with a pack of muddy kelpies.'

'Bless you both for being so sweet, but look.' I turn my phone around and walk over to the hayloft door. 'I've got my first guests out there, so I'd better go and feed them.'

Thea turns the phone onto herself. 'You all right, Mum?'

'Well, it's all a bit raw, and those people out there are arrogant as hell, but yes. I don't want you to worry for one second about me. Gotta go – love you both, love to Orson.'

I clutch the sink, close my eyes and let my head drop. Adultery. It's a lovely old-fashioned word and the cornerstone of many a novel. *Forty-one long years.* There was me thinking it had only been three.

25

For a while those words, *forty-one long years*, had me reeling. I even thought, death and an unknowing of all future matters had some merit. But luckily, I've found alternative solutions. For example, people say you can leave compost alone, but today it feels cathartic. The garden fork spears deep, then I heave and twist the putrefying mass. Again and again, I thrust the fork through yesterday's cabbage leaves, lawn clippings, cheese rind, and mix them in with last week's scraps. Dead peony stems tangle between the tines and need to be yanked free. I launch the fork once more into a different area of the bin.

Forty-one years. If they have known each other so long, maybe their affair started back then. Was I alone in my marriage? Were they the couple? Questions go round in my mind, intersect and collide. The painting in our sitting room, which I came to hate; did she give it to Simon? She's Japanese, it's Japanese. When I took the painting down and he wanted it back up – what did that say? I can go, she can't.

Now, what to do? I came here thinking Simon would miss me dreadfully, and we'd make our way back to a time when we were happy. Ha. That script is redundant. But bizarrely, I feel calmer, like this is the truth and all that niggling which went on in the back of my head has been satisfied.

'Lift your head above the slime of self-pity, woman. And yes, I'll talk to myself if I want to.'

Composting is a challenge, or a nightmare, depending on your tolerance for fecund smells. Using the wooden side of the bin as a fulcrum, I push down hard on the fork handle to bring up a black mass from the depths. Here is where the good stuff happens. Pale, indignant worms writhe in the haul, determined to go back south, back to turning vegetable scraps, garden detritus and chicken shit into the perfect catastrophe.

I pick a worm off the fork to study his segments.

'*Coucou.* Audrey, do not eat that worm, you look feral.'

Tata scoots across the field, a little electric cavalry, and brings herself parallel to the compost bins. The worm turns up into a U, so I release him to join his family.

'You should run the fork through your hair, couldn't do any harm.' Tata turns the scooter off and shuffles her legs around.

'I thought you were away for the week.'

'I know the lawyers are out today, so thought I'd pop in. How are you coping with them?'

'They're tolerable if I stay out here in the field. Plus, there are more pressing things on my mind, like being single is a state I've forgotten, and it's best to familiarise myself with it while busy.'

She pats her heart. 'Maybe you won't be single for many more weeks?'

'Tata, it seems I've been single all along. It seems likely Simon and Midori have not let his marriage to me get in the way of their affair. I don't know for sure, but I suspect my husband and Dr Midori Crump have been at it for forty-one years.'

'Oo, *la vache.*'

Suddenly her eyes are rheumy. Her arthritic, knobbly fingers look like a wounded creature. I lean in and kiss her forehead, note how dry her skin is.

'Don't worry, single is only a label. And, yes, my heart feels muddled by the freedom, but there are plenty of upsides.' I prop the fork against the bin. 'I have learnt a lot this week. For example, did you know when you delete a text from your phone, it remains on the recipient's. Lilou told me.'

'Who did you text?'

'Simon, it was the first I might add, but written in a bad mood.'

'Good for you.'

'And Lilou told the lawyers I'm an artist. The more I scuttle off to hide, the more it whets their appetites. They read my skittering off as the antics of a charming, reclusive savant – which I'm not. I'm burning off an intense heat that Simon generates in me. But we're not talking about him.'

Tata swivels on her seat and glances around the field. '*Alors*, what's this about you being an artist? You're not referring to moving the rocks, are you?'

'I am *moving* rocks, Tata, but you could say, as Lilou does, that I'm creating an installation. Come with me.' I brush compost straw off my trousers.

'*Pardon*. What's your *installation* called?' Tata dismounts from her scooter. 'Give me your arm, Audrey.'

This display of frailty, her bony wrist against my upper arm, the maudlin pace, are almost too much. I lift my chin high so she can't see my face. I know I will forever remember this moment, the quality of light, the rustle of her skirt against my jeans, the delicate weight of my lovely Tata.

'Right, the installation is called, "Sisyphus was an Idiot". I am converting your large pile of rocks into an elegant barrier, which will hide the compost bins.' I sweep my other arm back and forth indicating where this oeuvre will eventually manifest. 'Come and see where I began, against the pear tree.'

Tata bends a fraction to peer between the stones. 'Nice, neatly stacked.'

'You can sit on it. This end is very stable.'

She looks at it dubiously but gently lowers herself onto the top of the wall.

'Excuse me, this job is noisy. No-E showed me how.' I squat, take the metal spike he's lent me, and place it strategically on my stone of choice. Then I give the spike a hefty wallop with the mallet. The flint succumbs to reveal its belly. I run my fingers over the smooth surface, chuffed to bits. 'Magic, isn't it?'

'Should you wear gloves?'

'Probably. Bit late for some of my fingers. Limestone is a breeze; pretty much flops open with a tap. Red granite just won't give. And to think Sisyphus spent so long at war with just one rock. Didn't he realise there's a difference between perseverance and lunacy?'

'How far do you think your wall will go?'

'Until the rocks run out. Stone masonry is therapeutic. You know when I was laying those rocks you're sitting on, they heard my confession – I miss good sex; I've only had three orgasms with Simon in the last ten years.'

'Should you be telling me this?'

I put a few lumps of limestone in the wheelbarrow and walk back over to where she sits. 'Sorry, Tata, but I don't care who I tell anymore. This next, two-deep, vertical row will harbour truths about how bored I get when Simon goes on and on.'

I hold a limestone up for her to study. Put it down and split the poor thing open.

'You know I memorised the periodic table as a technique for surviving his monologues. Had it written out on a bookmark and surreptitiously revised it while he droned – Harley Health

Like Beautiful Body, hydrogen, helium, lithium, beryllium, boron et cetera.'

'This section of your wall is going to be very long.'

'As were his rants.'

'Take me back to the scooter, Audrey.'

'Are you …'

'Some days I'm wobblier than others, that's all.' She eases up from her stony perch. 'Will your children feature anywhere in the installation?'

'Certainly. I'll choose beautiful rocks, kiss them and lay each one carefully.'

We walk slowly. Tata forces a breezy normality into her pinched features. Then she climbs onto the scooter, leans back and closes her eyes for a moment.

'Well, Audrey, I'm glad you've found a way to avoid the guests rather than running around after them.'

'Lilou told them this whole *installation* will be reconstructed in a copse on the grounds of a château. Apparently they want to take photos, but she says it's a private, commissioned work and they should not.'

Tata puts her hands together. 'Lilou is a good woman.'

'Indeed, and now I must get on.'

'Audrey, are you sure you're all right?'

'I am. The worst I feel right now is monumentally silly. I just spent thirty-seven years like a basking whale, swimming in my own ecosystem of husband and children. I was happy to absorb myself into that small world and it into me. Wasn't it a pretty notion to think my husband felt the same?' I stoop and choose my next piece of limestone. 'Three months ago when I thought about Simon, I brimmed with the milk of human kindness; today my feelings have curdled.'

26

Checkout is 11 am. The lawyers leave at 5 pm. I may sue. I wave a cheery goodbye from the side of my snaking wall. When the rear lights of their vehicle are no longer visible, I leave the field, change out of my gardening clothes and hop into the cottage to get it ready for tomorrow's American guests doing Mont Saint Michel and Saint Malo, with a particular interest in Celtic music.

At home I have a system, which will be applied here. Strip the beds and put the linen in to wash. Spray the bathroom. Then into the lounge, bedrooms, corridors etc. Back to the bathroom, kitchen, and then out of there. No matter which room I'm in, I start at the top and work down – it's foolproof.

In the bathroom, oh my goodness. Their London bodies have thrown up a greasy film of flotsam and jetsam. The glass shower recess is so milky a shaving canister must have exploded. The wall and floor tiles are strewn with the dark, thready remains of a barber's floor put through a centrifuge. All that head and pubic fur must be vacuumed before I can even start. I back out of the room and apologise sincerely to the hoover. He tangles his cord in protest and puts up quite a fight before I can get him all the way into the house of horrors. In the absence of PPE,

I retrieve my gardening gloves and napalm the whole place with a eucalyptus–bleach mix.

At least the bed linen wasn't so bad. Washed and white, it jostles happily in a light breeze, blissfully unaware this freedom is only temporary and tomorrow they'll be incarcerated again, stretched around mattresses, buttoned up against duvets, plumped out with pillows. Fly free, my white beauties. Enjoy the moment.

———

Tata's bedside-table-chair was no longer big enough, so I swapped it for a cardboard box. Then last night I knocked over my glass of water, and this morning everything is soggy, and the box sags in the middle.

Inspired by my successful renovation of the bird table, I'm lured to make bedroom furniture. I cut some wood, and nail four legs together with cross-pieces. I think it has potential. I put my mug down, nudge a leg, and the coffee oscillates. When the surface is still once more, I note a marked slope to the liquid. This tells me one leg or legs is/are longer than another/the others, but which? I bend low to calculate the issue from the angle of the coffee.

'*Quisiera encontrar un hombre que pueda hacer eso.*'

No-E's voice, but it isn't French.

'Spanish,' he says, in French, 'and it means, I'd like to find a man who can do that.'

'Do what?'

'Make a flat surface.'

Technically he's right. No-E moves from the doorway into the darker interior of the *remise* and establishes himself at my workbench. He moves things, tucks random stuff up in the roof space, shifts tools. I retrieve my coffee and sip it. He takes my *masterpiece* and places it on the bench then, agenda apparently satisfied, he asks me to join him. I do. He gives me a look which says, *Put your mug down and pay attention.* I do.

He circles suspiciously around the construction. 'What are you trying to make?'

'A bedside table, from spare wood.'

'Just one?'

'Just one.' I stroke my project.

'You must change your language. Wood is what you burn in a fire. You will make this from timber.'

'Right.'

'Each leg of a table has to be exactly the same length.'

This much I know, but I think it best the student remains silent.

'Also, use the Japanese saw for fine pieces. It cuts on the reverse and is more accurate. You will measure everything in millimetres not centimetres, and good lighting will help.'

No-E rummages in a cupboard and produces a dusty lamp which he clamps onto a shelf above the workbench. Then he picks up a pencil and drops it into an old tin.

'You must not use pencils when you mark timber for a cut line. A pencil, in the trade, is as thick as a thumb print. In the future use a Stanley knife for all markings on fine work.'

'Is this fine work?'

'Yes, compared to your wicker hoops, the wall in the field, this is indeed fine work.' No-E has a mischievous grin but doesn't look at me. 'If you want to undertake any bigger projects, like enlarging the chicken coop, you can use a biro.'

He produces a biro from his shirt pocket and a Stanley knife from his back trouser pocket. The man is a boy scout. He places both items in front of me and I pick them up to examine their properties with respect.

'Please sweep the bench.'

153

'*Oui, monsieur.*'

The metal dustpan is battered, the brush has seen a lot of work, or has the onset of alopecia – I do as I'm told.

No-E picks up the wobbly construction, deconstructs it, and lays the legs out in a neat row along the back of the bench. He then takes a spare piece of *timber*, marks it with the Stanley knife and clamps it into a vice. He hands me what is apparently the Japanese saw.

'With regard to making an acceptable cut, start by going slow. Tell yourself not to apply pressure on the saw during the backstroke.' He demonstrates with his empty right hand: it moves forward with purpose then retracts slowly. 'Gradually apply more pressure on the backstroke.' He mimes the action again. Then he juts his chin forward to indicate I may start. 'Get into a rhythm before you increase the speed.' His right arm pumps back and forth. 'Concentrate on cutting to the mark; blow sawdust away in order to see your line.' He blows and a puff of sawdust skitters away from the blade.

The cut at the end of my first try looks much smoother than my earlier work. No-E holds it up against a set square, to show me why I shouldn't be wearing a satisfied grin.

'It's a good start,' he says, 'but I insist we mark out several more cuts and continue. Soften your wrist and get your head over the line.'

He puts another scrap in the vice for me to try again. 'It's a good thing you want to learn new skills,' he says, 'it will stop you being sad. Day after day we put up a brave struggle because what we touch and feel is only an imperfect imitation of a higher existence.'

Oh lord. Today in particular his body and mind are behaving like a dressage pony on crack; gorgeous, intelligent precision, gone haywire.

'Does your husband make you happy?'

Can I lie to this man? 'Not for a long time.'

He raises one bushy eyebrow, congratulating himself on a private suspicion. 'Never mind. After all, what constitutes happiness?'

'Indeed.' I straighten up. He gives me a little nod which I gather means he's satisfied with my last attempt.

'Pascal, may I ask you a question, please?'

He's poker-faced.

'Where do all your truisms come from?'

He puts both palms down on the bench and stares out of the window. 'I was a psychiatrist in Paris for many years, but then I started drinking because the more I heard, the less things made sense. My wife left me because of the drink. I became resentful, because we never spoke about it, and resentment is the silence around an unresolved thing. Then I got psoriasis and moved to Brittany.'

'Wow.'

'I have no psoriasis now.' He unbuttons his cuffs, rolls up both shirtsleeves and shows me his unblemished forearms. He clearly decides this is enough for now, spins on his polished boots and scuttles to the door. 'You should practise your cuts.' And he's gone.

Years ago, my brother sent me a postcard from Italy; a picture of Brancusi's bird. The sculpture's abstract swoops and lines are more birdlike than any realistic representation – and more inspiring. While I was turning compost – lifting my head above the decaying, cloying smell – I wondered how that experience of the compost could be reproduced? With barbed wire and bark perhaps. And when I miss the sea at home, I think I might attempt the flicker of a shoal of fish with cut up plastic bottles or tin. I'm not sure. The *remise* is full of boxes and bags of neatly saved oddities, and they beg to be used.

The cure for some of these *itches* is to let myself loose. And I'm quite confident that, after making this table, sinuous, flamboyant, lucid lines will come more easily. I may start with a simple scarecrow – an effigy of Simon. I'll give him a paunch and spittle in the corner of his mouth. And I hope birds will poo on his head.

27

Everyone's courgettes have gone mad and giving them away is impossible. I've learnt a lesson – never grow more than one courgette plant at a time. I think No-E may have mentioned that when I first arrived. But I now find myself having a lot of incidental conversations with neighbours about courgette etiquette: when to pick them, how many flowers should be left on the plant, what to do with a courgette. The many options include ratatouille, cake, soup, stuff them or freeze them for the harsher months when you're happy to see a courgette again. You can also blend a courgette with any number of herbs and garlic for a pesto. Or use them instead of eye pads during a siesta. Or perhaps pose a courgette with a kitchen utensil and a glass and paint a still life.

In another few weeks I'll be able to write an equally fascinating list on spaghetti squash, greengage plums, apples, pears and mirabelles.

There are new guests in the cottage. They arrived at 1 am by car from Schopfloch, which I've located on Google maps to be in the Black Forest. Every vowel they utter is hurled forward and pronounced with their tongue against the roof of their mouths. Every consonant is boomed. I think they're happy but it's hard to tell.

I'm heading back from another bout of gardening when I pass the guests mid two-hundred-decibel breakfast. Haricot has decided no attention can be too loud when there are buttery chunks of croissant on the table.

I try two cheery German words, '*Guten morgen,*' and am immediately shunted across the gravel as a reciprocal soundwave hits me.

I keep walking and my wrist buzzes. The little black screen lights up. It's an email, from *him*. Banana cake. Make one – now. The overripe fruit on the kitchen table is suddenly incredibly important.

Only when I've lined up all the ingredients, and the oven is on, do I stop, sit down and open the computer. The first line and a half is a general greeting with a non-specific enquiry as to how I am. I read it twice. Yes, it's a cut-and-paste opener and an elevator plummets in my gut. The next thirty-two lines are dedicated to what he's been doing – minus any mention of Midori.

I take up the whisk, smash the bananas, bully the butter and sugar to become one. I can't remember if I have already put two or three cups of flour in the mix, so I add an extra egg in case. The ad hoc mixture goes into its tin, and I slam the oven door shut. The urge to scream marginally overwhelms my desire to cry but I sit down again. I wrap the computer lead around my fingers and reread his email. My rule of thumb has always been to be polite. If someone speaks to me, I reply. If someone writes a letter, I write a letter.

Simon,
I was surprised to receive your email. I'm not ready to start corresponding with you until you've told me the truth.
Audrey

Extremely reasonable, given I feel out of control. I cover the butter, put away the scales and flour, set the cake timer for thirty-five minutes and … There's an ominous ting on my wrist. Another email.

> Audrey,
> Your curt reply is not helpful. When do you think you will come to your senses?
> Simon
>
> Simon,
> It's been five minutes since I wrote. I'm _still_ not ready to correspond, you need to tell me the truth.
> Audrey

My brain crackles and smoulders. I dread/want another email. What elicited his first one? Does he expect me to send a rapt, whispering plea for him to please reconsider his options and pick me? Does he hope I'll turn a difficult moment in _his_ life into a taut piece of great beauty. Does he want me to set him free, graciously?

Email three arrives ten minutes later. This one outlines the discussions he's had with our children. Of course, I already know their version of those conversations. I choose not to reply and sit down feeling like I've been sucked into deep ocean by a rip-tide.

Then email four appears saying he's forgotten to ask what I think about him going ahead with some study grant thing, which he'd mentioned in email one. Jesus. Four emails and the only civility dedicated to me is the first line in the first email, and there's nothing about his history or plans with Midori.

Eventually the smell of cake draws me away from the laptop and I open the oven. The top of the cake has split nicely, and the edge has started to come away from the sides. I place the bronzed success on a cooling rack near the window; there's a *House & Garden* photo opportunity if ever I saw one. In the past, when Simon and I were apart, I might have sent him such an image, a sort of cutesy, *look what you're missing* shot. Or I'd send a photo of the kids with their mouths full of cake. Where was he all those years when he looked at my happy snaps? In bed with Midori, at dinner with Midori, on a plane with Midori? I really have no idea, and I have no desire to send him an intimate image of my life now. I don't want him to know anything about my world. I bend in low to the cake and let the warm aromas soothe my skin.

> Simon,
> Make university plans as you see fit.
> Obviously, you're keen to hear my news, which will probably come as a surprise to you.
> I appear to be locally recognised as a substantial bassist. I attribute this to all those evenings spent playing Guitar Hero with the children. There is a slew of local musicians who want to jam with me. Furthermore, it has been suggested I may be able to establish a respectable solo career when pantomime season is over.
> Audrey

I shut the computer and put my smart watch up on the dresser.

What I have not anticipated is a WhatsApp call. Pathetically, I can't resist answering, or is that a knee-jerk reaction? I'm not sure.

'Audrey, these emails aren't getting us anywhere.'

'Us? I thought you and Midori were the *us*.' I know my voice sounds peevish.

There's a long sigh. 'Okay, is this what you need for a clean slate?'

'I'm not sure the slate will ever be clean, but understanding might help. Put your camera on, please, I want to see you for this conversation.'

There's a moment or two and then the home office comes into focus. I see the bookshelves, a glimpse of the garden through the window – still no lawn, which makes me smile. Howard is asleep in the doorway, and I want to call out his name. Simon's face is stony, jowly. I adjust myself and the phone so he can't see much of me, nor my surrounds.

'So? And, Simon, don't tell me some fiction about the last three years.'

He looks into the camera for a long moment and swallows.

'During my first degree I did a year's exchange in Edinburgh. Going overseas for a year was the done thing. Midori and I started a relationship. We knew it would be frowned upon if anyone knew. She was seven years older than me and my professor.'

Simon reaches out to his glass of water but doesn't drink, just wraps his long fingers around it.

I want to say, 'I expect she's still seven years older,' but don't. He looks at me once more and I raise my eyebrows in response.

'I had decided that friction was going to be my specialty.'

'She's the one who inspired you to become a tribologist?'

'I suppose, although her area is concerned with the increase and control of friction for various applications. For example, she revolutionised shoe soles for the elderly, to reduce falls.' He clears his throat. 'I was besotted. But halfway through the first year of my PhD Midori ended the relationship. She didn't want to get married, didn't want children.'

'I met you during the first year of your PhD.'

Simon's gaze fixes on something to the left of his screen and he nods slowly.

'You never mentioned her.'

He takes a sip of water. 'Didn't I? Probably not, no. Not long after you and I met, Midori married Jack, a Professor of East Asian Music. He was much older and offered what she wanted; a glamorous, globetrotting, intellectual life.'

'But you kept seeing her?'

He doesn't reply.

'Did Jack know about you?'

Simon drops his head and plucks at the stubble on his chin.

'Would it be fair to say Jack was tolerant of you and Midori because he was so much older and their world was so divorced from the mundane, Simon?'

He nods.

'I've looked through my diaries, and I can see you had three or four opportunities a year to catch up with Midori. That's in person. God knows how many letters and phone calls you two exchanged. Am I right?'

There's a pause.

'Yes.' This is directed to his fingers.

There is precious little satisfaction in having my suspicions confirmed. Howard shifts in his sleep in the doorway. The bend and dip of branches outside Simon's study window tell me there's a strong sea breeze blowing.

I haul in a deep breath through my nose. 'Simon, are you going to continue? I can't sit here all day.'

'Jack died four years ago.'

'Did she kill him?'

He lifts his head. 'That's not helpful, Audrey.'

I will not apologise. I think it's perfectly reasonable for a cuckolded wife to imagine the perpetrator is capable of atrocity. I think my quip was funny.

'You know as well as I do, Audrey, when the kids started to leave home, we rattled about the house together.'

'Are you saying that without our common denominators under the same roof there was nothing? I thought we were both in pain together. I thought we'd both mourn the loss of that life and make another one. I was also contending with menopause. Children leaving at the same time as plummeting hormone levels is a cruel time.'

Simon's chin drops slowly, and he looks to one side, moves a sheet of paper.

'Perhaps you were waiting for the kids to go?' I add. 'I believe this can be the point of no return for many couples.'

'No, you're simplifying.'

'Well, of course I am. My role in the world has been upended, my children no longer need me, I'm unable to breed, I have no employable skills; not much going on there for a woman who's devoted herself to her family. Of course you would think it was all horribly simple.'

It's clear Simon has nothing to say to this because he simply fiddles with the paper some more.

'Oh, just carry on with your story for god's sake.'

Simon lifts his head. 'Jack died about the same time Orson moved out, and that's when Midori and I got a huge grant to write this latest book together.'

'You and I might have taken up something together, you know, Simon.'

I watch the tears slide from under his drooping lids and a sob escapes into his cupped palm. I'm shocked and part of me wants to soothe him, but a stone is lodged in my gut, and I haven't finished.

'I have another question, Simon. Did she give you the Japanese painting? The one you said I obsessed about.'

A silence dominates my kitchen, his office. The smell of cake is faint now. Muscles in his jaw pulse.

'She painted it.'

I gasp. His sobs deepen. I push open the kitchen window so that his self-pity is sucked outside, away from me. Those tears are not remorse. The water on his cheeks isn't regret. This is confusion: he has the children he wanted, all grown up and independent. Midori the widow available once more, what should he do?

I say nothing and push back in my chair to be as far away from his image as I can. When his eyes dry, he looks up and I see he's oblivious to my pain. In fact, it appears he feels a little better now he's offloaded the terrible time he's having. I want to launch myself through the screen and slap his face. It's an odd feeling. I sit with myself in the silence. The desire to help him, to be gentle, is absent now. I will not create a rationale for his actions, and I feel no pity. This is all alien.

He slides his elbows towards the screen, interlocks his fingers. 'Audrey? You have the whole story now.'

I preferred the silence. 'Right.'

Simon's head jerks forward. 'What do you mean, "right"?'

'Your story erases much of the life I've been living. I will have to process our marriage differently. I must include details, such as how you lay in bed with Midori while I took your mother out to lunch, played with the kids, typed up your work. I need to reconcile you sharing blurred intellectual, romantic intimacies with another woman yet you wore headphones at home around me. You made me feel crazy about hating that picture, Simon. And now you have the gall to sit there wanting me to blow smoke up your arse? I'm not going to.'

Arse, I regret. It's what he expects from me, an emotionally driven expletive. He opens his mouth and I lift my hand.

'Simon, do unto others as you would have done unto you is our most highly developed morality.'

Simon leans closer to the screen. His skin is dry and there are lines I haven't noticed before. I can see his pale scalp, and a tension pulls tight across his nose. He looks weakened. 'Audrey, listen—'

'Simon.' I cut him off.

'Yes.'

'Fuck you.'

28

Standing back to appraise the papier-mâché sculpture, I'm surprised to see I haven't created courgettes, but a man's privates heavily outlined against his trousers. No amount of green paint is going to redeem it. Nor is the tap dancing coming along as well as I'd hoped. My right knee objects to a few of the moves, and I haven't found the correct ratio of drawing pin to sole of shoe. Result; the sound I make is occasional rather than rhythmic. And I had to take François back to his field this morning. Tata said he often drops in to eat the fallen fruit off the lawn and I need not worry. She says the council know where to find him.

'Do you want a drink with us?' Lilou's voice wafts into the *remise* from the direction of the terrace.

Us? Is Pierre back, is the wedding on again?

'You've got a surprise.' A different female voice.

Mysterious. I wipe my hands on a damp cloth and descend the few steps to the terrace. Lilou, in a rhinestone-heavy denim jumpsuit, sits opposite Rose. Their heads are close, and Rose weaves a strand of Lilou's hair around one finger. I see not all the lawyers left. Or Rose returned. Either way, her presence explains Lilou's less frequent visits.

On the table to the right of them is a bucket, and from

this rises a huge mixed bouquet of flowers in layers of purple cellophane.

Lilou leaps up and kisses me twice.

Rose twists around on the bench and smiles. 'Evening.'

'Look who got flowers!' Lilou pushes the bucket over.

'Who?'

'You, silly. We bumped into the florist at the end of the lane. I said I'd bring them down. Read.'

Lilou extracts the card from its plastic faux-twig stick and hands it over. 'Who are they from?'

The garish bunch sets off a slow creep of disappointment inside me. If Lilou and Rose weren't here, I wouldn't open the card. I'd sit with this emotion and then ... I don't know what, but alone I would give myself time. However, they clearly want a romantic conundrum solved. They want to see an older married woman get flowers from her husband after all these years. How little they understand.

I make my fingers open the envelope. My gut concertinas. Then I read the message out loud, with a smile on my lips so the words don't sound ungrateful.

'Hoping France is treating you well. Happy anniversary. You're missed. S.'

'That's an underwhelmed response if ever I saw one.' Lilou sits up straight. 'What anniversary? Is S your husband?'

'It's the first day we met.'

I flip the card between my fingers. Is S my husband? Excellent question. Do I still have a marriage? I don't think I do. I put the card down, turn my head between Lilou and Rose.

'Ungrateful, aren't I? Rude. Never mind. So,' I look at Rose, 'you didn't leave?'

Lilou jumps in. 'No, she didn't, then she did, then she came back, and it's not the point right now.'

Faced by two kind women, it appears I have a choice. Brush my feelings about the flowers and Simon off, which I'm an expert at, or be open. Dr H said I should talk to nice people. Would it kill me to try?

'I don't like mixed flowers, unless they're roses picked from a garden, or in a garden.'

'Good to know, I'll make a note. Go on.' Lilou pretends to type this into her phone.

'Simon should remember. My wedding bouquet was freesias. The vases at home are only ever filled with one bloom: sunflowers, agapanthus or lilium. When I take flowers as a gift, it's one type only. I have never mixed flowers, never, in thirty-seven years, and he should know. The fact he doesn't annoys me.'

'I can tell.' Lilou studies my face very carefully, drums her fingers on the table. 'So, Pascale's accident is not the only reason you're here?'

Both women wait for a reply. I've questions too. What is this thing between them? They say to assume is foolish, but I think it is perfectly reasonable to assume there's romance afoot. If that's the case and I tell them about Simon's infidelity, it might be the pot talking to the black kettle.

'If you'd rather I went, so you two can talk?' Rose shifts along the bench.

'Stay, please.' I take a couple of deep breaths. 'Let's have wine, then I'll tell you my version of an age-old story.' I flip-flop my hand between them. 'I'm a little worried. It might be awkward. Because you two … But what do I know?'

I push the white slip to one end of the table, pass around glasses. Lilou tears up a baguette, and Rose pours wine.

Lilou leans forward, her rhinestone sleeves send shards of light in all directions. 'My story is moot for today, but, yes, we will discuss, I promise. Meanwhile, Audrey, spit it out.'

'Right, okay.' I press my palms flat on the table. Rose lays a hand on mine, Lilou follows suit; we're a tripod.

'In May I was at home alone …' Regret sets in and my words slow as I try to think of a way to retreat.

'Well, this is a suspenseful opener! Reminds me of a Scandi-noir film.' Lilou leans up onto her elbows and plants a kiss on my cheek.

'Right, I asked my husband if he was having an affair, and he sort of said yes.'

'Sort of?' Rose's voice is soft, encouraging.

'He said *they* were thinking about it.'

Lilou's chin pulls back into her neck. 'Shit.'

'Since then I've had the facts updated and the thing I find particularly shitty is he's been in love with this woman for forty-one years. I've only been with him for thirty-seven. Worst of all, I had no idea about her.'

I stop for a minute. They probably think I'm stupid for not knowing. I think I'm stupid for not knowing.

'You're not saying anything.'

Lilou takes her hand down from her mouth. 'Audrey. My god! What a shock. You had no idea?'

'None, not until weird things started niggling at me, but I used empty nest syndrome as a blanket excuse for everything.'

'What niggles?'

'Many.' I stare at the card.

'He sounds awful; they are both horrible people.' Lilou clasps my hand tight.

'I agree but, and this is me attempting to understand why he *needed* a lover, it isn't self-pity, it's self-analysis. Okay?'

They both nod.

'I have been *doormatty*. I've apologised for every discordant thing at home. A million times I've said, *Daddy's not cross, he's just worried.* I should have said, *Simon, explain yourself to the kids.* But no, if he was angry, I thought it was because I wasn't playing my part well enough. It was my job to care for the kids and remain patient. *Daddy's under a lot of stress. Sorry, Simon, I'll take the kids out.* For hours, months and years I made sure their noise, my noise, didn't disturb him. For fuck's sake, I've shooed birds away from the tree outside our bedroom window when he needed to sleep in. What was wrong with me?'

'You were being kind, Audrey. Considerate.' Rose squeezes the back of my hand.

'Do you think? That's what I hoped. I hoped letting things ride for the sake of peace was a good thing.'

Lilou flings herself back and the rhinestones flare. 'Bloody hell, wanting your partner to love you is normal.'

'Maybe so, but I became one of those women I don't like. A vacuous shadow, self-conscious and excruciatingly awkward.'

'You? Not possible.' Lilou looks cross.

I lift my hand to stop her. 'I'm afraid it's an easy trajectory, which I started early on. At first, I had an overriding need to be liked, to have Simon's and his colleagues' approval. I became adept at giving people what they wanted and I created wishy-washy Audrey. I guess that boils down to a sense of shame in the real me – how sad is that?

'Then I spent years being Orson, Thea and Gus's mum. My existence was validated – without me no them, and vice versa. It was lovely until a few years ago when I looked up and the three of them had gone off to lead their own lives, and me a mourning vapour trail in their wake. Finally, I acknowledged the need to move on from mummyhood, it was time to look at the bigger picture, but guess what? It seems I missed the boat.

'Nothing is expected of me in Australia, where everyone wants to stuff Granny in the wardrobe. Except,' I raise one finger, 'it's okay if I'm not a burden.' The second finger goes up. 'I am allowed to help out here and there.' Three fingers up. 'Oh, and please keep a low profile because no one wants to be reminded of what's to come.'

Rose tilts my chin up so her blue eyes address mine. 'Those rules are *merde*, Audrey. You're in your prime.'

Haricot glides his soft flank along my legs.

'No-E said something to me during one of his visits, *Resentment is the silence wrapped around an emotion.* I do not have time for resentment.'

'True, and you must not remain silent, in fact you should roar.' Lilou throws her head back and lets out a sample of what that might sound like. Rose offers a more rounded version.

We pause to sip wine, nibble cheese and lick our fingers.

Lilou twirls the flower bucket, the cellophane crackles softly. 'Do you think these flowers are his way of saying he wants you to go home?'

'I don't know. Perhaps he wants to soften me up so I don't take him to the cleaners financially.'

Lilou's hands fly to her jaw. 'I do not like this man.'

Haricot hops up onto the bench next to me and works his way onto my lap. He presses my thighs rhythmically, purrs loudly and settles against my belly. I hold my wineglass in two hands and stare into the ruby liquid.

'Do you think he'd have told you if you hadn't found out?' Rose's soft enquiry again. I can imagine her with a client, nurturing, cajoling them. I hope she works in family law and not something like mergers and acquisitions.

'I don't know. I could have gone to my grave none the wiser. On the other hand, maybe he'd do anything to be with her, I don't know.'

Lilou runs her finger through a spot of red wine on the table. 'Have you cried?'

'I think I'm still in shock. The effort and ache of … it's hard to verbalise, except to say, I haven't lived the life I thought I had, and it's unsettling.'

'So,' Lilou slaps her palms down on the table. 'What are you going to do?'

'Theoretically I'll go home at the end of August, after the last guest, but I can't imagine being ready then.'

Both women applaud, rapid little claps high in front of their faces.

'Don't go until you know what you want. Do you know what you want?'

'I know I want you to take those flowers with you when you go. And I know I don't want quiet Sundays and perfect lawns.'

29

I let the days come and go like coincidences; only the different guests distinguish one set of days from another. The most recent people, birders, were out from dawn to dusk in pursuit of choughs, hoopoes and so forth. Then they spent the evenings 'listing' and never used the kitchen – I liked them a lot.

Of course, I'm still a domestic goddess – fabulous with grout, fridge drawers and so on, but in between I've mastered three tap steps without checking the video and can cut timber in a straight line. Things are looking up.

I know it is late July because the current guests are lotus-eaters. They're young and loll about getting stoned. The rolled joint has been replaced with vapes and oily liquids. These young folk tell me it's much healthier than mixing pot with tobacco. The only downside is this group have masses of long, floppy hair and I've developed a late-onset, shower-drain sensitivity.

This morning the outside table is strewn with a variety of large crystals. I am considering how and where to move them so I can lay the breakfast things, when one of the soft, bed-haired lotus-eaters emerges from a downward dog to my right.

'Good morning.'

'Morning.' She beams at me and raises two salmon-pink arms above her head, then descends again.

'Shall I leave these things on the side?' I lift the tray up a little so she can see it from the yoga mat.

'Please. The crystals must stay in the sun to be refreshed.' There's the sound of an exaggerated breath being taken in through nostrils.

'Excellent. Good weather for it, I'd imagine.'

'Perfect.' She balances on one leg. 'My friend has had some, *uh* issues and, well, we're all taking the opportunity to, to *um*.'

'It's a good place for that.' I decant the contents of the tray and make sure the marmalade doesn't cast shadows on the quartz.

'Join me, Audrey?'

'I couldn't.'

'You might feel you can't but look at you: two blackened nails, a bandaid on your right arm, bruise on your left and a significant scratch across your cheek.'

'I'm very clumsy.'

'Have you considered it's your inner turmoil manifesting?'

The answer is no, but she has me lie on my back, put my feet together and spread my knees. I feel like I'm waiting for a gynaecologist examination.

'Comfortable?'

'I'm sure I will be in a minute.'

'You know, Audrey, this is the first time you've been still since we arrived. You're here, there, scuttling about, in the field, the garden, baking, out the gate, back in. You're never still.'

'Good point.' It is much easier to sit back with a book when no one is here.

'Right, five minutes. Count backwards from ten. Every time you notice you're thinking about something else, start again. Be gentle with yourself.'

Five minutes to figure out why I gave in to her so easily. Ten, nine, eight – can't remember if I watered the radishes yesterday.

Ten, nine – will I finish the bespoke bedroom furniture today? Ten – must get the kids to send me a picture of Howard. I give up, how much longer do I have to lie here?

―

The table may be a little lower than I'd imagined, but it doesn't matter. The frame is around the legs, and all that remains is to install my beautifully pre-cut slats across the top. I'm optimistic the surface will be flat.

There's the distinct sound of a cordless drill coming from the *remise*, which brings me to an abrupt halt. If No-E has done *any* work on *my* table, I will be unhappy. I take a deep breath, continue across the gravel and enter.

A low-slung shard of sun lights up dust motes, and they loiter, aimlessly, moving on invisible currents. My eyes adjust to the relative gloom. There, taking up nearly all the floor space, are two wood-panelled, Tardis-mated-with-Swiss-chalet constructions. They're held together with clamps and No-E is drilling screws into a hinge.

To the left of these is Tata, on her bicycle, which is now static because one wheel has been elevated, and she's pedalling nowhere.

'*Coucou, cherie.*'

'Should you be doing that?'

'This is good for the hips, and there is no risk of falling.' She wobbles on the seat to demonstrate how stable the bike is. 'Isn't Pascal clever? And, if I pedal for twenty minutes it also helps the brain, right-left coordination and many other things.'

'Who told you this?'

'Oh, I don't remember.' She stares ahead.

'Of course you don't.'

'Look, I promise it isn't one of Pascal's ideas, if that's what you're implying. It was a health professional.'

I shrug and look past No-E's structures to the bedside table. It is untouched. My shoulders return to their usual position.

'What are you making, Pascal?'

'They are dry toilets, for bucolic weddings.' There's a loud buzz as another screw is driven into timber. 'My sister,' he mumbles, screws clamped between his lips, 'is the florist. She does a lot of weddings and we're going to rent them out.' *Buzz*, another screw, and then he gingerly opens and shuts the now hanging door. 'Not just weddings, parties as well.'

'Inspired.'

'You can be the first person to use it,' he says proudly.

I know this is meant as a compliment.

I'm briefly tempted to ask what the plans are for sanitary disposal, because I hope they're adequate. I have become an expert on guests' bodily functions.

He fills his mouth with screws again, and asks me, muffled, if I think someone I've never heard of has significantly altered the landscape of contemporary jazz. Tata pedals on, offering nothing. I tell No-E I couldn't say, and he says that's a shame because it's a question we could all bandy about for months. Then he hands me the drill.

I feel the weight of the Bosch, note the warmth of the handle, squeeze the button so the little engine roars.

'I can do the toilets anytime. You finish your project,' he points to my table. 'Are you going to make another one?'

'No. One's enough.'

'Maybe, maybe not. Nathalie, my sister, wants to meet you. She's unhappy you didn't like the flowers. You'll go to her shop, *non*?'

'It wasn't the—'

Tata slows her legs. 'You will go to her shop, Audrey. She wants you to choose something lovely.'

They both stare hard. It's obviously a matter of floral honour. I agree. No-E beams, then looks at his watch and helps Tata off the bike. I pass her the cane.

'Thank you, *mes chers*. I'm so much better, I'll help you with the cottage tomorrow.'

I see: No-E and I are both her *cherie*; she is feeling better.

'I don't want you to help. I'd rather you did another twenty minutes pedalling if it's so good for you.'

'May I ask you a favour?' Tata straightens out her skirt. 'I've always wanted to learn backgammon.' She fumbles in her pocket and produces a small plastic disc. 'Friends lent me a board, but these pieces are too small for my clumsy fingers. Now that you're a carpenter, I wonder if you would make me bigger pieces?'

I feel the smooth plastic disc between my fingers. We will need thirty. Perhaps I can make half with the old pear tree timber and the other half with bucolic toilet scraps – time with the drop saw is imminent.

'Certainly. I'll paint a board as well; bigger discs will need bigger diamonds.'

'Audrey, you are a natural.' Tata puts the piece back in her pocket.

I curtsy. 'Maybe I'll paint it directly on the terrace table, the guests can—'

'*Pff*, the guests. Paint it on the kitchen table, we can play when it's cold outside.'

When it's cold outside I may not be here.

Some three hours later I have thirty lovely pieces, which need more sanding. And my table is finished. The top planks aren't the same length, but the oiled wood looks rich, and the surface is flat. On goes the lamp, my books, water glass, spectacles. I take a few photos for Mumsgoneawol and Tata so they can all see. The only thing missing in this picture is an electric socket. Having the extension lead coiled under the bed, dangling down the stairwell, then across the kitchen floor is annoying and a trip hazard. I need an electrician.

First, however, Tata reminded me to top up the water butts, then I'll visit No-E's sister. I haven't written these things down; I don't do lists anymore. The urge to justify my existence feels less pressing and I simply recall things because they are a pleasure. If I forget something? Well, that's the great thing about forgettery, I won't know.

I lug the old pump, which is surprisingly heavy for such a small thing, into the lane and put it down next to the well. The grey stone structure is ancient with a domed roof – I'd like to be able to build curves like that. The wooden door is rotten, and the rusting hinges means it must be opened with respect. I turn on the pump and its phenomenal throb ricochets off every surface. I feed the hose down into the gloom of the shaft to attach it to the pipe on the wall and see an immediate problem – an entire community of frogs is down there at the bottom of the well. Obviously, I don't want to suck them up. But what's not so obvious is how I can prevent doing exactly that.

Eventually, with wire mesh and tie solutions in hand – I will not be thwarted by a few frogs – I lower myself, headfirst, further and further into the well until my hips are just over the hard stone rim. It's dark down here and my position is precarious. Above ground my foot flails around until it finds the old door and I manage to hook an ankle underneath. This is tricky.

I had planned to fix the wire mesh over the mouth of the well's pipe to act as a frog barrier, but the task is harder than I imagined. I dangle in the gloom, trying to do three things with two hands, because getting out again is possibly going to be harder than staying here. Drowning in a well attempting to save some frogs is not how I pictured my end.

Then a narrow beam of torchlight pierces the dark and throws the frogs into disarray. It appears I don't have enough muscle strength to pull myself back up so all I can do is watch the frogs dart and dive in the black-green water below. I'm so stuck.

A body presses itself alongside mine on the wall, then a head and two arms descend. I can't see the person's face as their torch is glaring in my eyes. I shout over the roar of the pump and point to the frogs but cannot hear any reply. In the twitching beam I see the person clamp the torch between their teeth. The forearms are masculine, as is the hand which signs for me to hold the mesh in place. I watch deft fingers thread wires behind the pipe and twist them through the mesh. The ligaments in those forearms writhe under the skin, which is darker than my own arms. The pump roars, the frogs settle, and I feel the soft movement of someone else's ribs against my flank. The man removes the torch from his mouth and checks the ties, then his body glides back up. I feel a hand on my ankle and, hoping he's connected my pump above ground, I attach the hose to the pipe, and watch water eddy towards its mouth.

Both my ankles are clasped now, which I'm grateful for. It makes hauling myself up possible, albeit inelegant. After the gloom amongst the frogs, the afternoon sun is blinding. I use both hands to shade my eyes until they adjust.

The man shouts. 'The pump needs oil.'

'*Merci.*'

I nod, and eyes watering, squint at two feet walking away. A car door slams and then I hear it drive off.

When blinking is no longer necessary, I rush over to the first butt and watch the stream of water bounce off the dry bottom. Childishly I feel the same splashing jauntiness inside my belly. Perhaps it's because I didn't drown. Maybe it's because not five minutes ago a male body was pressed against mine. Or maybe it's the two new accomplishments for my CV – hydrology expert and frog preservation.

'Okay, Nathalie, I'm on my way.'

30

Presumably the woman outside the florist's is Nathalie. She's surrounded by vases, some of which appear to be taller than her. I wait across the road. François, his cart, and two council workers are busy watering the communal pot plants. Nathalie's arrangement of glass receptacles on the cobbled pavement looks precarious. It is also after four thirty and the post-school rush is on. Parked cars block the road, vases block the pavement, parents clutch small children and hustle to the *boulangèrie*. There's the additional hazard of heavy-laden tractors rumbling through the village centre. The diminutive, red-haired Nathalie *bonjour*-kiss-kisses people, shunts vases, dodges baguettes.

I wait again, this time for a combine harvester to lumber past, then cross over to her shop. She has coltish limbs, perfect skin and a distinctive, retroussé nose planted centrally on her lovely face; a smooth, plumped-out, younger version of No-E.

'Ah, *bonjour*, Audrey.' She comes in close, offers a cheek.

'*Bonjour*, Nathalie.'

There's no time to protest about her wanting to replace Simon's flowers because she pulls me into her shop. I'm worried about the vases outside. A customer intercepts us and proffers a bunch of flowers. Nathalie stops, chats, clips stems, slices tissue paper, curls ribbon. There's a long exchange as the customer writes out a cheque and Nathalie writes out a receipt, and then he leaves the shop.

She shoos me over to a computer in the little office at the back. Her fingers stab at the keyboard a few times as she brings up the order my husband put in. I read, stiffen, the compressed earth floor cold underfoot. I am not surprised to read his order, *Mixed bunch, colourful.*

The desk starts to buzz. Nathalie feels amongst slips of paper and eventually unearths a phone. She tucks the receiver between her ear and right shoulder to flip through an order book. The phone slips, she gives in and puts the caller on speaker as she rifles through papers. A woman with a vibrato to her voice wants to check an order.

'The funeral, perhaps in two weeks.'

Nathalie moves her hunt from the dandruff of slips on her desk to the pile on the chair.

'Yes, it may be longer, but aquilegias will still be available in two weeks.'

The woman wants to know what will be around in three or four weeks. I listen to the conversation, and it becomes apparent the deceased is not dead yet but keen to organise her funeral exactly how she wants it.

There's the sound of a vase being knocked over. I rush to see if anyone is haemorrhaging to death. No harm done. A young father reprimands his child for not being more careful with their backpack. I assure them it's all fine, no problem, then find a broom, dustpan and brush and sweep up the glass.

A woman in her twenties with pendulous breasts approaches. I assume she assumes I work here, because she hands me a small pot of African violets and a ten-euro note. I commend her on her choice, wrap the plant as I've seen Nathalie do, and give the woman three euros change. Nathalie is still mid phone call with the not-dead customer.

Death is not a dark secretive thing here, like it is in Australia, and I like it. A long history of epidemics, wars and shipwrecks have accustomed the Bretons to contemplate the end. In one of my aunt's books the French Romantic writer Mérimée states Bretons can eat or make love with their mistresses in graveyards. He thought they were endowed with a certain fatalism. I prefer to call it wisdom.

Nathalie ends the call and beckons to me. She doesn't apologise for the interruption, which is impressive. I would have apologised repeatedly if I'd kept someone waiting.

'My brother tells me the flowers didn't make you happy?' Her look is impassive.

'Your bouquet was beautiful, really it was.'

She says nothing, just keeps her eyes on mine, until I'm obliged to continue.

'I like bunches with one type of flower, or just one colour – all white, all blue.' I shift under her steady gaze.

Nathalie plunges both hands deep into her apron pockets. 'He should know this, *non*?'

'He was probably busy,' I say before I can stop myself.

She knows that's pathetic, and her gaze is relentless.

'Yes,' I say, 'he should have known.'

'Good. So now you will make a bouquet for yourself.' She releases me from her optical hold; something inside has been satisfied.

'Thank you.'

Nathalie sashays across the shop to greet two new customers and there's immediately a great deal of activity. Everyone talks at the same time and six pairs of hands flutter in grand gestures. Nathalie finds her order book. The group peer and nod, jazz fingers writhe over clipped photos from magazines. Their voices fade as I wander amongst the buckets, touch the heads of garden roses, pale dahlias, lisianthus, zinnia, foxglove. The low light in the shop, the damp earth floor and the fecund perfumes are hypnotic. I decide on a small, handheld bouquet of the palest pinks and turn the bunch from time to time to insert a stem. My fingers are wet and droplets trickle around my wrist.

'Like those, *Maman*. Exactly like those.' The younger of the two women stands in front of me.

'Oh *oui, oui, ouais*.' The older woman grabs her daughter's arm and squeezes it. 'Perfect.'

Nathalie arrives in the narrow aisle between the cold metal buckets. Her lips twitch briefly into a subtle pout, and she gives me a conspiratorial nod.

'Oh yes, Audrey is *fantastique* with flowers.' Her right hand brushes my hip.

I smile humbly, arrange my face to look at ease in this perfumed cave. There's discussion about the colour of the bride's dress, and the ribbon for the flowers. They bundle me outside with the bouquet, which is to be held up, down, sideways, while photos are taken. Then I'm shooed inside to tie the flowers so the bride can try the bunch. She takes it, giggles. Holds them piously against her chest. More photos. Then the bouquet is put into a glass vase and accompanied by short asthmatic inhalations of pleasure. Finally, Nathalie herds us all into the office. Details, details; dates, table arrangements, mother of the bride, grandma of the bride, witnesses, buttonholes, church vases. My hand scrawls notes, the mother's neck cranes to ensure nothing is missed. They want to know my opinion on everything. They produce pictures of the dress, grandpa, the backyard, their dog, the mayor. The groom looks like he could be Jakob's twin; I hope his voice doesn't break during the ceremony. The bridesmaids will have to get a day off school. They're going to use the village horse and cart, and want the harness decorated. And, yes, they'll take advantage of the purpose-built wooden loos for bucolic weddings.

'Do you think a pink or white cake will look best?' The mother eyeballs me, with the eagerness of someone waiting for exam results.

'If all the decorations are pale, I wonder would a deep purple croquembouche be more striking?'

The bride-to-be and her mother are on the verge of fainting at that idea. Nathalie beams.

I can't help thinking about the earlier telephone call. That customer was a deceased-to-be, not a generally recognised group. A bride is only a bride for one day in Western culture, but she's the bride-to-be for weeks and weeks beforehand. How long before you die are you a deceased-to-be? Days, months, your whole life?

The bride-to-be and her mother kiss me enthusiastically and move off, fizzing.

Nathalie slumps onto a bench outside the shop, invites me to do the same. 'My stock is low today, yet you made something beautiful from very little. You'll do the wedding with me, *non*?' She pulls cigarettes out of her apron pocket and offers me one. 'I'll pay you, naturally.'

My fingers curl around the papery tube. We put our heads together over the lighter's flame. I inhale, once, then hold the cigarette between my thumb and fingers, roll it slowly. I lean on the stone wall to feel the day's heat against my back. I don't know much about flower arrangement, what if I can't repeat today and let her down? I don't want to smoke the cigarette, but I do like the school girlishness of holding it. I let my right foot stretch out carefully and touch a vase with the tip of my toe.

'Yes, I will. It'll be fun, but you don't need to pay me.'

'Yes, I do.' Nathalie keeps her eyes on the passing cars, smiles, and pats my thigh. 'With a husband like yours, you might need a job.'

31

Audrey,

Too little perhaps, and certainly long overdue, but I ordered flowers. You haven't said if they were delivered. Let me know because I can always chase them up.

    Yours, Simon

He'll *chase them up*. I know that means he'll go on the warpath.

Simon,

I did receive a bouquet. No need to sue Interflora.

    A

Yours, Simon. Really. I'm anything but. Perhaps, *yours* since you discovered Midori doesn't do dishes, has her own intellectual needs, and gives you no attention at all.

Lilou crashes through the gate wearing a concertinaed cardboard box with gossamer sleeves. She throws herself down on the bench, thwacks both arms on the table, then starts to bang her head on the wooden surface.

'Audrey, I need to grumble.'

I shut my laptop, push it to one side, and collect my thoughts from the bin of marriage.

'Okay. Grumble away.'

'The whole of Paris is cross with me for not wanting to marry Pierre, and everyone is gossiping about Rose.'

'The whole of Paris, huh?' The hairs on my arm align themselves with her ex. 'Tell me, what does Pierre think about you and Rose?'

'Oh, he's great, he understands completely. You see, I was with a woman before Pierre and I started dating. Everyone else is just annoying. Gossipy idiots.'

She shifts so she is sitting cross-legged. Her right hand on the table flips her phone over and over. Her left hand dangles off the cliff of her left knee.

'My mother is also very unhappy, and I feel like *merde, merde, merde.*'

'Unfortunately, it's human nature to gossip. But if Pierre truly is okay, isn't that the most important thing?'

'Do you believe me when I say Pierre is not upset with me?'

'Lilou, I don't know much about your boyfriend. You're of a different generation. People have different expectations, boundaries. If you've been honest with him then he's a grown-up and can make his own decisions.'

'If Simon had told you about Midori earlier, would you have been okay with it?' She rests her chin on her knee.

'I really can't say. I'd like to think I would have said, "See you later." But I was such a putz, he may have alluded to her many times and I didn't hear. For me, now, it's the emotional betrayal – him in love with someone else while married to me. That's what kills me. Your situation is quite different.'

'And what if I haven't been completely honest?'

I reach out and touch her cheek. She leans into it for a moment.

'Dear Lilou, in general, being general is not helpful when

trying to understand. Of course, you don't have to tell me anything.'

There's a silence and she doesn't move. Five or six well-camouflaged hedge sparrows lift off the gravel. Incredible, here we are, mid-August, and the lazy little things still come to the table to eat. They should be out seeking gnats and flies, grubbing in old wood, lifting seeds from stems. But why would you when it's all neatly laid out for you on a table?

'I will no longer moan,' Lilou says. 'Thank you for listening. Now, everything is ready, and we must go to make a video of chocolate and children for Jakob.'

I don't know why I'm surprised but I am, and yet this is a typically random thing for Lilou to have remembered.

'Okay then. One second.' I take my laptop back into the hayloft.

'Audrey, why are you clicking?'

I lift a leg, show her the drawing pins in the sole of my shoe. 'Tap dancing.'

She drops her head and peers over the top of her sunglasses. 'Why?'

'I'm planning an *Australia's Got Talent* audition, and it's fun. Look.' I break into a little routine then curtsy.

'Impressive.'

'I'd like to learn a more romantic dance at some point, but right now I couldn't fit anyone else into the kitchen.'

—

As we approach the last house in the lane, Madame Potdevin pops into her garden. As always, her timing is impeccable. I'm convinced she has a periscope in her kitchen to monitor the lane for passers-by.

'Audrey, the courgette-nettle pickle was interesting, good with cheese, not so good with meat, but thank you. My jar is nearly empty.'

'I'll have strawberry and pear conserve next week, if you like?'

'Ah, *oui*. Do you have time to come inside?'

Lilou is polite but says nothing.

'I'm sorry, I don't today.'

'Eh *bien*, next time, I have things to show you.'

Belgian placemats, her husband's tatting, who knows what else she has in mind. Lilou and I walk in silence until a final turn onto the playing field by the *Marie*.

There, out the front of the sports pavilion, is No-E, looking unusually smart in a Sunday shirt. He's even brushed his hair. Next to him is a long table laden with boxes and flowers, juice bottles, biscuits, cakes, chocolates. On the other side of the table are maybe thirty children of varying heights, all in their football kit. They mill and giggle, eye up the contents of the table, point, squeal and check in with two adults who I assume are teachers or coaches. A few parents off to one side bob their heads and wave.

'Now, to make this authentically French, I thought Pascal and I would be the servers, and you can do the filming. Use my phone, it has a very good camera. The parents have all given permission, so everything is okay. The children are excited to star in an educational film for Australia.'

Lilou double kisses every single child, who all line up to double kiss me. I am placed, precisely, on one side of the table, she takes up her position alongside No-E, and there are sincere discussions about technique and dialogue.

At last, Lilou presses her palms together and slowly, deliberately, lets one finger after another fold down like

synchronised swimmers, until she has the pious fist of a vicar.
Then she nods.

'*Bien, mes enfants*. Ready, Audrey?'

I have never seen a school volunteer wearing an haute couture
cardboard box, but *vive la difference*! I press record and the
grown-ups release the first child.

A little girl looks straight into the camera and waves.
'*Bonjour, Jakob*.' Then she walks over to the table. '*Une canelé,
s'il vous plaît*, Monsieur Nédélec.'

'*Mais bien sûr*, Isabel.' No-E's face is serious as he hands her
the sticky pastry. Then there's an exchange of pretend money.

'*Merci*, Monsieur Nédélec.' The girl beams like an angel.

'*De rien*, Isabel.'

The whole group follow this pattern, in ones or twos.
Occasionally a child tries to break with the script and buy a
couple of goodies. Lilou will have none of that.

At some point she stops the 'shoot' and suggests I film the
rest of the transactions from behind the table. Proud parents
ruffle the heads of their children. Food is eaten. One of the kids
offers me half his marshmallow.

When the last child is clutching food, and the table is virtually
bare, Lilou indicates we're done. Everyone thanks everyone,
the last few items are distributed, and once again the children
double kiss Lilou and I goodbye.

'*Fantastique*. I will compress the film and we can send it to
Jakob's teacher. That was fun.' Lilou rearranges the crevasses in
her outfit.

Every cell in my body feels fuzzy, warm. 'Lilou, thank you.
I'm really touched. Mrs Kay and Jakob are going to be thrilled.'

Cars filled with children honk and wave to us as they file out
of the carpark. I feel replete.

'Two things, Audrey. One, you said you wanted to get a socket wired into your bedroom – there's an electrician, Dominic, he often goes to La Pointe for lunch. Two ...' She, stops walking, squeezes both eyes shut. 'It's like this. I've completely got a thing for Rose.' Lilou opens the eye nearest me, slowly. 'Cross with me?'

I wait for both eyes to open. 'Did you expect to find me collapsed on the road?'

'Maybe.'

'You're a funny girl. We can't control who we're attracted to. Rose is single, I remember her saying so. I like her a lot.'

'I like her a lot, but I'm not single, am I?' Lilou's grin is lopsided. 'You don't think I'm awful?'

'What for? Having emotions?'

'Am I mad, then?'

'Let's just say I don't think your baguette is cooked in the middle.'

She wraps her long arms around me.

'You're a daft thing, Lilou.'

32

An assortment of white vans is parked outside La Pointe. None has an electrician's logo, and none is sign-written *Dominic Something-or-other Enterprise*. Perhaps he parks round the back, or isn't in today?

The last time I was in here with the children, Gus discovered a soda called *Pschitt* in the drinks' fridge. The kids could not contain themselves and begged, almost daily, to drop in for a bottle.

Today I enter the bar alone. Its charm has been gutted during a recent renovation. It is shiny and new, but some might say soulless. Despite the wide-open windows there is the distinctive aroma of yesterday's illicit cigarettes after closing, mixed with today's *côte de veau*. It's the sort of cloying perfume that lines your nose and lurks there until you're sick of it. Half the tables bear smeared dishwasher-safe plates, empty cider bottles, water glasses, dulled stainless cutlery, scrunched napkins – all proving food and people have been united.

It feels like I've arrived at a time when the hum of conversations dim as lunch comes to an end. Workers shift their seats back and shrug into fluoro vests, ready for the afternoon. Four tables to one side remain occupied by the village elderly. They will no doubt stay here with their chocolate mousse and *fromage blanc* until late afternoon.

When I asked Tata and No-E what Dominic looked like, they were frankly useless. *Breton*, was all I got. Simplistically this means short, swarthy. I'm the only person in the bar who isn't. I could ask to look at everyone's hands for tell-tale wire cuts. Or I can ask the barmaid.

'*Bonjour.*'

'*Bonjour.*'

'I'm looking for Dominic, please.'

Nothing. Her face is completely still. Perhaps there's more than one Dominic. 'Dominic the electrician?'

She wipes a glass and tips her head north along the bar.

'*Merci.*'

Well, she's not having a good day. As I look north, four pairs of eyes look back. I'm starting to think I might wire in the socket myself. Then the third person along shifts his bar stool, stands, and comes towards me.

The approaching man offers me his hand. It is warm and dry, solid, comfortable. His hair is uncombed and his skin creases around his eyes. Oh my, those eyes, dark as blackberries. I'm drawn in. Intrigued, I try to find the pupil amongst the dark iris. He doesn't move, as though accustomed to his eyes rendering people speechless.

'*Bonjour*, Dominic.' His grin spreads, pulling the stubble on his chin into an arc.

'*Bonjour*, Audrey, Madame Pascale Nessler's niece.' I have entered a bizarre staring competition; I cannot drag my eyes away.

'*Enchanté*,' he continues. 'We have met before.'

I am puzzled and must look it.

'At the football ground yesterday. Also in your well, saving frogs.'

Both my hands reflex up to my mouth. 'Oh my.'

The image of ample buttocks wobbling on the top of the little stone wall; the memory of being pressed against a body in those dark confines throws me completely.

'Would you like a drink?'

No, I don't want a drink. And *enchanté*, really? I, the fair-haired frog lady, want to get away quickly.

'I'd love a drink,' I say, 'why not?'

What is wrong with me?

Two other men at the bar get up and shuffle around, put their wallets back in pockets and finish the last of their drinks. I've broken up a male enclave. Dominic doesn't look bothered. I do represent potential income after all. The men briefly discuss how many metres of conduit are needed for the back of the school, everyone wishes everyone a good afternoon and I'm left alone with Mr Hasn't-stopped-grinning.

I order a rosé, which is pretty to look at but so dry my taste buds reel in horror. Dominic has a small beer. I wonder how many he's had this lunchtime. Why do I consider his alcohol consumption, and all the cider and beers that have been drunk today, and how those people will work this afternoon? I'm still uptight, despite being here for weeks. No. I'm rattled because my body has been pressed against his in a dark tube. *Audrey, that's all it was. It is not like you were at a party and had a drunken fumble with this man on a car bonnet.* Goodness. I take a deep breath and try to shake formal-was-married-to-a-serious-academic me into a more laissez-faire version.

Before we perch on neighbouring stools, I notice Dominic is only marginally taller than me. This explains why his eyes are so disconcerting. I literally eyeball his eyeballs with their metallic flecks of purple, their dark green rim and two strangely cool deep-sea pools. Now I also take in his smiley fit-as-a-fiddle, I-live-outdoors physique. How old is he? I wonder. Hard to tell;

European skin is less thrashed than Australian skin, forties maybe. I make a fuss about adjusting myself on the stool and apologise for the disruption to his lunch break. He just smiles.

'So, I hoped you would be able to finish off the wiring at my aunt's, please?'

'Your aunt is a wonderful woman. She was my *notaire.*'

'I think she was everyone's *notaire*, wasn't she?'

'Possibly. At the booth over there,' Dominic turns, points to a table by the window, 'Pascale gives her advice informally, freely. She says she offers common sense in matters of boundary arguments, lease arrangements and discontented partners. Mostly we – this village – don't have complicated legal lives.' He returns his gaze to my face, takes a sip of beer. 'You've come to help her?'

'*Oui*, just the guests in her cottage. So much to do in the garden, the chickens.' I wave my hands as though I've been overwhelmed by important business.

Dominic looks back down at his glass and turns it in his fingers. He probably thinks I'm some rich Aussie who irresponsibly flies around the globe churning up air-miles whenever my silk-screening classes are on a break.

'How long will you stay?' Those eyes are up again.

Perhaps he thinks I'm being extravagant. Why would I want a socket for a few weeks when there's a perfectly adequate extension cord? Or he thinks I've got more money than sense.

'Do you think it's a bad idea, the electricity? Is it a difficult job?'

'No, it's easy. I wired all your aunt's renovation. Do you like it?'

'What?'

'The cottage, the hayloft, living here?'

'Yes, yes and yes. Except I would prefer my aunt hadn't had an accident.'

'If she hadn't fallen, would you be here?'

'Well, no … maybe. I might be. Yes, I would be here.'

He waits for something else. Dominic's beer is down to the last centimetre, and I've politely matched him with the rosé. Who will finish first and bring this interview to an end? He takes a deep breath, or is it a sigh? Does it mean he's reluctant to do any more work now Pascale can't manage the stairs? He lifts his glass. I finish my rosé and turn rapidly to pay the barmaid. She's hesitant about taking the money. I've probably broken any number of Breton traditions and am still none the wiser as to whether he's prepared to do the job. I don't think I'll mention it again. His not answering is answer enough.

We step outside. The air feels fresh, and I'm surprised it is still daylight. On the rare occasions I've been to a matinee I've had the same disoriented reaction. Dominic walks over to a small *sans permis* and asks me to wait. On top of this tiny car, sold to people with no driver's licence, are two extendable ladders, which overhang the length of the vehicle by some distance. He stoops, puts his hand through the passenger door window and opens the car door. Then he pulls out an invoice book and flicks through it before he tosses it back onto the seat.

'I'll come next week.' He fixes me with those eyes.

Out here the colour is even more extraordinary. I wonder when exactly next week but feel it would be too anal to ask. 'Perfect, thank you.'

We take our leave and I watch him put the car on. Yes, *put the car on* like a shirt, because it's what a man with shoulders that wide, who drives a car of those proportions, must do.

33

'Flap HEEL heel SPANK heel TOE heel. And one and two and ...'

My children want me to send a clip of a tap-dancing routine. I will soon, there has definitely been an improvement. They'll have to promise not to put it on social media for general public humiliation. My tap is for therapeutic, not comic, purposes.

This morning I am tightly focused on the 'Alexander Clunk'. It involves rolling the ankle and putting down the outside of my foot – a little precarious. I like the rhythm though. I like the acoustics out here on the terrace, where I practise when the guests are out. Rod, my favourite tutor so far, is loose, convivial. I learnt the 'Double Buffalo' last week. The 'Alexander Clunk' is kind of repetitive, but snappy, and I do it while waiting for the kettle to boil. Have I turned my former feelings of redundancy into art? No. But tap is a joy.

Despite the racket from my feet, Haricot is low down on his haunches, poised motionless. He stares with intent at his reflection in one of the *Vide Grenier* mirrors. His position hasn't altered for twenty minutes. Until today his primary focus has been the exhaustive process of sleeping between meals. Maybe he's taken up loftier considerations? The other option is he's only just noticed the mirrors. I stroke his glossy back and it arches against my hand in pleasure.

'*Solvitur ambulando*. A little exercise wouldn't do you any harm, pussy cat.'

He merely looks at me and settles back down into repose with the idle twitch of an ear.

It's changeover day, again, and I find it harder and harder to work up enthusiasm for my guests who are, to be honest, a dreadful interruption in my life. However, if I don't get on, they will sleep on mattress protectors and dry themselves al fresco.

The current intruders are cyclists. I expect there'll be chain oil on everything. The guests before them were four very American Americans. They had also *done* the Normandy beaches, Dunkirk and Honfleur, and came here to *do* Mont Saint Michel, and the bed linen. The men augmented the colour of their hair with dyes and went to bed while it was still damp – the pillowcases became hapless victims. The women, big fans of blue eyeshadow and orange foundation, did a number on the towels. Tata said it was a trait amongst many guests. If they didn't have to do the laundry, they felt no compunction to be careful.

Because all the linen in the cottage is white, and we're not on mains drainage, I googled environmentally friendly ways to keep linen and towels virginal. I found a well-meaning, softly spoken blonde who wafted about her vlog barefoot in the dark. Her strenuous washing lines bore an assortment of ghostly – presumably white – laundry. Ms Vlog meandered between her anaemic props and stopped occasionally to caress a sheet, or stare lovingly into a petticoat's depths. Then she said, all breathy with ecstasy, 'Hang your whites at night since the moon and the *Oh-zone* combine to be more effective than any laundry detergent.' I won't be trying this.

Sufficiently hot and sweaty, I stop my tap-dancing tutorial and shut the screen.

'Haricot, I'm going for a walk. You should do the same.'

Nothing. Haricot and the cat in the mirror are busy.

'*Bonjour.*'

My head swivels sharply like a tacking sail caught in an unexpected gust. 'Jesus Christ.'

'*Non.* Dominic.' He extends his large palm towards me.

'*Bonjour*, Dominic. I'm sorry.' I wipe my palms down the sides of my jeans and shake his hand.

'Your aunt said you were home at this time.'

'Of course. Would you like a coffee?' This is just a formality, surely he's already had a few. I'm sweaty and disgusting and his eyes are disconcerting; he has to get on with the wiring then go.

'With pleasure.'

Bugger. 'Good. Let me put the kettle on.'

Perhaps he'll come inside and look at the wiring while I make the coffee? He doesn't. From the kitchen I see him sit down on the terrace bench and lean his back against the table. Sod it. I fill the metal kettle and light the blue gas flame underneath. I wipe my face on a tea towel, set a tray. The kettle ticks and stretches. I fan myself with an electricity bill and tuck my nose in the neck of my t-shirt to surreptitiously sniff both armpits. The kettle takes an age. Should I go back outside and talk to him about the job, or stay here and possibly appear rude?

The decision is made when Haricot gets up from his snooze, stretches his spine into a perfect U, then saunters over to Dominic and headbutts him. Dominic twists slightly to scratch the cat behind its ear. The cat in turn leans his whole body weight into the hand.

The coffee made, I take the loaded tray outside.

'Dominic, sorry it took so long. I hope I haven't held you up too much?'

I feel agitated, and wish my hair was clean. He did say he'd come last week. Never mind, I am pleased he's here now. Perhaps I'll be able to plug my bedside lamp in tonight. Then again why am I getting a socket wired when I may be going in a few weeks? I've forgotten the cream for the coffee ...

I like to think my trajectory prescribes a beautiful balletic curve for onlookers to marvel at. But I fear what Dominic witnesses is a post-menopausal woman, in a sweaty t-shirt, falling not only from grace but onto the terrace. The cups shatter in twenty different ways. Sugar fans out from the spinning bowl like magnetic filings. The espresso pot bounces and coughs brown liquid until it comes to a halt, empty, under the table. And I'm on all fours, at Dominic's feet. My wrists hurt; my pride is in agony. I can't put my hands out to pull myself up without clutching the electrician's thighs, and I cannot back away because my knees are strangely numb.

Two strong hands are under my armpits and suddenly I'm upright, lifted effortlessly like a toddler. A hand goes under my chin and tilts my face. I keep my eyes closed.

'Did you bang your head?'

I glance up. His expression is pure concentration. He is focused on me. Water starts to come out of my eyes.

Dominic takes me by the shoulders and sits me down. He pushes back my hair and runs his hands over my face, then takes my chin again and turns it slowly, first left then right.

'Does it hurt?'

I drop my head to hide my face. 'No.'

He lifts my left hand and examines the graze, moves my wrist. I flinch at a sharp pain.

'This hurts, *oui*?'

'Not really. Well … a bit.' In fact, it's bloody sore.

He purses his lips, tsks and lays my hand on my lap as though he were putting a sleeping baby in its crib.

'The other one.' He repeats the examination.

I now sob as his fingers walk from my wrist to my elbow. The skin hunger this sets up in me is agony. I pull away as soon as seems polite but my tears won't stop. My right hand is hot, and the wrist a bit stiff. I roll it around with my fingers playing imaginary scales to prove just how dandy this arm is. I need to wipe my nose on something. I want to vanish. As I move to stand up, Dominic puts a hand on my shoulder, exerting just enough pressure to stop me. I'm stuck, emotionally, physically, on the bench. He bends to look at my knees. Mortification clings like a grasping wetsuit. I can feel the slow descent of snot. Within seconds it will drop out of my squeaking, overfilled nose. I am sure my sobs are quite loud now.

'Don't move.' Dominic heads off to the kitchen.

A moment later he's back and puts a box of tissues near my right hand. I snatch one quickly and honk noisily into the flimsy paper. The wet gurgle is so vulgar I wonder whether I shouldn't have just let my nose run. Dominic deftly secures an icepack to my left wrist with a tea towel. This done he goes back into the kitchen and reappears after a few moments with a broom. He retrieves the coffee pot and asks where the first-aid kit is.

'Oh no, please don't. I'm fine. Don't trouble yourself.'

His look is patient. 'Your jeans are ripped, and your knees are bloody.'

He's right. I don't know if I feel like a child who just came off her bike, or an old woman who didn't make it to her seat before the bus took off.

'Oh please, it's nothing.'

'Move your legs.'

I oblige, to prove they still function.

Dominic lifts my foot, examines the sole of the shoe, and turns his eyes on me.

'*Punaises?*'

If I wasn't so sad, I'd laugh. The French word for drawing pins sounds, in the mouth of a Frenchman, like he's trying to say penis politely. '*Oui, punaises pour la danse à claquettes.*'

Dominic removes my shoes, turns me 180 degrees, slowly, until I face the table. He lifts my ice-packed arm up onto the wooden surface and starts to sweep the broken crockery to one side. Tissue after tissue, I mop my nose, dab at my eyes. The kettle's petulant screech calls him back inside and gives me a chance to recover some dignity.

By the time Dominic returns with coffee, this time in the Bodum, my face is hot but dry. My eyes feel puffy, but they don't overflow.

'Thank you.' I keep my head down to spare him the splodgy red fright of my remnant weeping.

'What for? *C'est normal.* But walking about in drawing pins is not so normal.' Dominic takes a seat on the bench opposite me.

I try a smile, which probably comes across as wind. It's the best I can do.

'I've seen this before.' He pushes the plunger steadily through the brown liquid.

'What, women falling at your feet?'

'*Ouais*, many, many, times. I'm irresistible.' Coffee ready, he pours two mugs. 'Sugar?'

'Today I need sugar.'

'I coach two football teams, under elevens and a women's team.' He snaps a sugar cube in two, puts one half in a mug, stirs, then pushes the warm sweet liquid towards me. 'Often,

I patch up injuries. Collisions, sprains, they're a common part of the game. The boys, they don't make so much of a fuss. I'm the coach, they want to look tough. But the women, they cry when they're hurt.'

I sit up straighter. Dominic stirs sugar into his coffee. Surely this man is not implying … I watch the back of his hands, the way the veins and tendons make a spaghetti junction. It isn't possible he's about to tell me women are weaker. I pull my left wrist in closer to me on the table.

'They cry, not …' He looks me full in the face, emphasises the *not*. 'Not because of the pain, but because of the kindness. I've learnt this over many seasons.'

'Oh.' I had not expected that.

'Mothers cry because they get so little back.' He leaves the spoon in his mug, holds it to one side with a thumb and takes a sip. 'You spend your life giving everything you've got to your family. Everything: your time, your energy, the last banana in the bowl. Then your children drift away, and they don't look back; not often, not even if they're good children.' Dominic takes another sip. 'My theory is mothers aren't used to people caring for them, being gentle with them. It makes them cry.'

I have no reply. Eventually my eyes drag themselves away from his blackberry gaze and I observe my motionless left arm. I dig dirt out from between the table crack with the nails of my right hand. We sit in silence, the coffee levels drop. I beg my tears to stay away.

'And now.' He puts his mug down.

'Ah yes. Now, the wiring, the socket. Thank you.'

'*Non*. Now we get your wrist X-rayed. I think you have broken it.'

34

A slip on a small step. A break. It's not possible. There's so much to do. Indignant, I move to stand, but my thighs ricochet off the underside of the table, which slaps me back down onto the bench. The sudden movement sends a sharp pain through my wrist and I'm sure I yelp.

'I can't have a break. I have cyclists.'

Dominic looks confused and comes to my side of the table. 'Cystitis?' Then he bends, and almost whispers so as not to startle me further, 'Audrey, your French is excellent, but I don't understand you.'

'No, I have *cyclists*, guests, and they're leaving today.'

What doesn't he understand? I've got to clean, and there's a birthday party booked in tomorrow. He pulls the bench out as though I were no more than gossamer.

'Dominic, I don't want my aunt doing any work. The cyclists go today, and I have guests arriving tomorrow.'

Dominic brings me gently to my feet and we walk to the gate.

'The new ones want a cake and candles. And they're arriving early.'

He ignores my domestic anxieties and bundles me, and my full bladder, into his tiny car. This is too awful. I can't move because I need to concentrate on holding my wrist still.

Dominic gets into the driver's seat and leans across to do up my seatbelt. His hair brushes my face, no matter how far back I recoil in this baked bean can. As he drives, our shoulders jostle due to the absence of space and poor suspension. From the feel of it, I'm sitting on a pile of receipt books, and a couple of pens. Every bump plays havoc with my arm, and my desire to pee.

I try to focus on things outside the car: the way summer has eased her tendrils out and the hedges are more densely packed. How tentative, fuzzy fields have reared into the first crops of hay and are being harvested. Kindergarten corn is knee high. But my bladder is persistent and, as we draw up under the ambulance bay of the emergency department, I really do want to cry again.

'Lilou can take me.'

'Audrey, we are here already, I'm with you.'

I must have hit my head after all.

Two orderlies stub out their cigarettes and come to greet Dominic; there's quick-fire chatter and hugs. One of the orderlies disappears to return a moment later with a wheelchair. Dominic puts his arm through my car window and opens the door, which just goes to show how useless I am because it hadn't occurred to me to get out. In the circumstances a wheelchair is overkill, but it's backed behind my knees, and with the pressure of a palm on my shoulder, I sit.

At the reception desk Dominic receives the same visiting-dignitary welcome. Two middle-aged receptionists stand and lean over their desks to kiss and *bonjour*. He leans into them but never takes his hand off the wheelchair. Entirely thanks to his popularity, I'm whisked straight through the department doors, and into a sparkling clean examination cubicle.

My preoccupation with the pain in my wrist, and my fear of being incontinent, have rendered me mute. Dominic understands

I lost my composure some time ago and helps me onto one of the narrow beds.

'Dominic, I don't have a *Carte Vitale*, or insurance details with me, nothing.'

'It's okay. I wired the hospital's cardiac monitoring system, they trust me.'

Almost immediately a doctor emerges from a glass office and slaps Dominic on the back. Then he introduces himself and nods as Dominic recounts my fall. I want to protest that I can tell my own story. But a conversation starts up about how the doctor's son is doing as left wing in the football team. The two discuss offside rules and raising money for new goalposts, while a man in a white jacket wheels me off for an X-ray. At no point along the corridors is there a sign for a bathroom, and my bladder is close to bursting.

When I am returned to the cubicle, Dominic and Dr Left-Winger emerge.

The latter looks at me sagely. 'You have a crack.'

'I have to go to the bathroom.'

'No, you have a significant crack in your distal radius.'

'No. I have to go to the bathroom.'

'Oh, I see.' The doctor looks around for someone to facilitate this.

Dominic swings my legs off the trolley. I want to dispute the diagnosis, and I don't need his help, but the warmth of his hand on my shins is a comfort. He helps me down and walks with me to the bathroom, then shuts the door. I struggle to undo my jeans and sit but can't wee in case he's still out there. And I'm afraid I may fart. It's awful. I am desperate, but I can't relax.

'Audrey. Are you okay?' His voice is muffled by the door.

'Mm.'

Gawd. I turn the tap on to camouflage the sound of peeing, to give the impression I'm on the way out. I sit as far forward on the seat as I can and let my bladder empty silently down the side of the pan. Sweet, sweet relief.

It's now, with one functioning hand, I realise how tricky jeans are to navigate. I stick a hip out to the side so they don't slide down but the zip won't budge. My t-shirt is in the way. I hold the bottom hem of the shirt between my teeth and fight with the zip once more. At last, I emerge.

'Excuse me.' Dominic reaches towards my waist and does up my jean's top button.

I look deep into the far distance, suck in my belly, and pretend this isn't happening.

The doctor has set up a trolley with plaster of Paris bandages.

I hold my arm possessively against my chest. 'I can't have a plaster cast. I just can't. I'm here to help my aunt. My hands get wet all the time because I must scrub the shower.'

Dominic lets me protest a little more, then comes to my aid. 'Perhaps a Futuro splint will be better?'

He and Dr Left-Winger exchange a look.

'Okay. It won't be as secure. You will have to be more careful.'

'I'll be very careful, thank you,' I tell the doctor.

I don't recall exactly what is said after that. There's talk about care of the injury, and analgesia, and how lucky the football team are to have Dominic for a coach. I am pretty sure I smile, and nod, and agree with everything.

Back at the hayloft I insist on a shower, and Dominic insists he'll wait until Lilou gets there, in case I fall.

When I finish, Lilou and No-E are at the kitchen table, Dominic has gone, and Tata is apparently at physiotherapy.

The departing guests come to the hayloft clad in lycra,

hair plastered to their heads with sweat. They squeeze in the doorway and insist they want to help; they'll do anything to be of use.

Lilou decides there's nowhere comfortable for me downstairs and marches me up to bed. She fluffs my pillows then goes home to find more cushions for my arm.

It feels like there's a constant stream of people, up and down the clanking stairs as they bring me tea and take it away again. Do I want water? Have I got a book?

The cyclists come back and shout up the stairs about how they've done their sheets, cleaned and vacuumed. Do I want anything else doing? No-E assumes the role of guardian and tells them not to shout at me, because I am asleep, which I'm not. They don't understand his French. Lilou translates for everyone.

Before today I'd felt myself relaxing here. My grip on the old Audrey was softening. Some mornings, instead of leaping up, driven by a bunch of *should*s for the day, I'd lie in bed, and bask in the satisfaction of watching clouds through the Velux window. Or I'd go for a bike ride, make something, walk for ages. Right now, though, it feels like the emotional equivalent of brawling cats have moved into my head. I reckon it is because all the kindness downstairs is doing me in.

The stairs clang again.

'I've been to the pharmacy.' Dominic opens a paper bag and pulls out painkillers. 'Have you taken anything already?'

'Not yet.'

He sits on the side of my bed and pops two pills into the palm of his right hand, then offers them with a glass of water. 'Take these now.'

I pluck at them, so as not to touch his skin, and try to smile a thank you, while I swallow the white torpedoes. I succeed in producing an impressive dribble. Excellent. Dominic takes a tissue from the box by the bed and wipes my chin. It just gets better. Then he slices the packet and separates two more tablets.

'These are for later tonight. About ten o'clock. No more until the morning. They are every eight hours.' He puts the rest of the tablets back in their box and drops them into the closest basket.

'Oh, Haricot sleeps there.'

He grins and picks up the box. 'Of course. I don't want you to take more during the night because you're confused. I'll take them downstairs.'

He thinks I'm an idiot.

'How much do I owe you, for the tablets?'

'Nothing. It's fine.'

'They didn't cost nothing. I insist, Dominic, please.'

'Audrey, *c'est normal*. You know this, you would do the same.' He grins once more and disappears. The stairs chime out his descent.

I don't know if my family would rally; I've never needed so much as an aspirin from them. This, by contrast, appears to be such a tightknit community we may as well all look into each other's sitting rooms. I shouldn't be uncomfortable but being central to everyone's generosity does me in. I feel an excruciating humiliation. I'm going to have to think about this more, develop a modicum of grace. I understand Tata's recalcitrance a lot better now.

This morning Lilou and No-E are in the cottage, and actually have the nerve to shoo me out when I arrive to set up for the guests. Tata insists I go back to the hayloft, saying I fuss unnecessarily.

'You expect me to be reasonable, Audrey, now I expect the same of you. How's the arm?'

'It's not too sore, if I keep it still.'

'Your fingers are very puffy, are you moving them?'

'Yes, like the doctor said. Look, an inky creep has already started to emerge from the splint. It's like a slow sunset. I'm supposed to be helping you, but all I'm good for is watching flesh discolour.'

Dominic has remembered the incoming guests are a birthday party and delivers a cake from the *boulangère*. It's big and looks like Carmen Miranda donated a headpiece for the top. He and Tata then start a discussion about when he's going to replace the switch in the town hall. Apparently it currently gives everyone a little shock when it rains. Tata says she's going across to the cottage to fold towels and I'm to stay put.

Dominic makes his way upstairs and there's a lot of banging above my head. I'm redundant, and full of guilt, which pulses to the not-so-tepid beats of his hammer.

—

The phone burbles for a while, until Orson answers.

'Hello, darling.'

'Hey, Mum, give me a second.' He walks across his office, down a glass-lined corridor and into the tearoom. 'What's up?'

'Nothing's up. Well ...' I lift my arm. 'It appears I've broken a bone in my wrist, and thought I'd show you I'm fine, rather than have anyone read a message and think I was in pieces. It's nothing really.'

'Hold it up again.' He pokes his head forward to study the splint. 'A broken bone is hardly nothing.'

'Don't ask how I did it.'

'How did you do it?'

'A foolish stumble while wearing drawing pins, but I'm fine, just bored with my stupidity. Does that make sense?'

'Because it's you, yes. What on earth did Great-Aunt Pascale say?'

'She was characteristically unsentimental about my wrestle with gravity. Tell me about you. How's your sweetheart, sweetheart?'

Orson moves over to the window before replying. 'Joolz is fine. She's got me free tickets to a Wagner concert.'

'If the tickets are for the *Ring Cycle*, she may not be your girlfriend for much longer.'

Orson pulls a terrified face. 'That is a distinct possibility anyway. Joolz is intense and I'm intense; two of us together may well be too intense.'

'Oh. I was only being flippant. You make good decisions, you'll be fine. By the way, I made a point of listening to that singer you recommended to keep me "relevant". She's very lowering on the mood. In one song she waits for a lover to go because she can't stand it anymore, and two verses on she's waiting – over-optimistically I think, for him to come back. Maybe you could avoid "sad girl" and "slapyourbitchup" genres, pick something more upbeat.'

'Mum, you're the one who insists I need to broaden your horizons. Don't suppose you're going to like black metal either, but I'll text you band names.'

He sweeps the camera around the empty room. A cappuccino machine, white cupboards, padded chairs, an enormous bookshelf full of large books and a pot plant all whizz past like items on a merry-go-round.

'Go back to the window. Oh, look at the river – it's black under those clouds. How fantastic. Twilight sailing will be off tonight. I keep forgetting it's winter over there. Are those university buildings there to the right?'

Orson keeps the camera facing the river for another minute. 'Are you missing Dad?'

'I'm not.'

'You would have liked being a fly on the house wall yesterday. He went mad because someone had been in and taken most of the rose bushes. Then his anger altered course and he said maybe you had a point and a waterwise garden could be a good thing. He asked if I thought he should get someone to plant the garden ready for when you get home. He's scared, Mum.'

I smile.

'No comment about Dad's changing attitude?' Orson asks.

I continue the upturned lips.

'Are you all right?'

'I am. I feel a bit sorry for myself because of this arm. No one will let me do anything. The last guests are about to arrive, and I just wanted to see one of your lovely faces. And now I have, so all is right with the world. Tell Gus and Thea about the break, tell them I'm fine, just clumsy. Tell them I'll ring soon. And good luck with the Wagner. Give Joolz my love.'

35

'Fruit is a great thing, but it's not advisable to tell people they have a great pear.' George's mouth is huge when fully open to laugh. 'It must be the one drawback of living here, not being able to play with the language, double entendres, word games. Unless of course your French is excellent, Audrey.'

His false teeth slide comfortably back into place amongst the few originals which remain upright and yellowing. Then his fleshy lips close into a permanent smile.

I've noticed the top lip can disappear with age. Simon doesn't have one anymore. There's his nose, a dipped slope of skin, and a thin line before the pale arc of his bottom lip. This too has started to roll out and collapse.

I think codeine makes concentration tricky.

'Well, my mother was French, but sometimes I'm stuck for how to say exactly what I mean, in the way I'd like to say it.'

My eyes roll around slowly over the scene at the outside table. These people will be here for a week, artists, according to Tata's diary notes. The main guest, George, eighty-five today, sits at the head. He has a large knife in his hand and waves it above the cake. He is a big man. Strong enough to wear a pink Lacoste polo-shirt with the collar up at the back. His muscular arms have the drooping skin of his years, but the movements are lithe. His head goes back frequently to let loose beautiful baritone guffaws.

To his right is Jane. His wife, I gather, although she looks much younger. She either applied a thick layer of factor 50+ sunscreen or is the palest woman on the planet. Her fingers flutter around her mouth, often. Then there are four other people whose names I've been told, but those monikers evaporated as they were being spoken. Everyone wears a version of pastel, and all of them have vast amounts of untamed hair. So much hair; I can just imagine the shower basin.

An orange balloon escapes from its string in the rafters and drifts slowly down. It bounces once on someone's plate, sways briefly, tips egg-like to the left and continues to the ground. Fizz is drunk, cake eaten, 'Happy Birthday' sung. Two people roll away from the table to unpack the cars. Lilou arrives, a limby gazelle in a lot of tulle. She bounds onto the terrace and shakes everyone's hands. *Lilou, hello. Delighted. Pleased to meet you. Welcome. Happy Birthday.* She comes to a halt near George and points with long fingers over the hedge to indicate exactly where her cottage is. Everyone peers and nods sagely. Then she says they must call her any time of day or night if they want anything at all because *Audrey has got to take it easy.* I could die. There are kind glances and mumbles of agreement. Plates are stacked and clank in the hands of others because everyone insists that I do nothing. The afternoon stretches ahead of me looking a lot like a siesta.

—

The next morning starts with an iambic pentameter throb of pain in my left wrist.

'Morning, morning.'

The harmony of two overlapping voices wends its way up the spiral staircase.

'Stay there, we're bringing your coffee up.'

'No.' I shift to the edge of the bed.

'We're coming up. Rose, go up there and stop her.'

Oh god. Footsteps rattle the metal treads and I shuffle back under the sheet, pulling it up high over my breasts.

'Hey, Audrey, sorry to hear about your wrist.' Rose's mouth lifts at the corners.

'Thank you, Rose. It's nothing, really. I'm sorry, what is your real name?'

'Astrid. I've never liked it and am delighted to be Rose.'

I clutch the sheet as she plops down on the end of the bed, crossing her legs effortlessly.

'Painful?'

Lilou's voice pierces the bedroom. 'It's very painful. Yesterday her face was grey. Don't ask Audrey anything difficult because she's a bit addled.'

Rose's dimple deepens. She strokes the top of my foot. 'Poor you, really.'

I like Rose. She's gentle and her smiles come from a genuine place. The staircase rumbles and Lilou appears with three mugs. She hands Rose one, puts a second down on the bedside table for me, then drops down onto the mattress. I wasn't ready, and her movement dislodges the sheet and exposes my somewhat flimsy cotton nighty. I give up. I was only trying to protect them from the ravages of old age.

'First of all, I have to thank you.' Lilou crosses spaghetti legs and twiddles her toes so they caress one of her lover's knees. 'I rang Rose to tell her about your arm, and we agreed it was an emergency.'

'I was at work. I finished the call with an expression of shell shock, yet stoic.' Rose demonstrates the look. 'As predicted, someone asked, *What's wrong?* So I explained my friend, who lives all alone, had had a terrible fall. *Oh, how awful, do you think you should go and help?* Hesitating long enough to give them the impression that my loyalty to work is as deep as my devotion to my friends, I then, in a rather weedy voice replied, *Well, if you're sure it's okay, I'll work remotely for a week or so.*'

'Ha.' Lilou was grinning. 'So, here we are. We're going to wait on you hand and foot, and you can't say no because I'll involve your Tata if you misbehave.'

'You're sweet but I'm not broken.'

An image of Pierre, alone in Paris, floats up. What strange bedfellows we are. Me: ageing, winged, on the outskirts of life. Them: bouncing, vital, all options still available.

'When you're ready, we'll take you on a little walk. Only twenty minutes, slowly, and you've got to wear your sling.' Rose leans over to squeeze Lilou's hand.

Their stares dare me to object.

———

Wednesday starts much the same. Lilou and Rose escort me on a short walk along the towpath. From time to time I hold back, feign a protracted interest in something like a butterfly zigzagging over a plant, a lizard flattened on a rock. I want them to walk and talk together, use this precious week for each other. Too diligent for my ruse, they stop almost immediately, until I'm once again sandwiched between them, and on we walk.

I feint left and try again. Three ducks fossick along the bank, the brown river water white around their diving feet.

Within seconds I'm aware of two people alongside me. I don't move my eyes.

Lilou crumples a fistful of my t-shirt in mock protection. 'Don't jump.'

'You do know I'm perfectly fine to walk by myself? You don't have to waste your time babysitting.'

'Does it feel like a waste to you?' Lilou cocks her head to one side, eyebrows nipped.

Rose rubs her chin with her thumb and index finger. 'Mm, I don't think it does. Being outside, on a sneaky week off, by a French river, with two lovely women – might be hell, I suppose.'

Lilou nods sagely. 'Audrey, you'll just have to get over yourself. Okay?'

'Would you please walk side by side, hold hands, and make me feel less of a drag.'

A damp towel is thrown over the mood. Lilou thrusts her hands deep in her converted-tablecloth-culotte pockets and takes a few small steps in a bid to turn around, casually. I look between their faces. Only then does it occur to me that it's early days and I've put them on the spot. Maybe handholding is a declaration too far?

I remember I could not say or do anything right before Orson's first date. Where are you going, darling? Do you have enough money? Do you want a new shirt? *No, Mum.* The exasperation and disdain in his tone were acidic. *The date is nothing, I wish I hadn't bloody told you.* But his behaviour had said the opposite. It was as though his life, his manhood, his kudos at school, *everything*, hung off this evening with Tessa Duhig from Year 11. At meals during this period he ate with a violent hunger, was intolerant of his siblings, argued with his father. If he left his bedroom, it was with headphones clamped over his ears and to skulk in front of the fridge. He would open and shut the door in search of something, anything, to satisfy the chaos in his head. I remember suggesting he have a mango, *they're delicious this time of year*. His look said I'd offered the maggot-ridden remains of a dead wombat. I decided to keep quiet, let him be. The time to scoop him in my arms and make it better had passed.

But keeping out of his way was wrong too. If I was outside, he'd come out and slump onto one of the garden chairs. I would continue what I was doing, pretend I'd not even noticed him. Then he'd sigh and huff until I looked up and asked if he was okay. *I'm fine. God. I just want some peace*, and he'd storm off, tormented. My very existence was torture to him. Walking on eggshells doesn't cut it as an adage for this time in our relationship. Luckily things have changed, and these days I am allowed to ask how a girlfriend is without fearing for my life.

The gap between my thoughtless comment about holding hands and the three of us stretches painfully. To say something or not – perhaps I'll get it wrong, but here goes.

'Evidently ducklings follow their mother at a distance while her head's up because all is good in the world. When she tucks her head down, they know to swim in close because of potential danger.'

'Interesting.' Rose lifts her chin, drops her shoulders and starts to walk again. 'Come on, follow me.'

We walk and Rose weaves between Lilou and me in figures of eight. Now on the outside next to me. In the middle. Next to Lilou.

'Okay. Bench now. Sit everybody.' Lilou leads us to a granite seat under a large oak. We sit in a row like birds on a wire and look straight ahead.

'I'm sorry, Rose,' she says. 'I've never been the affectionate-in-public kind. I want to be. I envy couples who are.' Lilou rubs her palms back and forth along her thighs. 'Put it this way, it's truly not you.'

'I'll take that.' Rose brushes Lilou's arm with the back of her hand.

'Ten weeks ago, I was a fiancée, engaged to a nice man, who I've been with for five years. Now, bang, I've gone mad, I'm smitten with you. I don't understand myself, my motives.'

'I get it. It's okay.'

'Is it?' At this moment Lilou looks about three years old.

'It is.'

'Now you, Audrey. What's your excuse for having a carrot up your bottom?' Lilou drops a hand onto my knee.

'Carrot, do you think so?'

'Yes. I think you need to speak up. You're so nice to everyone, so considerate. Those finickity guests mewling and demanding, *Audrey, Audrey, Audrey.* I can't understand why you don't shoot them.'

'Well, I'm here to honour Tata's bookings.'

'In part. It's also an excuse because your husband is completely unworthy of you.'

Unworthy, what a lovely thing to say. I feel light-headed.

'You're asking me to brandish my underwear on this towpath for any passer-by to see?'

Rose and Lilou look at each other, then me. '*Oui.*'

I look away and watch a brown spider clambering over his still dewy web, busy with the climb.

'I have unpicked all the facts and can produce a concise list. I have been bored since the kids grew up. My husband is self-centred. I'll turn sixty at the end of the year. I'm scared witless about my ability to make a decision. And I've been utterly invisible.'

'So, because no one here knows when your birthday is, you'll stay fifty-nine?'

'Exactly.'

'When is your birthday?' Rose's tone is seductive.

I give her a look which says, *I am absolutely not going to tell you*. Lilou reciprocates with a glance sliding down her aquiline nose saying, *I will find out, one way or another*.

My watch vibrates. 'Right, I'm going back to the cottage. The guests need a model.'

'Jesus.' Lilou leans back, feigns a fall from the bench, then sits upright again. 'Do you want to be their model?'

'Evidently George is well known and some gallery or other is putting on a family exhibition, and the remit is to paint the same things.'

'My question was – do you want to help them? *Want* is the operative word.'

'When they asked me to model for them, I wanted to say, *No, sorry. Busy, busy. Not my thing*. And those words ran on a cue card, but I said, *Okay*.'

'Lordy, you're hopeless.'

'But I'll get better, and now I'm going – *alone*. I will not fall and kill myself. You two, stay. Stay.' I pretend I'm instructing Howard outside a supermarket, and they lift their palms in mock paws.

36

Sitting still and posing will be difficult, especially with my wrist. I have friends who can go to a bar, clutch a drink, and chew the fat for hours with conversations which peak and dip like overlapping heart monitor traces. They don't seem to notice that the chairs dig into every fleshy part of their body, or the way stools wobble. It is impossible to get comfortable when sober. Plus, to lean on a pub table is to have its sticky surface adhere to your arms like a sycophant. And, without fail, when you get up to leave there'll be a single potato crisp shard attached to your flesh, even if you didn't order any. Anyway, I don't want to spend a morning sitting still, and I certainly don't want to be gawped at; just the thought conjures deep feelings of inadequacy. But all of this is moot because I said *Okay*. It's my own fault.

An arc of easels borders the terrace. Two people sit on shooting sticks and lean in close to their respective works. Another straddles a chair. George and Jane stand, feet planted more than hip width apart. It looks very serious. Jane makes a beeline for me and pulls off her hat. A heavy curtain of hair is released as she plants a kiss on both my cheeks.

'Oh super. We were just working on yesterday's paintings. Have a look.'

She leads me to her canvas and her face is so expectant, there's no getting away. I clench my jaw and focus on the canvas – a skull with an Elizabethan collar, I think.

Jane taps her bottom lip with a bony finger. 'I want it to capture the state of rumination in one's mind.'

'Ah.'

'I was overwhelmed by the history of Saint Malo. All those pirates, oceanic voyages, it's the contemplation of coming home from out there. Immense.' Her hands lift, splayed fingers twirling around her head.

'Immense, indeed.'

I angle my spine forward, drop my glasses over my nose and peer into the fine white lines of the Elizabethan collar. Up close it appears more like caul, the fat-dotted lace omentum used by French butchers to cover meats. It screams dystopia. How did she get this composition from the green blues of the Emerald Coast? Where are the rocky outcrops, the perilously perched forts, lighthouses, and stone walls?

I stand up straight again and slowly shake my head from side to side. It's an action I know works well in conveying I'm lost for words, while implying being impressed. Jane's eyes dart around my face. Good lord, she needs more. I shift back a foot or two and remove my glasses completely to continue the appraisal. There seems to be a swirl of diaristic text about cosmic furnaces. And a dangling marionette.

'Wow.' I stress the W for a long moment and do some nodding.

Jane nods too. 'If it isn't finished before we leave, I'll send you a photo.' She slides a finger slowly down the side of the canvas. 'I really need to connect Saint Malo's throbbing energy with death.'

'Jane, come on. We need Audrey. The light's perfect.' George leans his Saint Malo canvas down by the cottage door and secures a blank one in its place. Other canvases go up onto easels. Jane sits me on the bench. I'm asked to bend my front leg. Put the toe of my back foot on the ground. Left arm up on the table. Fingers curled; fingers flattened. Where is it comfortable to put my broken wrist, do I want a book? Head slightly to the left – no, right. Eventually there's a *yes*.

Prunella, an easy name to remember, comes and straightens my blouse. 'Oh, this is lovely, Audrey.'

A consensual ripple trickles from the group.

George's head pokes out from behind his canvas. 'We'll need this posture for a couple of hours.'

Holy mother of.

'We'll give you a break every, what, twenty minutes?'

My left buttock is already uncomfortable. 'Okay.'

Someone takes photos of me from every angle for *continuity*. It's unnecessary. Rigor mortis will set in shortly.

It's at this moment I resolve to do some serious otherising. It isn't these people, this bench – it's all the times the word *yes* came out when I would have preferred to decline. My head is still packed tight with the threads of other people's lives, and I need to cut through the Gordian knot I'm living in. I must use these two-plus hours to revolutionise myself so I'm never in this position again.

I can't think though. Having my body clamped in position seems to have frozen my brain. Just my eyes are at liberty to roam around a limited field. I see Tata come in the back gate and go into the *remise*. The dry scratch of pencils on canvas sounds loud. Six heads duck around the sides of their canvases again and again, in and out, unsynchronised cuckoo clocks. I can feel my hair tie giving way. Haricot weaves between my ankles, slowly. I know his I-want-more-tinned-food dance. A pigeon crash-lands on the bird-table roof. Are the muscles in my face starting to slide? Haricot's tail coils up the back of my calves. The temptation to bend and stroke him is strong. He won't understand why I don't; he'll think he's being punished. My hair tie descends further. The hanging baskets need to be watered. Pencil whispers. Haricot. Numb buttock, a strand of hair falls. Did I turn the bedside light off? A fly lands on my bottom lip. I let out a sheet of ventriloquist's air to move it. Not a single revolutionising idea. Just my nerves fizzing like a cartoon fuse.

'Take a break, Audrey.' George's voice rises over the top of his picture.

Jack-in-a-boxing off the bench I sidestep between the easels and make for the kitchen. They continue to work. One uses a method of nose pressed close to fine-tuned fingers, and meticulously marks out teeny tiny lines. George has a large pencil clamped in an outstretched hand. Arms sweep the air, spines lean back at thirty degrees to the canvases, individual techniques derived from years of painting. I wonder, if today was hot and they were all hungover, would that affect what they saw, would the model appear differently on each canvas? Is it a complex coming together of circumstances, or will it be my fault if their paintings are bad? That pressure I can do without.

I feed the cat, have a wee, shrug out my shoulders.

'Audrey?'

And we're back.

I assume the position. George says I have *excellent muscle memory* because little adjustment is needed. After twenty minutes in one spot, of course I know my terrain intimately. Isn't it more about spatial awareness? The knot on the bench, which my left thigh all but covers. The crack between two slabs where my toes stop. The red wine stain on the table, just out of reach of the fingers on my outstretched left hand. But he's the model expert, perhaps it is muscle memory? This means I could have made a great pianist, or a rope – they have memory according to fishermen. Hosepipes too. After a year in the Australian sun, hosepipes are bastards. They develop a mind of their own and kink. My epitaph could read, 'Here lies Audrey with her excellent muscle memory.'

'Have a break, Audrey.'

'We're ready, Audrey.'

'Take a break, Audrey.'

The call rings out again and again. I'm a Norwegian skier plunged into ice before being steamed in clouds of suffocating sauna fug. I'm in an air-conditioned supermarket, out in a scorching carpark sun. Underwater, on the beach. My thoughts never come together except to form analogies. I feel myself boil with self-consciousness. Then I'm released to walk *for five* and petulance crawls its stiff boned fingers along my spine. After more than two hours of this oscillating, I don't know whether I dread the moments of freedom more than I hate the sitting.

'Well, that should do it. Lunchtime.' George brings the session to an end.

Exhalations, dropped shoulders, the ting-tick of brushes being banged against jars of water. Those who were sitting stand and those who were standing come across to the bench to sit. I just swivel slowly and take a deep breath. There's a version of post-coital disappointment draped over my shoulders, and typically they look self-satisfied. How to extricate myself from this relationship? I straighten my legs and drift over to the easels.

From behind the canvases, our roles are reversed. I crab-walk along the arc and listen to their post-mortem at the table. If I'd expected to see me, I don't. I see exacting textures in a highly stylised composition. Another shows hallucinatory attention to detail. The third reflects unabashed allusions to children's art. Number four, riots of colour.

I look back at George and his family. There's something deliciously ironic about this moment, and a grin builds deep in my chest then crawls up to my lips. For two hours I've been fully clothed, feeling naked and exposed. But nothing of the sort is on these canvases. The artists have done no more than interpret the day's model and in so doing have revealed themselves amongst the paint, the lines. It feels good to walk on.

Painting five is a virtuoso of darkness, someone has captured despondence – society's or their own? The last one, Prunella's, how to describe it? I, if it is me, look like a congregation of amoeba on a Petri dish.

37

Last night Orson texted to let me know that he and Joolz have split up. I checked he was feeling all right. He said he was. I slept. This morning the Kraken, the monster of anxiety, has woken in full force. Did Gus and Thea make Orson tell me? Is he devastated? Should I be there? When am I booked to fly back? Two weeks! Good lord, so soon, but is that soon enough? My poor boy.

Going down the stairs, I step out the sentence – fly back in two weeks, fly back in two weeks.

Waiting for the kettle to boil, I put my feet through a set of tap steps to block the sentence. Double shuffle ball change, double shuffle step, which I can't hear in sheepskin slippers. But it's an intermediate move and the beginning of 'Footloose'. I plan on being able to do the whole routine by Christmas.

The fancy footwork doesn't help because the *shoulds* have already arrived, sinuously wittering about all the things which need to be done before I go. I haven't had them in my head for weeks, and I don't like their tone.

'Knock, knock. Morning, Audrey.'

George stands at the hayloft doorway waving his fist in midair. He wears his going-out-for-the-day-painting hat.

This one has a chin strap and he's explained how that can be invaluable on windy locations.

'Morning, George.'

'I've woken with a fancy to do some French cooking tonight and wondered if you'd like to join us, and if you'd be able to pick up a few ingredients?'

No and no. I have so much to think about, so much to do, and only two weeks to do it all. But I experience a cognitive glitch.

'Yes, George. Give me the list.'

Goodness. I should be pandering to my poor son, not guests. I look at George's beaming face and the full force of reality hits me – this birthday party is my last summer obligation. Tata's guest season will be over in a matter of days. It's surprising how sad that makes me feel and a chill creeps under my skin.

I need to have a long discussion with Tata. She's got to tell me why she fell and how her recovery is truly going. Will she be able to manage the hayloft or the cottage stairs soon? We need to organise a gardener, not that there'll be much to do over winter. As I run through these practicalities it feels like this little corner of life is slipping away from me already.

Of course, Tata doesn't answer her phone, and she isn't in the *remise* on her static bike. I shoot down the lane to No-E's – he may well know her plans for the day.

The door and all his windows are wide open and the sharp bang of metal on metal pops out of every opening. I step down into the kitchen where the clattering noises from the roof space are twice as loud and shouting becomes necessary.

'Pascal? Pascal.'

A muffled voice from above my head advises me he isn't in.

'He has taken your aunt, in the florist's van, to the beach.'

'Oh lord, she's not safe. Who are you?'

'*C'est moi*, Dominic. Now you're here, can you see a dangling wire, near the oven?'

I've never been invited into No-E's house and it's surprising to see a few tasteful pieces of art waiting to be hung, beautiful wooden cupboards, and a very slick AGA – not at all how I'd imagined No-E's home.

'There is a blue wire.' I tilt my head towards the trapdoor. 'Do you know when they'll be back?'

'Please pull on it until you see a yellow wire as well. I expect they'll be back later.' There's some scratching and shuffling above. 'That's good, thank you. Do you see the yellow one now?'

'I do, I've got both. Can I let go yet?'

Dominic's face appears through the hole in the ceiling. 'Hold on for one more moment, please. I'll come down.'

I check my phone's calendar – the flight is in ten days, instead of fourteen. 'God.' My aunt's absence now feels critical.

'Am I holding you up?'

'Sorry, no, it's fine, I've got a few logistics I need to discuss with my aunt, they're kind of urgent.'

'Can I help?'

Why on earth would I discuss my problems with him? But as has so often been the case since I arrived in the village, words start to come out which aren't in keeping with what my head has in mind.

'My son has split up with his girlfriend, Joolz. She's an American opera singer and he was very fond of her. They dated for seven months.'

'*Fond*, that's an interesting choice of words, very controlled, is that how you or how he described their romance? I'm very *fond* of my girlfriend. My son is very *fond* of Joolz.'

Dominic's face is hard to read in the gloom of the attic's opening. I can't tell whether he's truly playing the semantic game, or whether he's joking. I don't really know why I'm talking about Orson and his girlfriend.

'Well, she seemed to make Orson happy. Except when she played her shamisen for relaxation – that drove him mad. He said when she dry-plucked it, it sounded like a rusty banjo. But you overlook these things, don't you?'

Two feet then two legs emerge from the trapdoor. I tilt my head to focus on the blue and yellow wires so I can ignore the workman's trousers coming down the ladder, and the way they hug his muscled buttocks.

The ladder's creaking flex stops as he steps onto the floor, and I can once again address Dominic and not the wires.

'Evidently, Orson sat through two hours of Wagner's fifteen-hour *Ring Cycle* and realised the world of Norse gods is not for him. He did say that if he was going to be an opera singer, he'd want to be a tenor – they get the best parts, and they get the girl, if she doesn't die.'

Dominic washes his hands and splashes his face at the kitchen sink. Cobwebs linger in his hair.

'Joolz didn't die though, did she?' He turns the tap off and bends down to a workbag.

'No, she's fine. I've always thought opera can stir the people singing it but not necessarily the people listening to it. Do you like opera?'

Dominic rummages through the canvas bag, finds some tape, then stands again.

'Not particularly but the subject is your son. He and his girlfriend had a relationship, which ran its course from soaring blissful art to a moody pas de deux, and now it's over?'

I look around the room. Note the double-glazed windows, the new bench, the stacked boxes of bathroom tiles and Dominic's face – waiting for my reply.

'Do you have children, Dominic?'

He shakes his head.

'Wise man – in some ways. The thing is, as a mother, I've always been there for everything. Every school certificate, every graze. I've changed every toothbrush they ever used at home. A mother is there for every everything. I think I should be there now, in case.'

'Do you think you were there for the first joint? The first kiss?'

'I was not. But I was there for the first hangover. I was there fifteen minutes after the first car prang. Here, on another continent, I'm so far away.' I stare into and beyond his eyes. 'That's the thing, isn't it? I'm here.'

I fiddle deliberately with the wires to remind Dominic I'm still holding them. His gaze is steady, but he says nothing.

'All right,' I continue, 'Orson is twenty-nine and he's fine, but I feel guilty because I don't want to go back in ten days.'

He takes the wires from my hand. 'Guilt is a terrible thing.'

'The guests are nearly done, Tata is more robust, and now I've got this silly broken wrist I'm not much help to her anymore.'

Dominic picks at the end of the roll of tape and shakes his head slowly.

'Pascale only appreciates your practical abilities? I think not. I think having her niece's company is significant.'

If Simon had said something like that, I'd feel chastised. Dominic, however, seems to be calmly posing an optional way of looking at the situation.

'How do I justify staying here though, having a carefree time? In Australia I always have a list of things to do; and I did leave home in rather a rush.'

Dominic twirls the wires.

I slump onto a dusty kitchen chair.

232

He isolates the yellow and blue with red electrical tape. A recollection of all the chores which await me in Australia descends like a fog, and my wrist throbs.

'You have cobwebs in your hair.'

Like a child he simply leans in for me to remove them. 'What is on your list that's so important?'

I remove the gossamer strands. 'Well, I don't really have a list anymore because everyone is so independent they don't need me to do things for them. But without a list I feel rudderless. I could concoct one, of course, because my lists used to be amazingly helpful.'

I stick one finger up. 'Things I know I'll have to do: Howard, my dog, will need his nails clipped; and I'm the only person he lets do it.'

I put up a second finger. 'I usually bake cakes for the October school fete.'

Three fingers up. 'And, you know, the night I flew out, I found a melted toffee in a jacket pocket, which I didn't pick out.'

Goodness, I'm ripping that list up. But I will have other things to attend to like, get a divorce, move house, find a job. However, I will not discuss these pointy matter-of-facts with him.

'My lists used to be longer than the Tour de France, Dominic, but I've realised I don't like the way they make me feel. They feel rigid, like I'm obliged. And patting myself on the back when I've ticked an item off is no longer rewarding. In fact, it's sad. Yet, without a list, I'm not sure how to proceed. More immediately, I need to give the guests clean towels. And George wants me to buy sheep's brains. And I want to talk to Tata.'

'Audrey, stop.' Dominic puts the palms of his hands on my knees, and stares directly into my eyes. 'If you want a list, we can make one and I'll help you. Okay?' He straightens up, rips a strip of cardboard from a tile box, locates a pen, then sits down next to me, exaggerates a pose to write. 'I'm ready.'

'You've missed the point, Dominic. It isn't really the absence of a list that's the problem. If I want one, I have many – on my phone, in my diaries. One goes back decades: file school drawings, finish the patchwork bedspread, wash the terrarium. There are many outstanding items on all my lists. And I've always felt I should attend to them in chronological order.'

That little outburst whorls around me, smudgy and ill-fitting. Those words belong to a different time when lists were helpful because other people were leading my life.

'I think, actually, the point is – I don't want a list, they make me feel exhausted. I like the way things come and go. I need the flexibility of this unstructured spontaneity. Here I can get up in the morning and decide what to do with the day. I have never felt wealthier.'

'That's good, Audrey.' He puts the cardboard slip and the pencil down. 'Would you like me to take you to Saint Malo to buy sheep's brains, before the market closes? When we're back perhaps your aunt will have returned.'

I hold a finger up. 'One second please.' I stand and walk about the kitchen, look across to his face a few times.

'Dominic.' I pace, look through the doorway and let the idea of a list for the next few days waft down the lane and out of sight.

'Dominic, my guests have three cars between them. They can buy their own offal. I shouldn't have said I would go in the first place. But you're very kind to offer. And thank you for listening.'

38

Tata scours Haricot's luxuriant coat for ticks. Her bruises have all gone, the walking boot is off, but she's still unsteady on her feet. She thinks I don't notice, but I watch her like a hawk. I see the way her gait shuffles for a few steps before she gets into a rhythm. Take note of how hesitant she is when moving from one surface to another. It's easy to keep an eye on her when she's here. The rest of the time my aunt remains an enigma – *physio, friends, more time by the coast.* 'I'll be back soon,' she says. I've given up asking if *soon* means she'll be back later the same day, tomorrow, or in a week. Sometimes I wonder if she'll vanish altogether and I'll get a postcard – *Snorkelling in the Antilles, back soon.* She says she's doing all the things she's ever wanted to.

One of these things is to learn to play backgammon. If Tata were a teenager, I'd say she's obsessed. She always chooses to play with the pear tree discs, and I get the bucolic toilet wood.

'You know Orson and his girlfriend split up.'

She sets up the pieces on the painted tabletop.

'It sent me into a bit of a tizz, feeling guilty about being here when perhaps ...'

She nods, shakes her dice noisily in an empty tomato tin.

'Theoretically I don't have much time left before I fly back and ...'

I wish she'd take up the thread of my conversation and help out.

'Why are you moving like a plank this morning, Audrey?'

It appears I'm alone on this one.

'Since Lilou gave me *permission* to walk on my own, I tackled a slope by the river which is better suited to mountain goats and I'm muscle sore. Are you going to roll those dice?'

They spill out onto the table – four and six.

I check emails. She fusses Haricot, considers her strategy, and the pigeons on the gravel outside coo and adjust their feathers.

'Did you read this email from Laurence?'

Tata shakes her head.

'He says he can't wait to get home from the film shoot. And look at this picture from little Jakob.'

I turn the screen. Tata borrows my glasses, leans in, then out, puzzled by the image. 'What is it?'

'Not sure. A laid-off van driver with a drug problem, perhaps? I won't suggest that in my reply. Mrs Kay says the whole school assembly watched the video of the French children and Jakob has become something of a star. Perhaps the van is his way of telling me to bring a lot of chocolate back.'

An email from Simon swirls into my inbox and my perkiness threatens to slide down the greasy slope of confusion and anger.

Tata makes her move, returns the dice to their tin, and peers into one of the cat's ears. 'Your husband?'

I shake my dice in their empty artichoke jar.

'It's been nice to have Simon on the outskirts of my life. The kids told him I broke my wrist, so I suppose it's reasonable he writes, but—' I scroll through the email. 'He says ra ra ra, and he'll be in Cambridge in a couple of weeks so perhaps he should pop over? He doesn't say he wants to pop over because he's worried. Or pop over to help. Or pop over because he loves me. There's no plea, no whining guitar riff to lyrics stolen from a post break-up journal entry. No. He's going to be an hour's flight away so *perhaps I should pop over?*'

'Your turn, Audrey.'

'Bloody hell, no. Apparently, I'm to tell him if his plan is *agreeable* to me. It isn't. I won't reply at all. That'll make my answer very loud and awfully clear.'

'Good girl, that's one way of saying, no. You do realise you can use the word on him. *No, Simon, I don't want you to come over here.*' Tata flips Haricot onto his back. 'I'd like to talk with you about—'

There's a tap on the door.

'Audrey?'

I can see a fist, an arm and I recognise the voice as Prunella's.

'Come in.'

Prunella comes as far as the mat and halts. She fills the doorway, superbly weird in so many ways. I'm drawn to her square jaw, overly large hands and ludicrous hair.

I lower the computer lid. 'What can we do for you?'

'I just wanted to say thanks again for modelling. I don't suppose you'd like to have another go?'

'No, I wouldn't, but once was fun.' Goodness, listen to me all decisive.

'George is having a wonderful time here.' One of her hands goes up into the shock of wire on her head. 'We all are.'

'I'm pleased.'

'The weather's going to change, you know.' She tucks her hand deep into a cargo pocket. 'The thing is, we wondered if we could extend our stay?' Prunella shifts her weight from one enormous foot to the other. 'I mean, do you have any guests booked in straight after us?'

I look across at Tata. She flicks her eyes across my face and returns her focus to the cat.

I nearly say, *No, you're the last,* but stop, pretend to flick through the cottage diary. 'No, not straight away. Why, what were you thinking?' So cool.

'Well, as long as you'll have us, really. A couple of days, a week?' Prunella drags down her cheek with three heavy fingers. 'Tata?'

My aunt lifts her head momentarily and smiles, no help at all. I turn over two pages of the diary then go back again. If my guests were still here, I could postpone my return to Australia. *Still have guests, you know, can't leave for the moment.* The idea twitches.

Prunella continues to put forward her case. 'Mummy has given me rather a lot of money to make sure George has a good time.'

Mummy! Prunella must be sixty-something, how old is Mummy?

'What I'm saying is, obviously I'm happy to pay the full rate, in cash, more if ...'

I'm not bothered about money right now; I am intrigued by *Mummy* though.

'Your mother?'

'Yes, Mummy was George's first *wife* if you like. Mummy is older of course, ten years. More of a benefactor, I suppose. She modelled for him way back. They had me when George was still wet behind the ears. Well, *they* didn't have me. Mummy did, they were never really an item. Good pals though, always have been.'

So, your ninety-five-year-old mother is paying for you all to come here and paint? This is what I want to ask. Instead, I look back down at my diary – obliging Audrey is nowhere to be seen.

Prunella pulls her hand out of that bottomless pocket and rolls a stone between her fingers. 'Being here is a wonderful full-body experience.'

'A week you say?'

'It would be perfect. Unless you could do more?'

They could stay the whole of September, but I'm not going to say so. I return my gaze to Tata, who continues to study the auditory canal of her cat. I tap my finger while I calculate an idea. It's important I make the decision here rather than being railroaded.

'I can do eight days. I'll give you a change of sheets today and another on Thursday, but I won't provide breakfast. What do you think?'

'Perfect. Thank you.' Prunella's soft belly jiggles under her t-shirt.

She turns her bulky frame away from the doorway and sunlight once again flops across the floor.

I grab my phone and message Mumsgoneawol.

I know I said I'd probably be back 2nd September, but it seems I miscalculated the bookings. I'll have to take a closer look. Will let you know what's happening. We've still had no rain, although apparently, it's due. I hope so, I'm fed up with watering everything. I'll give you a ring later – when you're awake. xx

'Audrey, you do not have to have guests and domestic duties to justify staying. What were you thinking?'

Now she offers an opinion. 'True, I suppose.'

Tata points to two post-it notes on the pinboard. One says, *My children* = Australia. The other says, *Laurence* = Australia. They both catch in a small breeze and flap like discordant butterfly wings. 'Is that supposed to be a helpful list of reasons to stay and reasons to go?'

She puts the cat down and clasps her hands on the tabletop. I make my move and collect the dice, drop them into the jar. My mobile rattles with an incoming call. I answer and put the call on speaker.

'*Bonjour.*'

'It's Nathalie, I hope you don't mind me calling.'

'Not at all.'

'Am I disturbing you?'

'Not at all.'

'Madame Mitteaux did eventually die. It's her funeral, Saturday week.'

I have no idea who Madame Mitteaux is.

Nathalie continues. 'She's my mother-in-law, so I can't be in the church on the morning to do the flowers. I must be by my husband's side.'

'Of course.'

'I was wondering if you would please help my brother, Pascal. Make sure he puts the vases out properly. I will make the bouquets, he will deliver them, but I don't trust him to finish the arrangements.'

'I'm sorry for your loss, and I'm happy to help.'

'*Merci.* You are an angel.'

'Shall I come to the shop to discuss the details?'

'Perfect. You are a beautiful angel. The service is at ten o'clock.'

'I'll be there.'

'Thank you very much.'

'It's my pleasure.'

'You're very kind.'

'Not at all.'

And then she hangs up.

Tata chortles. 'Yes, you can stay longer. Yes, I'll do flowers. Yes, yes, yes.'

Indeed, it appears I have made my mind up to stay longer. I straighten, look around the room to see how it feels – it feels right.

'Yes, yes, yes. I said yes, but not to Simon, I didn't say, *Yes, come visit* to Simon.'

'It's true.' Tata throws a double.

'Sometimes doing things for people is about the opportunity to be kind, and that makes me feel good. I like it. Truly. Yes, I may have let things get out of whack. Yes, I've been taken advantage of, but I am not going to let one self-absorbed husband stop me acting the way I think is fundamentally right.'

'How many narcissistic husbands will it take?'

'The absence of one is enough.'

———

Midnight blue, the woman in the shop said; *black,* is what she meant. After weeks in jeans the silky fabric of my only respectable dress brushes against my legs and I feel like a little girl playing funeral dress-ups. I untangle damp knots of hair as best I can and haul the misshapen result back into a clip, which immediately pops off. I feed the cat, eat a banana, collect a gardening glove and a pair of secateurs then head out.

No-E is at the gate. 'Would you like a lift?'

I've had a lift with him before. 'No thank you, I'll see you there.'

His face crumples. No-E doesn't have a vehicle, nor a licence. He uses his sister's van to tow the bucolic wedding toilets to local venues. To see over the steering wheel, he has to sit on a large cushion. Then he pulls the sun visor down and rests his forehead against it; and that's how he stays for the entire journey. No-E doesn't think second gear is necessary and feels using the clutch is overrated. You can hear the distressed squeals of gearbox cogs as they're destroyed by his technique. But, perversely, he can back the trailer through the merest suggestion of a gap.

Low grey clouds move fast, and black jackdaws circle the church steeple, which is silhouetted against the gloomy sky, when I arrive. The van is already parked at the church with the back doors flung open. Rows and rows of freesia bouquets and metal buckets of lilies line its metal floor.

Inside the church, a woman methodically wipes the backs of the prayer stools. She turns her head briefly, then continues. No-E ferries the flowers in from the van and puts each vase down reverently. I count pews, watch the woman. I thought she was stooping to dust but see now that her back is bent. Her jowls droop, her eyelids hang heavy over beady eyes, and she ignores us. Her arthritic fingers weave a microfibre cloth between the slats, over and over.

No-E hooks vases over the ends of the pews, fills each one slowly from a green watering can. I follow behind him in silence to release the freesias from their elastic bands and install them in the conical glass receptacles. They fan out, oozing late summer fruit aromas towards the vaulted ceiling.

The font vase is perfect for Nathalie's arrangement, but calculations have gone awry for the vast bowls at the altar. No-E helps me scrump luxuriant green ornamental mimosa fronds and strands of ivy from the churchyard. He bats my hand away when I try to snip, and gets me to point instead, then he lays our haul out on the altar step. I then bat him away, and he leaves me to weave the sinuous curls so they twist and trail amongst the stems of white lilies and daisies.

The polishing lady gives a little cough, which breaks my concentration. I look across to her, and she gives the slightest nod towards the vestibule. Outside there's a moment of sunlight and I catch sight of a sea of people in black, perhaps the whole community. They part like the wake of a boat to allow the coffin through. There's no way out. The polishing lady kneels in the transept, and I join her.

The lament starts up from the organ. The church fills, the pews creak as bodies slide along their length. I hear a few high-heeled shoes clip over the stone floor. The coffin comes to rest. Organ notes drift until their last chord slips away. The priest and his aides settle, fluffing their robes at the front of the church. The rustle of jackets and stiff ironed dresses fades into silence.

Nathalie sits in the front row between an old man and someone I assume is her husband. I look again at the older man's face and recognise it now as Monsieur Whistler, the person who shared the doctor's waiting room with me weeks ago. A slight throb starts up along my forehead. I remember the way he waited, his wife's slippers, her sultana eyes. That minuscule shake of the doctor's head in reply to the old man's unspoken question. Today his face is impassive.

The church fills with standing, sitting, kneeling. The organ plays, people sing, the priest's lyrical voice rises and falls. The congregation fall into step with the rhythm of the mass. There are readings, eulogies, hymns. A stream of black ants makes their way to the sacrament of the Holy Eucharist, heads bowed. The agile kneel, the infirm are helped, children's hands are held. The mayor and his wife wait their turn.

No-E pushes Tata in a wheelchair to the altar. I'm shocked. Why isn't she using her cane? Tata's hands form a bowl and rise, slowly, as though her joints are seizing. Despite the fact she holds them close to her chest, I see a tremor, her fingers pill-roll and her jaw is locked in concentration. No-E slips his palm beneath her hands and lifts them further, to receive the sliver of wafer. I wish I hadn't witnessed any of that.

A silver chalice goes from lip to lip. Madame Potdevin walks with the Dandelion sisters. Dominic has brushed his hair and is barely recognisable. The *boulangère* clutches a cap in hand. The polishing lady and I sit quietly to one side.

The church bulges with the tiny bristles of everyone's memories of Liliane Mitteaux. I can feel how well she was loved. Then the pallbearers take the coffin once more and, led by the priest, they leave the church. I hang back, watch the holy water being sprinkled over Liliane's coffin before she's returned to the hearse. The gleaming black vehicle creeps away and the people of the village follow slowly behind her to the cemetery.

I don't know what, if anything, must be done with the flowers. The church is lonely without Liliane. The stained-glass windows have turned dull as the intermittent sun is covered by clouds. The polishing lady moves from row to row to collect the prayer books. I step outside the church, a few fat raindrops land and create little craters on the parched ground.

39

The rain didn't come to anything, and Tata has avoided me since the funeral – *physiotherapy*, she said, then a trip to Paris to see friends and go to an exhibition.

The birthday party guests go out early every day. They find a spot along the coast, draw, sketch, paint, take a long lunch somewhere, then start over before coming home about seven. Sometimes Prunella stays behind to work on her canvas. In the late afternoon we meet in the garden, drink Earl Grey, and watch the chickens.

Jane prepares a meal for us most nights, which is invariably some version of cucumber salad, tomatoes from the garden, baguettes, cheeses, butter and at least one bottle of wine per person. *Something light to go to sleep on*, George says. I always excuse myself early and go to bed, where I hear their conversations rise through the loft window like a radio play. The themes vary. Cultural transmission between those in their dotage and the thriving younger generation. The hazards of producing lithium batteries. Exhibition reviews; are so and so's drawings a frail word for diptychs? The scrape of chair legs on the terrace pavers tells me Jane is up and down, fussing over George, topping up the water, full of sentimentality about this time with her cobbled together family. George's voice peaks and troughs as he and his children mix bawdy jokes with the politics of geriatric care. Later, when the wine has taken hold, their conversations contain sentences like, *to spiral seems to be the only option*. These proclamations tell me their evening is coming to an end.

On the last day George and Jane thank me and take their leave in a battered white van. Three others are off to Rouen for a night or two. I hope my children like each other when they're of the same age, holiday together, cooperate with each other during my demise.

Prunella walks in some five minutes later. 'Got a sec?'

'Sure.'

I follow her big frame out to the terrace. On the wall she's hung a canvas and covered it with a large floral skirt.

'I want you to have this.' Prunella moves to stand beside the painting. 'I'm going to uncover it now, then leave you for a minute. I'll make coffee.'

'Goodness, you really don't have to give me anything, honestly.' I'm simultaneously scared of the portrait and overwhelmed by her generosity.

'I know. Thing is, it's for you, about you.'

Prunella hesitates a moment longer, then pulls the skirt off with a flourish, crushes the fabric in her hands, and lumbers over to the cottage kitchen.

When her back has disappeared through the doorway, I make my head turn towards the canvas, recoil, and sit down heavily. I drag in a breath because the portrait feels like being entrusted with a home truth.

The background starts camel-yellows, which bleed into a deeper, gritty orange along the bottom. A person leans left to right taking up the rest of the canvas. The face is photographic in style, me unsmiling. It's kinder, flattering, but me. The right side of my body segues into abstract cubism, like modular panels of uncertain function. The left side is represented by the most prosaic of kitchen items – the vegetable peeler. This she's executed so graphically that I want to pluck it off the canvas. My legs reappear from the knees down, photographic again, like the face, and on my feet, which dangle midair, mid-step, are metal-soled shoes. My eyes are obsessed with the whole picture, drawn from corner to corner, around and over, then back again.

The bench bounces slightly as Prunella sits alongside me. I can't turn to face her. She puts a mug of coffee in my hand. I take a sip, aware she does the same.

'You like it.' This is a statement made with the roundness of contented vowels.

'Oh, Prunella.'

More moments of silence.

'Prunella I … I just can't do justice to the connection I feel with this woman in the painting.'

'It's okay. You don't have to explain. I can see your reaction, and I'm happy.'

I drop my hand onto her knee. 'Tell me, if you can, what made you put these things together in that way.'

She pauses, breathes deeply. 'Life is a cyclical drama, waking and dreaming, brutal and beautiful, but whimsy outstrips dread.' Then she throws back her head and laughs. 'That's the art world's way of saying that what I see in you, Audrey, is a complex and fascinating woman who's yet to blossom.'

'I love that idea, that there's more to come. Does it have a title?'

'Tap Dancing on Sand.'

I swing my head towards her, tears lurk in their little ducts.

She nods.

'You saw me?' I drop my shoulders and suck in a deep breath until my belly is as taut as a drum.

'Yes, when I was looking for you one day, I heard this noise coming from your shed. It was the pop and snap of your bare feet on bubble wrap. You were holding your arm, mimicking the steps from a laptop screen.' Prunella pats my hand. 'I never made enough fuss, Audrey. Promise me you'll make some noise. Get some proper shoes and make some noise.'

———

A t-shirt dress puts up less of a fight than jeans and buttoned blouses, and that's what I need with my silly splint and reduced dexterity. This dress has blue and white horizontal stripes; very nautical. But probably not the best stretched around my hips. Never mind, it was on sale, and I bought two.

Lilou comes up onto the terrace carrying her own mug, of tea it appears, which is unusual. What is expected is her always unexpected wardrobe and today she wears several white fabrics, of varying lengths, like the tattered remains of *château* curtains.

'Audrey. You look sassy.'

I swivel, jut out a hip. 'Does it make my bum look big?'

'Succulent. You should wear fitted clothes more often.'

'Why thank you.'

She puts the mug down, saunters over to Haricot, picks him up and cradles him in her arms. His eyes close into slits of feline bliss. Something niggles. She's wearing the ill-fitting white interior of an airing cupboard, not something skin-tight, and she hasn't ignored the cat. She comes to a halt in front of Prunella's painting.

'*Zut*, it's brilliant. Weird, but I absolutely love it.' She squints into the portrait. 'It is amazing. *Ouais*, domestic, unformed.'

Her nose is an inch from my features on the canvas. 'The face is more you than you.'

'I look like I'm verging on miserable, don't you think?'

'No, verging on content.' Lilou slides along the bench, eyes fixed on the painting.

'So clever. I have a favour to ask.' She grabs her mug and vigorously occupies herself with the teabag. In and out of the mug, in and out.

'Looks like you're trying to drown a witch. What's the favour?'

The teabag, oozing clear amber liquid, is placed on the table.

'Can Pierre stay here for a night or two?' Lilou turns to look at me for the first time. 'My place, as you know, only has one bed, so he'll just sleep here.'

'Oh, sure he can. When's he coming?'

Lilou flips a wrist to look at her watch. 'In an hour or so, by train.'

'Do you want me to ask why he's coming? Because I want to. Equally I won't, if you'd rather not say.'

I force my focus around the terrace, up to the portrait, across the mirror wall. Perhaps she regrets the split, perhaps …

'I'm pregnant.'

'Oh my.' My arms fold around her. 'Wonderful.' I squeeze her to me, and she relaxes into my chest. My head runs on with this fantastic news and then it dawns, maybe this isn't what she wants. I stroke her silky hair, release the ponytail from its elastic.

'He knows?'

'No. He thinks we're going to talk about the flat, selling it or … I don't know. Do you think I can do this, Audrey?'

I kiss the top of her head. 'Absolutely.'

'Did you like being pregnant?'

'Loved it. It was miraculous, natural, unlike anything else. You know it's hard to describe, but pregnancy, for me, was like being filled with a laid-back ode.'

'So, this is okay?'

'Lilou, if you want this baby, it is absolutely the best thing that has ever happened to you.'

'I don't know what Pierre's going to say.' Lilou squeezes the soggy teabag between her fingers.

'Of course you don't, but the decision isn't his.'

She moves her head in little nods. 'You know it was Rose who said I should take a test. She's the one who verbalised the symptoms I'd been dismissing.'

'Clever girl.'

'Beautiful girl.'

'She knows?'

'Yes, you and Rose.' Lilou looks down and toys with the velcro on my splint. 'I think my time with her might be kaput. Quite an impressive way to end a summer fling, don't you think?'

'I don't know what to say.'

'You know what's stupid, it's probably hormones, but I was so happy to tell Rose about the pregnancy.'

'Hang on.'

I turn my phone and hunt for a photo. I took it the day the flowers came. Lilou and Rose sitting opposite each other. In the reflection from the terrace mirrors are three versions of the two women. Each one at a slightly different angle; but in each case Rose looks openly at Lilou who laughs. I push the phone across the table. Haricot swipes at it idly. Lilou grins at the cat, taps the screen, enlarges aspects of the image with two spreading fingers, lets out a short *hm*.

'It would be nice if we can be like that again.'

'Send yourself a copy. And thank you, for telling me.'

'No, thank you.'

'No, thank you.'

'Oh, do shut up.'

The sound of the gate's click puts an end to our volley. Lilou sees who it is before me and stands.

'I'm off to the station,' she says with a cheap movie wink.

Dominic comes into view.

'Oh lord, stop it. I left a note at the bar asking him how much I owe him.'

I stand, tug my dress down. Dominic and Lilou *bonjour* with a handshake, as I crab-walk the narrow gap between bench and table. He leans in to greet me. I'm taken aback. A beat behind him. His breath sweeps my face as we transition left to right to kiss the air. Something ancient begins with a slow trickle of heat into my belly.

Dominic walks over to the portrait. Lilou grins like an idiot and takes her leave. I swat in her direction, not quite sure what to do. The gate clicks and the air thickens on the terrace. This is ridiculous.

'I don't understand the half potato peeler, half something else, but the rest is magnificent. You can't leave it here, the water from the pot plants will ruin it.' He puts his tanned hands on either side of the canvas and unhooks it from the wall. 'Beautiful.'

His brown fingers cupped over the yellow edge look beautiful. What's wrong with me? I blame post-menopausal chaos. There are a lot of studies done on periods, getting pregnant, being pregnant, postpartum, but no one has much to say when you're done with breeding. I suspect the funding dries up for that kind of research and scientists have to prioritise. *You've done your job, kept society topped up, sorry, you'll have to deal with the next bit yourself. Oh, hang on: hot flushes, dry skin, look out for them and good luck.* No one writes articles that say, *Some of those remnant hormones will do their own thing; you're likely to become a raving strumpet for a few minutes, now and then. It's normal, don't panic.*

'You're right.' I wave my splinted wrist at him. 'I'll hang it properly, soon.'

'I'll hang it now. Do you know where?'

The kitchen, tiny at the best of times, shrinks with Dominic in it. I circle, in reverse, around the table, but really there's no decision to be made. Just one wall has enough space to hang the portrait.

Dominic goes over and holds it up. 'Here?'

'A little higher, please. Good.'

He appears to wait for something.

'Come and put your finger at the top, so I can see what height you want it.'

I look around for a pencil but can't find one and grab a biro.

'That will mark the wall, and then you'll have to paint it over. Just put your finger on the top.'

Heavens. I concede and take more time than is necessary to cover a couple of metres. I hesitate next to him and consider how to get my finger up at the top of the portrait, without touching him. It's impossible. This is now like a game of Upright Twister. I throw him a I'm-casual-about-these-sorts-of-things-you-know smile and move in. Sandwiched between the Dutch dresser and the hardness of his chest I lift an arm and slide it under one of his. His breath moves my hair, our forearms twine. A liquid warmth loops around the inside of my hips. This is an alive I've forgotten. I'm filled with startling emotional swings and dense orchestrations.

Dominic lowers the painting, moves away and I flatten myself like a moth against the wall.

'The cordless drill is on the shelf.' I speak to the wall, forehead pushed in hard.

There's the *tink* of drill bits in their metal box. The whirr of one being secured into the Bosch. And then he slides his finger gently beneath mine and I scoot across the room. A fine rain of plaster spirals from behind the screech of the drill and descends to the floor. Dominic finds a rawl plug. I note the arch of his neck, push my hips away from him into the sink's edge.

The painting is up.

'Thank you.' I'm sure my body is shouting, so I grab a tea towel and hold it against my belly.

He turns slowly from the painting, eyes cupped in the creases of a smile. 'My pleasure.'

'Dominic.' The words are sticky in my mouth. 'How much do I owe you, for the electrical work?'

'I do my bills every three months. You have an appointment at the hospital. Ten o'clock on Friday.'

'I haven't had a letter, a phone call.'

'No, I saw the doctor at football training. I'll take you.'

'Oh goodness, I can get there.'

'I know this.' He takes my wrist, undoes the velcro on the splint and tightens it slightly. 'I'll check some equipment while we are there.'

We. The word strums a chord. I just ceased being part of a 'we' and it was painful. Why on earth am I homing in on one syllable? But I can't say no again.

I don't want to.

40

The washing needs to be brought in. This is normally a mundane activity, but my mood carries me across the lawn, my body coursing with a long-forgotten frisson. A stiff breeze fills the pillowcases, which flap against my face. It's as if they're trying to bring me round from an emotional swoon. I unpeg one, fold it awkwardly against my belly, feel the slap of the next against my cheek. In the background the distinctive rattle of Lilou's Renault drifts over the hedge as she returns from the train station with Pierre. Fingers crossed for her, for them.

Who'd have thought hanging a picture on a wall would turn me into a romantic heroine? Walking along the washing line, unpegging pillowcases, inhaling the garden freshness in the fabric, has never been more enjoyable. Somewhere, in a recess of my heightened senses, I hear another car rumble down the lane.

When the next pillowcase comes down, right there, small suitcase in hand, is Simon. All my happiness evaporates on the breeze. I'm as pleased to see him as I would be the front end of an oncoming truck.

'Audrey.'

'What are you doing here?' I feel one second of surprise, one of disappointment, and then my core starts to hiss and spit like cold water has been flicked onto a barbecue plate.

'I told you I was coming.' He drops his bag and tucks the rental car keys in his pocket.

'You told me you were going to be in Cambridge.'

He stretches his head to peer into the field. He's looking around the garden for changes or familiarities, I'm not sure which, but either way he's blithely unaware of how I'm feeling.

'Yes, well, you didn't reply to my email.'

'Indeed. That was my reply.'

I tug at the next sheet and a peg pops off and twirls brightly onto the lawn.

He lopes over to the washing in his ironed chinos, ironed shirt. 'You'll break them.'

'Quite possibly.'

I'd forgotten just how contrived his look is and continue to yank the washing in silence. The pegs are my missiles. He bends and picks them up one by one, drops them into their bag. The last sheet is hauled off the line, and I'm stuck for an activity now. The basket is over full. I don't remember a time when Simon has ever deigned to be near a washing line.

'You can sleep in the cottage.'

His face flattens out like a sheet of paper. 'The kids said you still have guests.'

I stomp towards the cottage. The gravel hurts my bare feet, but I refuse to show it.

'Please bring the laundry basket.' I grab the handle of his overnight bag and drag it with me.

'I do have a guest. Just one. A neighbour's friend. There are three bedrooms.'

I park his case at the mouth of the corridor. He puts the basket on the kitchen table, looking aloof and splenetic.

'Take the room at the end.' I point and stand back.

He goes down to the room and returns almost immediately.

'Use some of these sheets.' I wave my splinted arm over the basket.

'There's no ensuite.'

'Correct. Settle yourself in. I'll be in the hayloft.'

I leave, feeling shocked, angry and confused. No ensuite – for god's sake.

———

Ruby tomato slices wait patiently on the plate for a drizzle of oil. The little seeds, innocently cupped in the belly of the fruit, are perfect. The thing is, do I cut up another tomato for him? Do I make salad for two, or will I give him a few things in a box to sort out over in the cottage? That's probably a bit harsh, although it is tempting. Salad for two then.

I pluck a few basil leaves, rinse soil from radish roots and become aware the room has darkened. And there he is, dwarfing the doorway. Prunella filled the space too, but she was more of a draught excluder. *Him*, he's a damp, oxygen-sucking blanket. Simon steps inside without an invite and casts his eyes around the room. It feels like an invasion of my privacy. I don't want him in here.

'Here, take this outside, please.' I push the tray with dinner things towards him. 'I'll bring the rest.'

He takes a step towards the table. 'Won't there be midges out there? I think I heard a few.'

'Probably. Light a coil if they bother you.' I'd forgotten his small bug phobia – swatting and spraying, scratching and moaning, *Oh they just love me.*

'I see I don't rate a mention on your list.'

Tray in hand he looks at the two yellow slips of paper on the pinboard. Just the children and my brother are up there.

256

I continue to crush sea salt into pink dust between pestle and mortar.

He turns. 'Oh, your portrait—'

'Out, out.'

I don't want him to make some wisecrack about the potato peeler. I will not have him tarnish the spot where my body, not two hours ago, came alive against the skin of another man.

There's a silent dome over us as we settle either side of the table. Each plate is put out, each knife and fork passed over with Edwardian formality. I keep my eyes down but see him scan the small bowls. Haricot, knowing a human meal when he sees one, jumps up onto the table. I tap a hard-boiled egg on the cutting board, peel the shell and think about passing it over. I don't.

He chooses an egg. Rolls it between his fingers and looks at me. 'There's a cat on the table.'

What possible reply is there to that? *Oh gosh darling, I hadn't noticed, very well observed, so that's what a cat looks like?*

'You don't like cats, Audrey, so why is it allowed on the table?'

He cracks the eggshell on the side of his plate, which tips under the force.

'Don't I like cats? I think it's you who doesn't like cats, and it's why we've always had dogs.' I help myself to lettuce and dressing. 'If you look behind you, there's a water spray. This is what guests who don't like cats use. Just the sight of it in your hand, and Haricot will be gone.'

Simon doesn't reach for the bottle, and for this I give him one point.

He takes a napkin, spreads it on his lap. 'Do you like cats?'

'Are you here to talk about cats?'

Holding a radish between his fingers, as though not quite sure what to do with it, he looks up. 'It seems your list and the portrait are off limits.'

'They are.'

He slices the radish, awkwardly, with a butter knife. I take a ruby white orb, dip it in the salt and pop the whole thing in my mouth. Radish wars.

'You look well, like you've lost weight, and your hair is longer. How's the wrist?'

How's the wrist? – half a point. Should have asked me on arrival. *You look well, like you've lost weight* – minus two points. He's really saying you were a bit chubby. *Your hair is longer* – that's disapproval so minus two points. This is the sort of comment I got when he thought I needed a haircut. *Are you due for a trim?* I think I'll give up scoring this conversation; he's a terrible loser.

'... do you?'

'Pardon?'

'You weren't listening. I asked if you knew when you'd be back, because the children really miss you, and they want to know.'

He pulls off a bit of baguette and starts to spread butter along its length.

'The kids and I message, a lot. We have a group, Mumsgoneawol. We also talk at least once a week and I write long emails. It's been valuable. If I write something and no one wants to read it, well then, it's no more valuable than a snotty tissue fit for the bin. But I can tell the kids read them because of the way they reply.' I take a mouthful of tomato and enjoy the flavour, but not as much as if I were on my own.

'They poke fun at me, laugh at my foibles, and I understand that's their acceptance of me. I've also learnt a lot. Did you know that telling a person they're clever is meaningless? To tell them something they did, or said, or wrote, is great because of how hard they tried is much more helpful. I didn't realise, did you?'

I'm just about to put another radish in my mouth but I decide I don't want him to reply so I put the red orb down again.

'I've learnt that when I told them they were brilliant and clever, and I did a million times, it can feel like pressure.'

I pop the radish in my mouth and chew. He chews too. There's just the sound of chewing. I take a sip of wine.

'I'm getting to know more about them from this distance. Sure, I don't know how much laundry they've produced, or whether the toothpaste is nearly finished, but I know significant things. Like Thea's love-life.'

His head jerks up.

'Did you know Orson is keen to get a skipper's ticket when he's finished his Masters?'

Simon puts his cutlery down as though it's too heavy and opens his mouth to speak, but I hold up a finger.

'I don't think they miss me. Not badly. I think this time is good for the children and me. It's a growth spurt.'

I fork pale lettuce into a shaggy pile, pop it in my mouth. I chew; now he can talk.

Simon swivels his head left and right, scooping up information he thought he knew. 'Surely you mean Gus is the one who wants to run away to sea.'

'Maybe he does, but it's Orson who wants his ticket.'

'And what do you mean we shouldn't tell someone they're a genius, or brilliant or clever if they are? Isn't that a new-fangled kind of ridiculous?'

I cut a slice of Comte and perch a large slice of tomato on top. 'You are talking about yourself now, Simon. You love the plaudits, and you strive for academic excellence, because if it isn't achieved there will be people who might think less of you.'

His mouth goes still. I glower and dare him to reply with a mouth full. He chews again, no retort. If I were still scoring, I'd give him half a point.

'You may not think of it that way, of course, but I'm telling you what my experience has been of your academic path. I was directly involved too, you know. If our home wasn't decorated with the spoils of a large salary, if we didn't serve the right wine, then we risked not being able to secure the respect of people you didn't want to look right through you.'

'I think that's very unfair.'

Goodness, he heard me out, he let me speak. I may as well continue. 'Simon, do I exist?'

'Of course.'

'Well then, it's my opinion, and I'm too tired for it to be up for discussion, not tonight. And if you don't understand, I may as well have spoken into a vacuum.'

I put my cutlery on my plate, the plate on the tray.

'I think we should leave it there for tonight, don't you? Make sure you put the butter in the fridge please. The cat really doesn't need the carbs.'

'Butter is fat.'

'Right.' Of course it is, and of course he had to point it out.

I stand, push the bench out. He's probably not impressed by the meal; his friends certainly wouldn't be. At this moment I understand there are many things I can do, and indeed may do, but I will never go back to the odious labours of trying to impress people who can't see me.

'Good night. See you tomorrow.'

I top up my wineglass and head off to the hayloft. What on earth can I do tomorrow to keep out of his way?

His voice breaks my departure. 'What time tomorrow?'

I swivel slowly. It's a reasonable question. He looks pale under the terrace lights and I feel a pang of pity. 'Shall we say four?'

'In the afternoon?'

'There's only one four o'clock I acknowledge in a day.'

'That's late.'

'I'm busy.' I pick up the cat and head into the hayloft.

41

The first thought on waking is *Simon is in the cottage.* There was a time when that would have thrilled me, but I sneak out of the gate, wishing my jeans didn't make a dry whisper at the ankles – as though he'd hear that. Then I duck down the twisting path to the river where a canopy of velvet green folds overhead. A blackbird lets loose from within a darker thicket. Leaves are turning rusty. Summer, with the long holidays, suntans and tourists – the season for ice cream, postcards, caravan traffic jams and beers on the beach – is almost over.

I used to love summer. But all that heat, the crowds, and exposed body parts, feel a little vulgar now. Perhaps my change of attitude arrived when irrational sweating became a newly acquired talent. Perhaps summer became annoying when I realised I'd forgotten to look after my body, and there were wobbly fleshy bits all over the place. A body better suited to heavy winter coats. The thought of returning to an Australian summer makes me shudder. Here it's perfect. The beaches are emptying, caravans have been replaced by tractors hauling corn and apples, the medieval towns and towpaths return to their locals, and the weather is delicious, volatile. Over the next months, there'll be blue skies, dark clouds, fluffy ones, no sky at all, rain, hail and a watery sun. This lack of certainty resonates with me. It's a theatre of possibilities.

The path angles sharply over a makeshift bridge. Below the split railway sleepers, a lazy rivulet idles, coating roots and rocks with a metallic glint.

'Audrey, you're procrastinating, turn back, go home. You could walk all day, but you'll still have to face the music. My word, you've not talked to yourself for a while.'

I force myself to turn around and go back to the cottage like a petulant child. This time I shut the gate with force. Simon's routines are predictable. He will prowl around the cottage for breakfast, find and eat a bowl of cereal but tut about the carton of long-life milk. He's most definitely not welcome in the hayloft so coffee will have to be on the neutral territory of the terrace.

There's a soft mizzle. The water hangs in drifts over the garden and makes the thick green hydrangea leaves more intense. Sparrows hide in the holly hedge and the seeds on the bird table turn darker as the damp settles in.

Simon emerges tentatively from the cottage, shrinks away from the weather.

'I thought you were going to be busy all day?'

'Yes, well, I thought I would go out, but I felt bad.'

'I did too.' He pauses to flick at imaginary droplets on his shirt. 'You looked horrified to see me yesterday.'

I look him in the eye for the first time and consider my words carefully. 'I think I was.'

'Isn't it reasonable your husband comes to visit?' He drops both hands easily into his pockets.

'That is a question now, isn't it? Yesterday I looked at you and asked myself, *Is he my husband?*'

I cup my palm over the top of the coffee pot and slowly push the plunger down. I do not want to hear another one of his self-righteous monologues.

'Do you still have questions?' He rakes his grey, combed hair with clawed fingers and sidles around the terrace, not quite sure what to look at.

'Are you going to sit down?'

There's the scrape of the bench and he takes his time to sit opposite me. He folds his hands neatly, then he asks again, slower this time, 'Do you want to ask me anything?'

He focuses on the coffee pot, turns it back and forth nonchalantly. I take a cup, think it's sad how we just flick our eyes over each other like strangers now.

'How's Howard?'

'You want to know about the dog?'

'I do.'

'Howard is Howard – hairy, moulting. I think he misses you.'

'It's mutual.'

I lift the spoon out of habit and beat out a slow rhythm against the side of the sugar bowl. 'I haven't decided what I want exactly, not for the long term, and it is not a decision you can help with.'

Simon looks around the tray and then up at me. 'Don't you take sugar anymore?'

Sugar habit changes are not high on my list of priority discussions.

He tries again. 'Don't you want to ask anything about Midori?'

'You made it quite clear it's been a long-term thing.'

'Yes and no. I was wrong. Midori isn't a fit. She doesn't sit comfortably with my being a father, the domesticity of family meals, obligations, Howard's hairs. We see that now.

264

Frankly it's been a difficult battle. It isn't going to work. I see it would never have worked. I wouldn't have what I've got, what I've achieved, the children, none of it, not if I hadn't had you.'

'Of course, you wouldn't. Unfortunately you should have appreciated that a long time ago. The benefit of your hindsight is too little too late.' I look at his pale, soft-skinned, manicured hands, and then at my own unkempt nails. 'You see, my idea of our marriage is, was, my husband and I would be sequestered off from other sexual partners. We'd live securely in our family. We'd be relatively safe from things which might hurt us, like infidelity.'

'Audrey, I—'

'Simon, you turned off the burglar alarm protecting our marriage before we took our vows. You also failed to mention you'd done this, that you'd decided it was okay for Dr Midori Crump to be a part of your private world.'

'It wasn't like that.'

He stirs his coffee slowly and I can feel his gaze, but I won't look at him, not yet.

'It is like that for me, Simon. Perhaps I've been boxed in by my own silly ideas, but I did think we were exclusive, and that I was loved. Based on this I subconsciously built a picture that we'd be *we. Us.* Off I went, with my somewhat myopic views, creating a home, a life, sharing my experiences. We acquired a history and things, and I believed, assumed, what we were doing, what was ours, would naturally therefore be for our children. Simplistic I know. I assumed there was a certain stability between us, and it soothed me. But I got all of it wrong, didn't I?'

'No, no, you didn't. I wanted those things.'

'Did you? Perhaps with another woman, or perhaps you thought you'd try to have it all.'

'Midori never wanted to marry me, never wanted kids. Our relationship is cerebral. We don't function day to day, and I made a stupid mistake thinking we could.'

Simon slides his hand across the table, and I pull back. His fingers stretch briefly then lie still and flat on the wooden surface. I fix his pale grey eyes with mine. His focus shifts to the right of my head for a fraction of a second.

'We've talked a great deal.'

'We? There you are, you and Midori are still we, which makes me, her.'

'No. She doesn't want the responsibility of upsetting our home, the children, everything. She feels bad.'

'Interesting. So, you bond beautifully when it's illicit and you can talk about volatile funding streams, technological advances in kelp protein extraction, friction in engine bays. But do the shopping, vacuum the rugs, and your affair loses its lustre?'

He looks away.

It's odd – I don't feel rattled. There's certainly a lemony bitterness to this moment but that's about all.

'This all started for you while you were a student, in love with your professor, forty-one years ago. It started for me very recently; when I knew something was wrong with *your* Japanese painting. And then I searched my diaries to see when we'd got it, and I found many other points over the years where I should have had my eyes open and didn't.'

He lifts his head, his face flooded with righteousness. 'You and the kids always came first, none of you wanted for anything.'

I feel such a bolt of indignation it tightens across my shoulders, yanking them back. 'Wow. I was living a lie, Simon. One I would not have agreed to, had I been given the choice.'

'But now, Audrey, now there is no Midori and me.' He looks at me. 'I know I've been a complete idiot and I don't know what to do.'

My anger builds so much I physically recoil. The way he flinches, I know he sees it too. We're pinging off each other and it's not good.

'When I arrived here, in France, I felt as though I'd been emotionally colonised by you, Simon. And I've only just started to see my boundaries again, to get me back.'

'Audrey, can't we …'

I pat the top of his hands once and then push his arms gently back towards his side of the table.

'For now, there's no you and me. No *we*.' I run my fingers over my lips until the required sentence forms. 'Right now, I don't know if I can, or want to, adapt to a different reality with you. I don't even want to consider it.'

There, I've said it.

His long neck strains out of his collar. 'People have started to talk, you know, to ask questions. I don't know what to tell anyone, about when you'll be back. There'll be rumours, and I don't know what to say.'

'There will have been many rumours over the years. Nod, nod, wink, wink, brilliant Midori and Simon.' I slide down to the end of the bench. 'Are you flying home out of London or Paris?'

'Paris, why?'

As I suspected. His email, which theoretically *asked* if it was okay for him to visit after Cambridge, was a nonsense, he planned to turn up all along. He would have assumed my hasty exit in May was a drive-by mood swing, and by now I'd be *back to normal*. Huh.

'I'd like you to leave, today, Simon. You can drive to Paris or take the train, leave the hire car in Saint Malo. I don't know

how long you thought you'd stay here, but you need to go now.'
I hold my hand up, flat and broad like a school crossing guard
on a busy street. 'I'll be back in Australia when I'm back. The
children will know well in advance.'

All my limbs are filled with wet sand.

'I'm sorry, Simon.'

Then I use what little energy is left in my fibres and walk
through the mizzle into the hayloft and shut the door behind me.

42

Lilou comes through the field gate in a pink flying suit, one hand over her belly, which is flat and smooth. I note how delicately her fingers cup what will be. My hand, by contrast, is midst one-handed willow weave; surprising what you can do with clamps and your teeth.

'Should you be doing this with a broken wrist?' Lilou removes the willow strands from my mouth.

'No-E set me up and I'm happy as a pig in mud. The bride wants four arches for her wedding. She saw the ones for my runner beans and simply must have some.'

'You don't have to make them, you know.'

'I want to. I'm happiest out here. Nathalie has ordered more for Christmas and asked for a reindeer.'

'You're mad, but I'm glad because it means you won't leave. I see you also had a visitor. Was it Simon?'

'Yes.'

'And?'

I flip the subject. 'How did it go with Pierre?'

'How about you and I both answer on the count of three, okay? One, two, three ...'

'Yes, it went well.' Our voices overlap.

Lilou cocks her head to one side. 'I meant it, but your delivery was laden with sarcasm.'

'You first.'

'Pierre was delighted, initially. Not so happy when I said I wasn't moving back to Paris. But, to sum up, he's happy about the pregnancy and he wants to be involved.' The skin around her mouth bleaches.

'What's the but?'

'I'm very lucky.' She crumples a dry leaf between two fingers. 'I wish I could be in love with him, not just love him, and the baby will hate me for it.'

'Yes, your child will hate you, sometimes, momentarily, when you limit the Anzac biscuits or insist it's bedtime.'

I pause then continue. 'Have you, amongst those love-not-in-love words about Pierre, come to feel you're in love with Rose?'

'*Ooof*, it feels like it. She has withdrawn a bit. She says it's so I can figure things out, but maybe she's simply not into Lilou plus baby. Or maybe I think I love her because sex with a woman is far more me than sex with a man. I don't know. Anyway, the point is moot. Pierre's going to be a great dad. Enough, I'm going round in circles. Your husband came over, were you expecting him?'

'Certainly was not.'

'Oh, cheeky. Romantic.' She pushes a frond through my creation. 'Or perhaps not, judging by the look on your face.'

'Definitely not romantic. He turned up expecting cooperative Audrey to be in residence.'

'And she wasn't?'

'For less than a millisecond. There was nothing there and I'm too, too cross.'

'Nothing stirred then?'

'Zip. Zero. Zilch. I love Simon, I do, without him there'd be no Orson, Gus and Thea. And I'd never wish him any harm. But there's always a *but*, isn't there? It's going to take time I reckon. People can change their mind, they do it all the time, about all sorts of things, but I'm not sure I will.'

'Good for you. You can stay forever.' The brilliance of this idea lights up her face.

'Tempting, but what about my children, my dog and my brother? The practicalities I'll have to face in Australia.'

'When do you think you'll go?'

'Oh god, I don't know. I can't work out what's going on with Tata.'

'You absolutely cannot leave your aunt all alone. And what about me? I need you. Then there's Dominic, are you going to break his heart?'

'You're evil.'

'I couldn't bear it if you left, Audrey. You're this baby's grandmother.'

'You have a mother; she'll want to help.'

Lilou glides around the arch theatrically. She stops, tosses her hair, puts one hand on a jutting hip and gives me an imperious glare. 'One cannot carry a baby while teetering on Louboutin heels. Dribble worn down the front of vintage Vivienne Isabel Westwood blouses is not in this year, or any year.' Lilou dabs at imaginary baby goop on an imaginary lapel. 'If you go, come back quickly, I won't cope without you.'

'The world isn't the same, we can't nip across continents when we want. Well, I don't feel like we can.'

'So, it is September now, can you hazard a guess, a ballpark date?' Lilou collects more stems for me, moves the clamps along the frame.

'I truly have no idea. It feels like doing flowers with Nathalie, tap dancing, being time rich and money poor is an excellent option. On the other hand, there's always the seductive blue skies of Australia. Perhaps I'll start to miss the ocean at the end of the road. I've no idea. So, the answer is who knows.'

43

'**M**um.'
'Hello darling, where are your brothers?'

Two more windows open.

'You all look a bit sombre; gorgeous but sombre. Are you annoyed I'm not coming back yet?'

Gus removes a toothpick from between his lips where it's been rolling back and forth. 'Not at all. The problem is, Dad's back.'

'Yes, grumpy, morose Dad is most definitely back.' Orson sips what I assume is one of his herb teas because it's late over there.

Thea leans forward onto her elbows. She's sitting cross-legged on her bed and puts the phone down on the mattress, so I see her face from underneath. 'He came back a week early, Mum.'

A week. He planned on staying a week with me – how rash of him. 'What do you want me to say? I'd like to know about what's going on with all of you.'

Gus looks up from the toothpick in his fingers. 'This is what's going on with us, or partly. Dad said he'd told you he was going to visit, and you changed your mind.'

I jerk my head back.

'So, it's not true then?' Orson has read my expression.

'It's not true, no. He asked if I wanted him to *pop over* after Cambridge and I didn't reply, thinking no reply was answer enough. But he turned up and, all I can say is, it was wrong.'

'I knew it. I told you Mum hadn't had a personality reshuffle.' Gus puts the toothpick back and talks around it. 'I get it, you're not ready yet. So what have you been up to?'

'Oo, let me see … this morning I got a bumblebee jasper crystal in the post from ex-guests and their note says, *Audrey, use this to remove blockages, relax and try putting your concerns out to the aether.*'

Orson snorts.

'So sweet of them.' Thea grabs the phone and flops backwards onto her pillow, the phone following the trajectory of this movement.

'I appreciate the gesture I do but …'

'No number of crystals will work on Dad, right?'

'Right, Gus. It's going to take more than a crystal to sort this one out.'

Orson grins, drops his voice so its sotto voce. 'Time is a great healer.'

'You've been reading Hallmark cards again, Orson.'

'Yes, Mother.'

'How are you, you know, post Joolz?'

'I'm absolutely fine, and I think it's cool you didn't indulge Dad, I'm pretty proud of you. And you stay there as long as you like.'

'Thanks, Orson.'

Three faces look at me in earnest. I wave my splinted arm at them. 'I truly am okay and am going to be more than okay soon because I've got an appointment at the hospital. I think this splint can come off today.'

Gus waves his toothpick at the screen. 'No more falling over?'

'Correct, I've given that up.'

Three faces blow me kisses, two hands wave, Orson feigns a salute, and the screen goes black.

My wedding ring twirls around and around, trapped in place by my enlarged knuckles. I spin it again, tingling with a strange, guilty anticipation.

There's a knock on the door, which makes me jump, although it is exactly what I've been listening for. I give the ring a final spin.

Dominic greets me with the two-cheek kiss again. A mingling of soap and coffee line my nostrils and I hope I haven't inhaled too obviously. I'm overreacting. This is schoolgirl foolishness.

His phone rings from deep in a trouser leg. Dominic pulls it from his pocket, notes the number and apologises. I brush away the interruption with a smile and follow him out to his minuscule car. I'm glad something mundane has popped the ludicrous bubble. I'm a grown woman with grown children – Orson Thea Gus, Orson Thea Gus – I run their names through my mind as I walk to the car. Dominic attaches his phone to the dashboard with a bungee strap and continues to talk as we drive away.

I'd like to buy him a small thank you gift for everything he's helped me with, but buying presents is intimidating.

We pass a flock of cream sheep and I want to put the window down, but from the general condition of the car, I don't know if it's mechanically an option.

A homemade gift might be an option for Dominic. But I'm not sure a homemade backgammon board or a bottle of stinging nettle vodka will be to his taste.

Dominic ends the call, and is about to say something, when the phone rings again. We raise eyebrows at each other.

Low stone walls line our journey now and their clinging lichen is the orange of synthetic burger cheese. I am very keen to look out the window, to occupy my mind with something other than the fact I'm squeezed beside Dominic in a car so tiny I can feel the rise and fall of his chest. Look at the cider press, Audrey; stop registering the honeyed-oak tones of his voice.

He is still mid conversation about conduits and the new legislation on fuse boxes when we arrive at the hospital. He collects a battered canvas bag from the back seat and walks with me to the outpatient entrance. He puts a hand over the phone's microphone and says he'll either come and find me in the clinic, or I'm to meet him out here on the bench. I watch him walk away and a wizened pocket of air in my stomach tells me I'd hoped to spend the appointment in his company.

The doctor's eyes, magnified by thick glass lenses, are round and earnest. He wants me to study the X-ray on his computer screen, shows me how the crack is healing well. Then he removes the splint and holds my wrist in his dry palms. He presses his fingers over the articulating surfaces and tells me I can leave the splint off for a few hours every day. I ask him about gardening. *Gently, with your splint on.* When can it come off completely? *Not for one more week.* Supporting my arm, he runs through a few exercises which are to be done every day, twice a day. I can't help but grin at the routine. He wants to know why I find it funny. I explain that the movements would look amusing if he was wearing finger puppets. His face says *I have no idea what you're talking about.* Remembering the French are better suited to tragedy than comedy, I apologise for my silliness. We shake hands. I thank him. Simple.

As the hospital sliding doors open to let me out, Dominic's car arrives in the drop-off zone. He leans across and opens the door. This isn't a chivalrous gesture, the handle on the outside is broken. I get in as elegantly as one can while navigating an aperture better suited to toddlers.

Dominic chuckles. 'I expect your car at home is bigger, *non?*'

'Your car is certainly *different*.' I pull my skirt down over my knees, keep my voice light. 'In Australia most of the vehicles are huge four-wheel-drive things. And we don't make cars for people who don't have a licence. We get a bike or take the bus.'

I know most people who drive *sans permis* have to because they lost their licence through *pissy drinking*. There are so many offenders the courts put together *Sauvignon sessions* to reprimand groups of drivers at the same time. I want to ask Dominic if that's what happened to him, but equally I don't want to know.

'I can't take a ladder on the bus. Are you busy? I thought we could have lunch.'

Weeding the gravel can wait. 'Lovely idea.'

Dominic pulls away and waves at a young hospital orderly. 'He used to be in my football team.'

His phone is nowhere to be seen. We chat about the appointment and drive straight through the village, past the bar. Odd, I'd assumed we'd go there. He talks about his job and then about the doctor's son who has great speed on the left wing. After another ten minutes of idle chatter, he pulls into a lay-by high above the river.

'This is where I often come to eat my lunch and have a swim.'

The brown sinewy river arches left and right below us, dotted with tiny ducks and skimming cormorants. Miniature people exercise miniature horses on the opposite bank. Three toothpick church steeples can be counted on the horizon.

Dominic produces a supermarket bag from the car and lays baguettes, cheese, wine, tomatoes and cold meat out on a picnic table. He pulls out a large pocketknife, uses the corkscrew to open the wine, then flicks open a blade, and wipes this on his trousers.

'You sit this side so you can see the river.' Dominic slices cheese and opens the plastic meat wrapper.

'There's enough room,' I say, 'sit next to me.' Brazen hussy.

Dominic passes the knife and sits. 'What else is different about France, apart from our cars?'

'Many things. I see it more and more, the longer I'm here.'

'Like what?'

'Commercial gain, prosperity, efficiency, they feel like they're secondary motives here.'

'In Brittany, maybe. Paris, Marseille, no. What else?'

'Cheese, butter, the names of wines, trains, beaches, the buildings.'

'I know these things from postcards, TV shows, what else?'

'The culture is fundamentally different. For example, my dad was sick for two years before he died, so death was discussed freely at home. But generally, in Australia, people don't talk or think about death nearly enough, and consequently they never get into the belly of what's important. Death is visible here. There are cows' heads behind glass counters in the markets – no one screams and runs away, no one covers their children's eyes. Pascal collects his own snails, purges them on thyme, lets them foam on salt. There's no squeamish flinching, no cellophane wrapping. And Madame Mitteaux planned the flowers for her own funeral.' I take a bite of cheese. 'But my ex-mother-in-law, who's already had an emergency cardiac bypass, is in total denial, won't go near the subject. And her attitude is quite typical.'

'Do you think about dying?'

'I think about living better because I know I will die. That's the point, isn't it? I'm acutely aware I'm closer to my death than my birth. When, *if*, I return to Australia, I'll trot along, withering away, being invisible, and then one day I'll drop down dead. If I stay here, where the attitude to older women is kinder, I'll exist, right up until the moment I don't.'

What on earth am I talking about? I grab a tomato and cut it, pierce the first slice on the blade and offer it to Dominic.

'Interesting. How are we kinder?' He takes the slice and pops it into his mouth.

'Australia applauds youth. TV series are filled with young, pneumatic women – youthful beauty is what fuels dreams, sells products. We're not very flexible in our views on what's beautiful. Getting older, wrinkly and misshapen reminds people of decay, death, and they don't like it. At my age I'm the fusty apple in a fruit bowl; the one you throw away. Society at home wants me to live carefully, neuter myself. That's quite an unsexy way to lead my life.'

Dominic looks as though I've just explained a sci-fi plot to him. '*Mon dieu.*'

Nodding sagely, I feel quite proud of my monologue, which is undoubtedly full of holes, but no one here is pulling it apart.

'French female protagonists on TV are often forty or fifty, beautiful, sassy, charming. It's a reflection of how differently your society sees ageing.'

He passes the bottle of wine across. 'Sorry, no glasses. *Bien dans son âge*, that's what we think, beauty is not dependent on having no wrinkles.'

'Exactly and we say, *She is attractive for her age.* It's awful.'

The icy rosé shimmies perfectly over my tongue. I take a second sip then offer him the bottle. I notice the horses across the river are doing figures of eight now.

Dominic looks at me very hard. 'Young or old, French women don't want to give up the experience of being loved for their beauty or sexual power. And it's not just on TV, or at home, or at work – it's everywhere.'

'We need some of that. My daughter, Thea, says her generation has a complicated relationship with beauty and sexual power. It must not play a role in the workplace and socially there remain a lot of stigmas. She feels on edge about these matters.'

'That's a shame.'

'It is, or is it? I believe the French think nothing of Mitterrand's long-term affair whereas Australians tsk-tsk.'

'During the 2006 World Cup—'

'You're not going to give me a French sexual mystique analogy in football, are you?'

I bite into the next tomato like an apple. It explodes and Dominic wipes away a few seeds which settle on my chin. Wearing lunch – Jesus, Audrey, you've just proved your own point about older Australian women being dismissible.

'I am going to talk about football. In the 2006 World Cup, the French team clawed their way into the final against Italy. Zinedine Zidane was our undisputed hero, and it was to be his last game in a perfect career. With just minutes to go, Marco Materazzi whispered something, and Zidane headbutted him. ZZ was sent off with a red card, and the French lost to the Italians in a penalty shootout.'

Dominic turns towards me, his muscles alive with the story. He drinks some wine and passes the bottle back to me. I notice we're not wiping the neck between mouthfuls.

'In the English papers, the headlines said, *Zidane Hero to Zero*. But in the French papers it was different; people only wanted to know what Materazzi had said.'

'What did he say?'

'There were several theories. He'd insulted Zidane's sister, his mother, but another said he'd insulted Zidane's wife. ZZ was having an affair at the time, with a young singer, but in France it's the *jardin secret,* you don't discuss it. However, by insulting Zidane's wife, Materazzi had insulted Zidane's honour. A wife is sacred in France, even if you happen to be cheating on her. So, you see, there was no hypocrisy in the footballer's outrage. ZZ was a hero. As President Chirac said immediately after the match, ZZ had merely shown himself to be *human.*'

Dominic has a faraway, happy look in his eyes. There's not a drop of resentment that the match had been blown because of Zidane's reaction. I munch on a piece of baguette for a while, thankful for its chewy disposition. Perhaps if I were more than half French, I'd have been more relaxed about Simon's *jardin secret*? Perhaps I'd have forgiven Simon if he'd come out swinging to defend our marriage.

'We call your charming *jardin secret* infidelity.'

'As you've said, many things are different. For example, remembering what you said about the apple, I expect an Australian husband would say something like, "Audrey, you look well."'

'He might, yes.' I think about popping the bread into my mouth.

Dominic spreads his hands wide, with a slight look of disdain. 'A French man would never say such a thing to his wife.'

'What would you say?' I take another sip of wine instead.

'I would tell you: *you are intoxicating.*'

Something low in my ribs contorts sharply, and my throat spasms. The wine shoots out between parted lips in a splendid fan across the picnic. I gasp, clamp my hand across my mouth, cough, splutter, dab uselessly at the table and laugh. My whole body shakes. I can't speak, I can't breathe. I look at Dominic who just smiles at me, pleased.

'Intoxicating.' I repeat the word and it sets me off again. He waits a long time until my guffaws settle to a chortle, then some deep sighs, and normality is restored. Normality that has been washed through with endorphins.

'Dominic.'

'*Oui.*'

I look at him and wonder how I'm going to put this so I don't come across as either an idiot or self-pitying.

'Dominic.'

'Audrey.'

I've no idea what possesses me as my hand lifts to touch the side of his face. It feels too complicated to exchange words, and anyway, they'd be inadequate. A deep-set honesty eases out each movement and I bring my mouth to his. His lips are perfection. It's so wonderfully simple. This contact with Dominic exceeds the last five months, which hurtle away as I disappear into the moment.

When I move my whole body moves away from his. My arms drop from around his neck. His hands part and slide down my back. My skin leaves his and every muscle in my body grins.

His blackberry eyes reflect a curiosity, as though I were one down in a crossword puzzle. 'Mm, I see.'

'Thank you, *Monsieur.* You've done me a great kindness.'

44

Tata's village sits near the first lock at Le Châtelier along the river Rance. Standing on the bridge, looking inland, the river is fluvial. Looking towards the coast, it's tidal. Today the tide is out and the riverbed heading to Saint Malo is a yawning, undulating mass of black mud. Lazy waders dot the sinuous trickle as it snakes towards the sea. Redundant, bleached wooden jetties with their disused fishing huts jut out across the morass like witches' fingers. I take photos and send them to Mumsgoneawol.

The children used to love guessing whether the water would be in or out, and they'd run down to Le Châtelier to see who was right. If the tide was in, we'd stay to watch boats snuggle into the lock and then spill out the other side. As they got older and learnt about the rhythm of the sea, the guessing games stopped. Instead, we'd wait for a high tide to go onto one of the precarious *cabanons* and drop lines into the muscular flowing water.

No fish today. Not that I'm walking the towpath to catch dinner. I know exactly where I'm headed, and yet hope to find a reason to back out.

It's been a week since the picnic. The kiss appears to have taken up residence in my body. It pesters my thoughts to such a degree I'm now ready to discuss the lunacy. Or is it loveliness? But discuss with whom – this has been the problem.

On the other side of the lock the river is full and wires tinkle against swaying masts. With each step I check my thoughts again.

Laurence: I could talk with him, but he's somewhere between god-knows-where and there. He did sell one of his cars at the end of the film shoot, and evidently cried when he handed over the keys. But the funds mean my brother and his husband are having a protracted road trip home.

The locks along the canal have closed for the season and the river moorings are full of boats, trapped, and under tarps for the winter.

My children: I absolutely cannot talk to them about kissing a man who isn't their father.

The woman with two Irish wolfhounds waves to me from the other bank. I often see her and I know she walks that side to avoid the boat ramps so her dogs don't skid down them for a swim.

Lilou: If I told her about the picnic, she'd have me married off and living here forever.

Tata and No-E: I have considered asking their opinion, and they'd probably have great answers, but they might not be relevant, or at least not obviously helpful. Anyway, Tata's very evasive around any topic which threatens to turn personal. The other day I asked if she wanted her trousers out of storage, now her moon boot was off, and she asked me to bring the geraniums in.

The worst thing about my need to discuss the situation is my usual, highly effective remedy of talking to myself out loud hasn't been effective at all. Frankly, on this subject, I've been useless, going round and around in unhelpful circles.

So, there remains one person I can entrust my lunch with Dominic to. I climb the wooden steps, past where the falcons sometimes roost, and head onto the cliff edge. I swing my legs over the picnic bench and turn on my phone.

Sister Naomi lets me into the Zoom meeting, smiling and adjusting her earphones. 'Audrey, I was surprised to get your email, but I'm glad you contacted me.'

Not as surprised as me to admit the professionalism offered by the Holy Order of Handbags was my best bet.

'Thank you for making the appointment.'

'Where are you?'

'Brittany, France. My aunt fell out of a cherry tree and badly injured herself.'

'Oh, I remember, that's why you cancelled. I'm sorry. And you're still there?'

'Ostensibly I came over to look after her summer guests, but being here has given me time to process a few things.'

'Excellent. Has there been a particular focus?'

'The fact my partner of thirty-seven years has been having an affair for forty-one years. And, by the way, the Japanese painting, which you may recall niggled me so badly, was painted by his lover.'

Sister Naomi wriggles forward on her seat. 'What a lot of grief.'

'I suppose it is grief.' There's a nip in the air and I can feel my cheeks pink. 'But I've coped. More than coped.'

She seesaws her pen between two fingers. 'Of course. But what a complicated time for you.'

'Multifaceted, that's for sure: confusion, doubt, misery. And it's been relaxing, challenging, fun.'

'So many emotions, but you must be gentle, Audrey, give yourself time to heal.'

I don't feel like I have time.

'That reminds me, I broke my wrist; slipped on my tap-dancing drawing pins.'

She looks confused. Well touché, not as confused as I've been by handbags since our last appointment.

'I've been experimenting with the pleasures of new things.'

'And tap dancing, is that new or something you did as a child?'

'New. I like it. I've also built a wall, a bedside table, made sculptures, been paid to do flowers at a wedding, and I kissed a man.'

Sister Naomi goes to say something but stops herself. She writes a couple of words, pulses her jaw, then looks straight into the camera.

'These, apparently random, choices are often detours we take. Detours which act as respite from the issues at hand.'

'Which is why I asked for this appointment. All those things I listed have added up, been beneficial.' I take a breath to read her face, and see I need to drive this appointment on. I don't want to talk about carpentry joints. 'Learning has been a great respite, a great awakening. And the kiss was not a *detour*, it was more of a bridge.'

Sister Naomi leans further forward and rests her elbows on the desk. 'If we're to focus on the kiss, permit me to suggest something. You felt hurt, abandoned, and needed to remind yourself you are attractive.'

I must cut her off. 'Permit me to try out an analogy.'

I wonder why on earth I thought this appointment was a good idea. I am not a teenager, gagging for some boy to ask me out.

The skin on her pointy chin tightens a fraction. 'Analogies can be helpful.'

'I'm a big fan of them. Anyway, here goes. When I'm hungry, I don't function well. Therefore, if I'm hungry and I eat some sticky date pudding, for example, I am happy, and no longer hungry. I would not cry because the pudding was gone. Being sated I'd carry on more effectively.'

'I see, so you're not hankering for more *sticky date pudding*?'

'No. I like to think I'll have more sticky date pudding in the future, I do. However, I also hope to have guacamole, crème caramel, Comte cheese et cetera. The point of my analogy is, because I satisfied a particular hollow, with the perfect remedy, I feel like I've bridged a gap between old me and current me.'

Sister Naomi writes on for a good fifteen seconds after I've stopped talking. 'This is interesting.'

'I think so.'

'Old you, who's she?'

'Goodness. The most obvious example is Married-Mother-Me. I devoted a lot of energy to help Simon's academic advances, which I was happy to do at the time. And motherhood is an exercise in compromise, joy, selflessness, pretence; gosh, it is far too complicated to discuss in one hour. Certainly, I'd have lived differently without my children, but without them I wouldn't want to live.' I wonder what she's hearing. 'Everything feels big, fuzzy and confusing.'

She writes, head up, looking into the camera.

'Current-Me is harder to describe, and post the kiss, post *the bridge*, it feels like outlines of recognisable objects have started to emerge from layered, abstract tangles. And, without forcing anything, if I relax and look long enough at the jumbled shapes in my diary entries for example, or imagine a new life, there appear to be even more ambiguous forms lurking.'

'I see.'

'Well, I don't see.'

'I see.'

Across the river, Madame Irish Wolfhound has turned and heads home. A falcon swoops on currents of air, the horizon's church steeples are fuzzed out by a rain-heavy sky.

'Audrey, I see why you might not see. The *things from your past, which are currently unclear* will emerge. For the moment you may not be able to trust yourself about which path to take, so don't force anything.'

'You mean I shouldn't decide on a career as a musician, for example.'

'Interesting. What genre would you adopt and what would your lyrics speak of?'

'Vulnerability, understatedness, domesticity, with a nod to fury.'

'Good.'

'Is it good? I don't want to be a musician, nor a decorator, nor a vet nurse. Should I shut down all these ridiculous, new internal swirls?'

'They're not ridiculous. They're moments which have been tightly coiled up in you and now—'

My hand goes up, and Sister Naomi stops talking.

'I'm sorry. I don't know what I wanted when I made the appointment, but you're telling me it's okay not to know.'

She leans back and smiles for the first time. 'It is.'

I whorl my hands either side of my head. 'So, this is an amorphous time, and things will become apparent?'

'I am sure they will.'

I let out a long breath and imagine it being carried downstream. 'Do you mind if we stop now?'

She lays down her pencil. 'Not at all. Judging by the sky behind you, it looks like rain anyway. You'd better get a move on.'

This makes me smile, so very Aussie to scuttle off when the sun goes in; a raindrop will not dissolve me.

'How do I pay for this?'

'Don't worry, I'll bulk-bill. You know where I am when you get back, or before, if you want.'

'Thank you, you are kind.'

She is, and if I see her again I'm going to ask her a question, which François, the village horse, was unable to help me with. Of all the things that send women to therapy, I bet the main one is a sense of being invisible to themselves.

45

A frog slips from the lid, plops into the rainwater butt, and hides himself along the edge. Haricot lurks outside the *remise*. When I approach to collect garden tools, he stretches slowly and eyeballs me. Blue tits hang off a peanut bag and a robin sits on a hazel bough, which has already shed its leaves. The chickens are unusually cavorting, and there's a cow in the field. This would have had me wondering a few months ago, but it will be something to do with Tata or No-E, and that's fine.

'A metaphor is a figure of speech which directly refers to one thing by mentioning another for rhetorical effect.'

I nearly faint to hear the chicken coop talk. I drop the spade and take a step back. 'Pascal?'

He pokes his head out from the side door, 'Yes, nearly done.' He ducks back in, and clumps of dirty straw fly out.

'Jesus, I had no idea you were in there.'

He re-emerges and wipes his hands on a filthy rag. 'My wife says metaphors are a great language tool.'

'Your wife?' What is he talking about?

'My wife, yes. She has Parkinson's.'

'I'm sorry, Parkinson's is a horrible disease. How is she managing?'

'I will manage everything for her.' No-E steps out of the chicken coop and straightens. He regards me carefully. 'Audrey, my wife is your aunt. She left me years ago when we lived in Paris and I drank too much. She came to live here, work here, and a few years later I bought the cottage down the lane. We've never divorced. When your Tata got the diagnosis, I said I wanted her to come home. I've built a ramp and made the salon into a bedroom for us. Next week the downstairs toilet and shower will be finished.'

I sit down. My understanding is once again in tatters.

No-E grabs a bale of hay and deftly cuts through the strings binding it. He then grabs a thirty-centimetre slab of yellowed grass and froths it onto the chickens' roosts. A mumbled something or other floats out across his back.

'Pascal, why didn't I know about any of this? Why hasn't she told me?'

He reverses and shuts the coop door behind him.

'Your mother didn't approve of our marriage, she was happy when her sister left me, and so I suppose we simply never said anything. It was easier, and the years just drifted along. As for telling you about the Parkinson's, Tata said you had enough to contend with when you first arrived.'

'Oh lord.' I clutch my head, fearing it might fall off as new pieces of information shuffle into place. 'Oh, my. I'm so sorry, Pascal. I'm so sorry.'

'My wife says they, metaphors, are a great language tool because they explain the unknown in terms of the known. Like the garden. A garden is one of the great metaphors for humanity. You could also use the river, of course, the ocean, mountain ranges, cities. There are a few.' He rakes the soiled straw into a pile. 'In winter all the leaves will fall off the trees, and the garden's nudity will represent the impermanence of all living things.'

'Is this how Tata explains her condition to you?'

'It's how we process the end. She says it's nicer to use a metaphor, which we both understand, than the medical terms her neurologist prefers.'

'Is she referring to this winter, or winters in general?'

No-E's face says he's perfectly happy with the non-specific reference to a winter, a death, and they haven't discussed when that might be. He collects the eggs he's balanced on the water trough, then stops with another thought. He points towards the weeds behind me.

'When you dig out those nettles, you are fighting your enemies. There are many enemies: snails, bugs, frost, time, even the chickens.'

'Parkinson's is an enemy?'

'Most certainly.' He puts the eggs into his pockets.

I pick two pieces of straw from his hair. If he wasn't wearing eggs, I'd hug him.

'But I told her, I want to pour myself into the garden, like I always do, and watch the beauty and the failures. My radishes are all gone now, the onions have died away. I know everything dies away, but I get back out there and keep doing it, don't I?'

'You do, Pascal, you do. You and Tata are lucky.'

The spade's smooth wooden handle twirls against my palm and the chickens make their way across the field. He flicks chicken poo off his trousers and slaps his hands together. 'Dominic is finishing the last of the plumbing now, I—'

'He's an electrician!'

Again No-E takes on the look of a long-suffering saint who must be patient with his wife's niece. He stops his exit from the field.

'He'll finish the electrical work when I've finished the panelling.'

Well, of course he will. I expect the baker will do the tiling and the village horse will pick out the paint. And Tata will die of Parkinson's.

No-E turns. 'Your aunt wanted me to tell you, and I have. We can all get back to normal now. She will move in next week and we'll be family.'

—

With each worm-rich sod I turn, Tata's condition becomes clearer. Her hands always clasped to disguise the tremors. Using a wheelchair in church. The way she has been so elusive. I think it's reasonable to assume the Parkinson's explains her fall from the cherry tree.

The chickens emerge from checking out their new bed linen and launch themselves at the worms. A light drizzle dampens everything, and the exertion of digging generates a deep-seated pleasure. It's as though the fibres running from my hands and through my arms are driven by an urgent territorial drive to plant, to provide food for the tribe.

The tough, yellow stinging nettle roots come out with a fight. I bang the soil off and throw them in a pile for the chickens to hunt through. A fecund chocolate brownie mix clings to my spade obediently, unlike the sand at home. The battered straw-bale vegetable garden might hold up for another few months if the cow isn't here long. There's still some summer spinach. Tata said, *Spinach is great for slipping in smoothies for those much-needed vitamins.* I tried a mouthful, and then slipped the mixture into the compost bin. Spinach is much nicer with butter; everything is nicer with butter.

I weed around the turnips, fantasising about a time when they will be ready to pull and how their feathery roots will hold on to their genesis. And the leeks will hide pockets of soil between their layers. They'll all need a lot of washing, and the hands that clean them will freeze under the outside tap. But the idea of them is delicious; the ancient romance of going out to pick your dinner. And if I'm not here, Tata and No-E will share them with friends.

It's October and deep red raspberries still bob on autumnal boughs. I pluck a few, taste the ironic edge to their sugary deliciousness. I used to dream of not having to cook, night after night, and now I see how very wrong I was. It's all about eating with people you like, the hunger in my children's eyes. Conversations about the day's achievements and catastrophes. Voracious appetites, cleared plates, licked plates. Simon hated the licking; he said it was vulgar. It made me laugh.

I play a raspberry over my tongue and slowly pop it between my teeth.

'Alone, dear raspberry, you are delicious, whereas if I were eating lobster with Simon, I would not enjoy it half as much.'

'Don't you like lobster?'

I swing around to see who's caught me talking to myself.

46

'I love lobster, I love most food, but alone, or with the right people.'

'Am I a *right person*, because I wondered if I may cook for you tonight?' Dominic moves deeper under the umbrella of the willow, away from the wet evening.

'Thank you, how lovely. You know I've often wondered why people bring you food when you're sick, and you don't want to eat. It's so much better to be offered a meal when you're fit and ravenous, or stoned.'

'Are you stoned?'

'Why do you ask? Because you caught me talking to myself? I do that, it's genetic, and I'm not stoned, no.'

The field has been plunged into darkness but, despite the gloom, I can see I'm covered in mud.

'I'm hungry, and dinner is a lovely idea, thank you.'

Immediately a reverb of untuned strings start up in my thoughts, which makes the idea of dinner unlovely.

'Ah ...'

I spin the spade's handle and concentrate on pushing its blade into the soil. I look up to see Dominic is grinning.

'What is your reservation? You think my house is like my car?'

The simplicity of his question pierces straight to a truth. I don't want to see his house, but not because it might be messy. I don't want to know whether it's messy or tidy. Both would be wrong. I don't want to know whether he lives in one of those ugly, thermally efficient new-builds, or in a charming old cottage. I don't want to observe his things because my head would start to put pieces together. *Oh, he has a lot of books.* Or, *Oh, he doesn't read.* I don't want to form a picture. I want to keep Dominic as a fantasy figure. Someone who appears from the unknown from time to time.

Head to one side, he inspects me for clues.

'I can cook it for you here. The food is in the back of my car.'

A sigh of relief escapes. 'Would you, I …'

Overhead the leaves start to bounce with heavier raindrops.

'It's okay, I understand.'

Does he? I think he does understand, which makes me feel like a clumsy, feral animal and he's an Audrey whisperer. I think back to the picnic: the poor man is probably used to women *wanting* to launch themselves at him. Equally these women will almost certainly behave with alluring restraint. Never mind, I'm new to my single freedom – live and learn. I expect he has suggested this meal to restore the balance of an appropriate village friendship. Well done him.

—

Seconds after I make my way indoors, Dominic appears in the kitchen and starts to unload a bag onto the table. I'd assumed we'd make a plan for when he'd return, and that would be later. But he's here now. None of this would be an issue if I hadn't kissed him.

'Can I help with anything?'

He turns his back on me so I can't see the ingredients. 'I am the chef.'

Normally I flick my trainers off, but tonight I undo the shoelaces very deliberately.

How do I take my clothes off, have a shower, and get dressed again in a bathroom when there is a relative stranger on the other side of the flimsy sliding wooden door? Ridiculous. I'm dirty and must get clean. Of course, I can use the cottage bathroom. No, the hot water is off.

'Wine, Dominic?'

The smell of frying garlic trails across the room. Haricot twitches long white whiskers at me from his bed on a pile of newspapers. The cork leaves the neck of the bottle with a soft *pap*.

'Chef, your glass.'

'Thank you.' He turns back to the bench, and there's the rustle of a paper bag. 'None of this takes long. When you're ready, I'll finish off.'

'Right.'

The stairs clang noisily, making my ascent obvious. I think perhaps I'll just change up in the relative isolation of the bedroom. But then I'd be horribly dirty. As if he's even going to pay attention to the functional ablutions of an older woman. If we were both in our twenties, then perhaps he'd feel a twitch of intrigue. A firm, young, naked girl just a few feet away through a bathroom door. He might picture such an image. He might even come into the bathroom and join me.

'Audrey, shut up you're truly behaving like a teenager. Stop.'

Bugger it. I'm nearly sixty. I have the scars of three caesars, cellulite for thighs and wobbly wing arms. *Bugger it* wins, and I descend with fresh clothes, knickers and a well-hidden bra.

The chopping at the kitchen bench is rapid. The bathroom is small, and everything feels awkward. Once my clothes are off, I've never felt more naked. The sliding door doesn't even lock, I might as well be washing in a bucket outside the *tabac*. I can smell myself and am repulsed so over-soap everything, while making sure I don't wet my clean clothes, which perch on the toilet cistern. Jasmine perfumes start to dominate the room, and steam builds to settle in a merciful cloud over the mirror.

The room is like a sauna and my dress judders over my damp skin. I yank the fabric straight around my hips, which has the effect of twisting the cloth around my shoulders. I open the louvre windows up at the eaves, and a blast of cold air drops onto my wet hair. The condensation on the mirror starts to descend in little beads of water to reveal a soggy reflection.

Dominic squats by the pot belly and encourages tentative flames in its metal interior. His t-shirt pulls tight across broad shoulders. The back of his thick hair is damp, probably from his own less troubled shower. He swivels gracefully and slides my slippers across before he returns to the fire. Of course, he thinks these are suitable attire for an old lady who's about to eat. I slip them and a heavy dose of reality on. Two large sheepskin-covered feet look back at me; their usual squishy familiarity affords no comfort at all.

The fire door closes with a metallic *thunk*, and Dominic stands. His body rises very close to mine. He lifts my chin with one hand, which he then slides lightly down my neck. The confusion of this moment floats like a single feather on a current of warm air.

'Hungry?'

The lightness of his touch delays my reply.

'Starving. No, not really. I mean if it's ready, sure. This is lovely of you, so kind.' I can feel my vocal cords vibrating against his hand.

Dominic lifts my hand up to his throat and holds it there. 'I listen to you. Your words sound on my eardrum and in the movements of your throat and tongue.'

A silent echo of his voice plays in my mind, and a vestigial pattern of its shape moves across his throat. He drops his forehead against mine for a moment then leads me to the table. I sit. He returns to the stove.

'Coquilles Saint-Jacques.'

There are so many things I'm sure I could say, if only I knew what they were. If I wasn't adrift. Instead, I scrunch my bare toes against the woollen lining of old sheepskin and touch the stem of a wineglass with one finger. Dominic brings over a plate of pale scallops dressed in crisp, translucent sheets of filo. He sits. We toast, the clink of glass on glass.

'*Bon appétit.*'

'Thank you.'

The delicate filaments on the plate beckon. Dominic waits for me to take one, but I seem to have forgotten how to put my glass down or lift my fork. There isn't a single sentence in my mind. And then he weaves the fingers of his left hand between mine and everything steadies, comes back into view.

'Dominic, in English we have an expression – the elephant in the room.'

No recognition moves across his features.

'It's when something obvious is not said.'

'Ah *oui, non-dit.*'

'Not said, indeed.'

The little pot belly ticks and creaks.

'I expect you mean when you kissed me at the river, Audrey, it was very disturbing.'

'Do I need to apologise? I don't want to. It was selfish, I know, but it was perfection, for me, at the time.'

'I don't want an apology, no. I wonder if you might do it again?'

I put a scallop in my mouth, buy time to think about a reply. The pastry explodes to release a sweet, salty softness. We chew in silence, fingers entwined. I take a sip of wine.

'I'm a thousand years old. You are so young.'

'Forty-eight, for what it's worth.'

'I'm married. No, I'm separated, and I'm renovating my life, fingers crossed.'

'Scallop?'

'Please.' I open my mouth like a bird and close my eyes to fully appreciate the flavours. When I open them again Dominic is looking down, thick eyelashes make new-moon arcs across his cheekbones. I tell myself if he looks up now, I will make one decision and if he ... He looks up.

'I'm grateful you kissed me back, I really am. The thing is, I don't know what I need or want, and I'm told that's okay.'

The sentence dies on my tongue, and I help myself to another scallop. It's my turn to look down and study the plate. He slides his hand away from mine leaving the remnant pressure of fingers.

'Your life is difficult, I understand. But, if you want to be wanted, even for a short while, let me say this. You're funny; very, very, beautiful; a little bit mad perhaps, which I like; and I want to be the one wanting you.'

There is no artifice in this statement nor in his eyes.

'Let me check: you *want* to spend some time with me?'

'*Oui.*'

'Well, how convenient, because there may be a temporary, casual position. Yes. Thank you. The job is yours.'

47

Can I talk about the details? How we moved from the table and up the clanking spiral stairs. Was a lot of alcohol involved or indeed was it necessary? Only close inspection would reveal such details and I'm not up for that.

For the first few nights, Dominic hides his car, concerned I might worry about gossip. I tell him people will do the proverbial two plus two in their inquisitive heads no matter where he parks. He agrees. The soccer mums' interest in him is no longer cursory. They sidle up, lean in, and are oh-so interested in how happy he looks.

By the second week of October, we acknowledge the village drums will not be silenced, and he parks his car in front of the *remise*. The miniature, battered *sans permis* has never looked bigger or bolder and the ladders on the makeshift racks collect falling autumn leaves.

This morning as I top up the bird table seeds; Dominic comes up behind me and puts his hands on my hips. I turn into him, drape one seedy hand over his shoulder and wave the other in loops towards the horizon. 'This is just the very best season.'

He kisses my nose then moves back a fraction. 'Is it, Audrey?' His hands slide to my waist, finding curves I'd forgotten.

'Yes, of course, very much. What's not to love?'

Two blackberry eyes hold mine. Confusion starts to scuttle like mice that are not sure where to start on a bag of wheat. 'Isn't it evident? Don't I look preposterously content?'

'But you don't ask for anything. I touch you – you respond. I ask if you want to eat or walk – you beam and agree. You know you could ask me for things. I'd like it if you did.'

I step back, feel the warmth from his palms slide away, inhale the cold air between us.

Dominic tucks his hands in his jacket pockets. 'Do you understand?'

I really don't and shake my head.

He stirs the gravel with the ball of his work boot. 'Okay. Yesterday, when I dropped you off so you could walk home, did you want to kiss me before I drove away?'

'Always.'

His head tilts. 'And yet you didn't.'

'I didn't want to hold you up.'

'Ah.' Dominic releases my gaze, brings his feet together, and then looks back at me. 'If I'm ever reversing, in the wrong lane, down a freeway – in this situation I may be too preoccupied to kiss you.'

I step forward. He doesn't move. I touch his beautiful face.

'Good, but you need more practice. Now ask me for something not so lovely. Go on, right now, the first thing that comes into your head, something you'd like me to do for you.'

His fingers interlock behind my back. I look over his shoulder and wonder what I could possibly want? I'm so content, it hurts to think I might be lacking something. 'Something I'd like?'

He kisses my jaw. 'Yes.'

'I'd like not to go into a supermarket; would you do the shopping, please?'

His laugh is round and pure. 'With pleasure.'

'And ...'

'Another request so soon? Good.'

'I'm converting a garden fork into a lamp – would you show me how to wire it up?'

'I will.'

'Thanks. And ...'

'And?'

'Do you have to go to work?'

Dominic tells me he's changed his mind. He says I'm demanding. I explain it's purely medicinal, that I'm unfamiliar with being nurtured and need all the practice I can get. He says he's happy to help in any way he can.

———

Quite apart from having the best sex of my entire life, the conversation at the bird table has become yet another pivotal moment. By asking what I wanted, Dominic effectively shone an interrogator's light on my past and I see I was never a victim. I colluded. I passively allowed the thirty-seven years with Simon to take shape.

When I first met Simon, he had many fine attributes, and the fact he pursued me was flattering. I never stopped to ask questions of him, or of me. Did I like the way he kissed? Did I want to be with him? I simply followed, Simon at the helm. He rang – I went. My father was dying and adored the world Simon offered. I wanted Dad to be happy. Simon was driven and had a passion – I didn't, therefore I could help with his dreams. He loved sex, which was flattering, and I blithely ignored the fact it wasn't amazing for me.

In retrospect I was infatuated with a package. It wasn't until we had children that I learnt what love is. Only after that seismic shift into motherhood did I begin to love my husband in a rounded, loyal, proud, appreciative way. By then our patterns were set. We were busy; he dictated the big picture, I kept the details going. And I certainly didn't look up to see the signs.

I still think Simon is a lying, selfish narcissist, but I don't feel like a poor little victim anymore. I understand how and why I fitted in.

Actually, apart from the children, I rarely think about my Australian world. I'm otherwise occupied.

Tata has never said a word to me about Dominic. Every now and then a satisfied grin spreads across her face and she says how healthy I look – and that's it.

Conversely No-E has become quite chatty with me. As we returned from the florist's yesterday afternoon, he said, in one very long, continuous sentence, 'Audrey, most marriages sink at some point, whether they're retrievable or not is another matter – have you noticed how your hair is very like the horse's mane.' The bit about François wasn't a question, and he's right. The horse and I both look like we get our hair done by the council.

He and Tata are over here most days. She loves to play backgammon, the score is forty-eight games to my aunt, twenty-seven to me. When No-E helps make up orders for Nathalie, or when it comes to teaching me a new technique for an idea, Tata does kilometres on her static bike. And next week they're on a boat going down the Rhine; another bucket list item being ticked off.

Then, of course, there's Lilou who never shuts up about Dominic, and I bat away her unsubtle prods in the way I'd shoo a fly. Speak of the devil.

'Audrey, what is that smell? I can't come in.'

She leans on the hayloft doorway, and a hand floats to rest over her belly, which, if she stands sideways and you squint, could be said to be growing. Mind you, she's ruched from neck to knee in a purple 1940s-style men's bathing suit. I wonder if that's intentional, or perhaps her sewing machine is protesting.

'Tata and I are wearing the paint off our backgammon board, hopefully this varnish will protect it.'

'Well, I hope the stink dies off while we're at yoga. Are you ready?'

'I am but …'

Lilou starts to ping various horizontal bands of elastic to demonstrate how practical her creation is.

'Guess what?'

I wrap the varnish brush in clingfilm, and am obviously too slow with my answer, so she runs on.

'I'm off to London at the weekend. To visit Rose.' This elicits a twirl. 'She's invited me to stay with her.'

'Now that's exciting.'

'That's it, no questions?'

'I am demonstrating appropriate restraint when it comes to the love-life of a friend. Something you fail to do, I might add.'

'Audrey, really, truly, you love my inappropriate questions. Go on, ask me why Rose has had a change of heart. Ask me if darling Pierre might have helped by contacting her to say he was seeing a policewoman. He said he wasn't trying to give Rose *permission*; it was more he didn't want her to worry. Ask me if I'm beside myself with gratitude to that wonderful man. Ask me if I'm terrified.'

'Okay, I will, but not while you're driving.'

48

Sitting in my warm bed of homespun contentment I'm aware there's zero control over time in my world, and that's the way I like it. I bimble: which is to walk, talk, read, eat, make things in no particular order. Even Dominic and his battered book of contracts don't add an order to my weeks. No, it's my phone which keeps me up to date with facts like October just sped into November. Outside, the deeper morning chill and the shorter afternoons confirm that fact.

Rose has been over to visit twice, and she's with Lilou now. Pierre and his girlfriend are staying in the cottage this week to *establish relations, for the sake of the baby.* All in all, all is well in their – plural – worlds, which I still find baffling.

Emails are something I incorporate into the bimbling, and I have two this morning.

Mrs Lamont
Sumtims you gesses ar not gud, this iz a crismas tre.
    Jakob

Nice to know, I would have said Martians with various identities, all pegged together. The last image he sent was, I thought, of more human eyes. He said it was a sleep-deprivation chamber. How does he know about such things? The second October drawing was apparently a netball game. I'd said Bangalore dancers. It's a relief he's not going to make me guess anymore.

Mrs Kay's PS on the email says the presents for the class arrived and she'll hand them out on the last day of term. She also comments on the phenomenal cost of postage.

The second email is from Susie. Since June, when she admitted to James's affair, we've exchanged rambling epistles. Usually both of us grope for words to understand how our roles in the world continue to change. However, this morning she's reverted to the short and sweet.

> Audrey,
> Occasionally gossip is useful.
>
> I gather, from your husband's displeasure, you're not returning to the marital home. Excellent.
>
> Our daughter vacates her flat sometime in January for a year in the States.
>
> It's basic, liveable, near the sea.
>
> Interested, for a few months? Rent free of course – just pay your bills.
>
> It goes without saying the dog is welcome.
>
> Love the idea of supporting you.
>
> Susie

I pull heavily on the field gate and lock it. I don't mind chickens in the garden, but the cow is a different matter. Dominic throws a workbag into his car and then shuts the door. I lean low to kiss him and wipe a heavy dew from his wing mirror with my sleeve. 'You know, I can imagine coming back next year to do another summer season. A lot will depend on timing for Tata, and her horrible condition. I'd like to be here for that. No-E might need some help caring at the pointy end of things.' I walk around the other side and clean that mirror too, then open the car door and sit on the side of the passenger seat. 'Anyway, I need to say these things because, if I do come back, I don't want you to think that you have any influence over my decision. Does that sound very harsh, arrogant?'

'It sounds truthful.' He runs a finger over my lips. 'You know there are some very low tides coming up.'

'Does this mean you'd have to take time off work?'

'I think I should.' He sighs deeply, leans his head back on the cracked upholstery.

'So, perhaps I could make a picnic, a flask of tea?'

Eyes closed, he nods. 'Life is an endless decision tree.'

I climb out of the car. He feigns the burden of his terrible existence, reverses, tyres crunch over gravel, and he heads out to work.

I follow his little car down the lane and turn into Tata and No-E's garden. They call for me to come in before I have a chance to knock. The interior is a mist of pot-belly heat, airing laundry and geranium plants which will see the winter out in here.

'*Oo la la*, your face, Audrey.' Tata stands, pushes gently down on No-E's shoulder to stop him leaping up. 'You stay, I'm perfectly capable of making coffee.' She turns towards me with a false grimace. 'He makes such a fuss, it's driving me insane.'

'Your aunt loves it. I tell her if she has, say, twenty meals left in her to cook, she should save them. Use them slowly over the next five or ten years.'

Tata rolls her eyes, giggles. 'And I tell him that the more I do, the longer I'll do things.'

'And I expect you two have this conversation several times a day.' I sit down, clear a few sections of the weekend papers to one side. 'My expression isn't awful. You're observing a woman who's made decisions, which in the face of so many options, was no mean feat. "Stay in the village indefinitely to wallow in bovine bliss" got the most votes by a considerable margin.'

No-E gives up on stopping my aunt making the coffee. 'Bovine bliss? The cow, yes. Have you noticed how she stares at the horizon until it blinks?'

Some images are perishable, that one though will remain with me forever. No-E is undoubtedly one of the most intriguing men I've ever met; affectionate, technically insane, and bizarrely observant.

'What do cows think about when they're chewing cud is another question. But right now, your decision is more important.' He focuses on me.

'My decision is to stay here until after Christmas, go ice-skating on that tiny rink in Saint Malo and knock over some small unsuspecting children. Then I'll be ready to go back. It all feels very satisfactory. And, Tata, please dig out your pâté recipe, Madame Potdevin has been hinting for a couple of weeks.'

———

December starts with the moon's gravitational forces at their very best. Dominic and I take advantage of the spectacularly low tide with the promised additive of high tides. They create a certain euphoria, and, despite the chill of winter, beaches fill with people who unite in this enthusiasm.

We start out around the headland at Saint Jacut exactly as the tide turns, which means there'll be two hours of hard sand.

A day can get away from you out here and we take our time. We stroll out to one of the small islands, flip shells with bare feet. The oyster beds start to poke through the water's surface like the fibrous remains of a huge sea creature. Families spread out over the exposed sandy flats with buckets and spades, digging for whelks.

As we turn down the southern side of the peninsula, the wind picks up, and the sea makes her decision to return. In the distance, along the water's edge, is a large object. We hypothesise what it could be, and when we're eventually close enough to see clearly, it's too late. A stranger, unaware of the thirteen-metre water shifts and huge sucking tides, has parked their vehicle here at low tide. With the speed of a galloping horse the sea races around its wheels, axles, bodywork. Dominic and I move higher up the beach to sit and eat dried fruit, sip green tea from a thermos and watch the now virtually indistinguishable car rock in the ocean. By the time the tide nears her peak, little waves foam around the rear-view mirror.

'That's such a shame.' I blow into the surface of the tea, letting a flurry of steam warm my face. 'We travel to ourselves when we go back somewhere that we've spent time. When I step outside the airport in Australia, I know familiarity will hit me. My skin will recognise the feel of piercing heat, and even behind sunglasses my pupils will recoil under the police-siren blue. I do keep warning myself about all this, that I must not revert.' I chew slowly on a dried apricot. 'You know, watching the car drown is exactly what I fear. What if my old life creeps up around me when I return to Australia and this new Audrey is no longer distinguishable?'

Dominic turns my head towards him with one finger and shakes his head in slow, tiny arcs. 'The water will go back down again.'

—

The sound of coffee being made downstairs is music to my ears. It doesn't happen every day. Dominic hasn't moved in after all. However, when he is here, six days a week, sometimes seven, he insists he bring me coffee. He says it's one of his pleasures. It's one of mine too. Last night I booked my ticket back to Australia and this morning there is a perceptible shift in the mood.

My computer pings with an email from Prunella. The stairs chime out and my coffee is placed, handle towards me.

'Do you think you would ever entertain the idea of a second bedside table?' Dominic sits beside me, mug in hand.

Wow. On the face of it, that's a harmless, practical question, but it has heavy overtones. It smacks of a reality I've been avoiding. We both look ahead and up through the Velux window to the patchwork sky.

'You came into my life really fast, and I like it.' I take his coffee mug and put it down next to mine, pull him in so he lies alongside me. 'With you I've had weeks and weeks where my heart is locked in the present. It's so hard to explain how it feels in here.' I tap my sternum. 'My interior world is the colour of ancient frescoes full of rich, purple–black figs for the afterlife, created by artists of mysterious origins and minor reputations. I can honestly say I never knew I could feel like this.'

'I think you're incredible, and slightly unhinged.'

'Possibly.' I don't know what else to say and twist my laptop slowly towards him.

'Look, Prunella says she'll come and look after Haricot and do some gardening until the end of March. And after that, I'll have to see what's happening.'

'Perhaps it's not to me that you want to speak about these things?'

I silently repeat his sentence slowly, taking it apart. *Perhaps, it's not to me, that you want to speak about these things.* 'Perhaps I'm sensible enough to know I can only draft an iffy horoscope for the beginning of next year.'

Dominic leans in and kisses my nose. We drink our coffee in silence, his body warm.

'I love this, Audrey. When you're gone, I will feel deformed.' He goes down the stairs and I hear the kitchen door close behind him.

Today it's like a limpid saxophone solo drifts through the hours he's at work. It is the exact pitch, not of anxiety, but of an intelligent worry which wants to be heard. How do I maintain me back in Australia, when everything there will change so much?

49

'Happy birthday, Mum.' Three faces, three waves and a lot of kisses are blown.

'Hello, darlings, and thank you.' I pull up a stool at the workbench in the *remise*.

Gus brings his hands up and gently rests the tips of his fingers together. 'We've gathered here today for an intervention, Mum.'

'Ooh, I'm in trouble. You don't want me to come back until Easter? You haven't bought my birthday present and feel bad?'

Gus wags a finger very deliberately. 'No, we're very organised and got you a wheelie frame for your birthday and matching hearing aids for Christmas.'

'He jests, you know that, don't you, Mum?' Orson leans forward. 'You can see your presents when we have our belated, January Christmas at Uncle Laurence's. He says the whole meal is going to be car-themed, but that might be a threat.'

Thea wriggles to the front of the sofa. 'What did you do for your birthday, are you celebrating?'

'I've had a special day, musing on the big things. Tata brought me cake and we played backgammon. No-E just finished explaining the intricacies of an ancient Breton biscuit design. And tonight a friend is cooking dinner.'

'That sounds lovely.' Thea leans back and there's an awkward silence. Then she sits forward again, and Orson tells her not to do something or other and she pushes him back with a *shhh*.

'Mum, you've gotta speak to Dad. He's driving us mad.'

'He's driving himself mad, it's not Mum's problem.' Orson looks straight into the camera. 'Don't think about it.'

'Orson, shut up. It's kind of about you, Mum, and it's pretty ugly. He's cross you're not coming back to the house when you get here. He got all uppity about you going to Susie's flat and said, *Tell your mother it's not going to help if she stays away.*'

'Darlings, going to cut you off there if you don't mind.' I lean heavily on the bench, dig my nails into the old wood, and watch my knuckles bleach. 'I'll ring your father when we hang up, but only because I don't like him using you to communicate with me. I'm not going back to the house and that's that. Laurence is going to pick up Howard for me and I'm so excited to see the old boy.'

'What, more than us?' Gus pulls at his mouth with both hands.

'Oh yes, much more than you lot. The first night I'm back I'm going to sit on the sofa with Howard and catch up on months of missed cuddles.'

Orson leans his elbows on his knees. 'Dad told us about, you know, all those years – knowing her.'

Three alabaster faces are caught in the headlights of a secret, which only thrived in the dark. Thank the lord it's out.

'That is very good, truly, I'm pleased.'

Gus drapes himself over Orson's shoulder. 'It's pretty fucking shitty.'

I look down the workbench for something to pick up and settle on a blunt chisel.

'It is. It's not the kind of heartbreak that slips away easily. But I have been having the best time doing nothing spectacular. I haven't written a book or got a degree. I've found lots of transient, fascinating things which please me no end. Honestly, I'm right as rain. Righter than I've been for a long time.'

'*Righter* – your English has deteriorated.' Thea sits back, relaxed.

'Thanks. This is why I love the dog more.'

A long silence ensues. Outside the dirty *remise* window I can't see much now the night has dumped herself across the field.

'Wish I could hug you all right now.'

'Happy birthday, Mum.'

—

Headlights swoop across the door to the *remise* and I watch a couple of startled bats flit in agitation. When the outside world is dark again there's the slam of a car door, followed by crunching feet on gravel. Dominic stands in the doorway, finds me flipping my phone over and over on the dusty bench.

'I'll be in in a minute. Got another call to make.'

'Everything all right in Australia?'

I grin.

He clicks his tongue and cocks his head in sympathy.

Simon answers on the second ring. 'Audrey.'

'Simon. Don't use the kids as messengers.'

'Well, you don't tell me anything.' His voice drops an octave. 'Surely after all our years of marriage we can get through something like this on the same property?'

Surely after all our years of marriage you might remember today's my birthday, but it's not on the calendar so I guess not. Anyway, I didn't ring for that.

'I don't know, Simon, you're the one with the liquid bonds, liquid love.'

'Audrey, what are you talking about?'

'I've told you not to expect a cosy, coddling redemption.'

I can hear exasperation in his inhalation, so I wait for a moment.

'If you asked Freud—'

'Don't quote Freud to me!' His voice has now gone up an octave.

Again, I pause.

'If, Simon, you asked Freud, he'd say society traded freedom for security; everybody coupled up, married, had babies, hung in there together out of duty et cetera and today it's the reverse. Yes, I left Australia wanting togetherness, but now I fear it will bring burdens and cause strains which I'm either unwilling or unable to bear.'

'This is hopeless. We need to talk.'

'We will.'

'Okay.'

There's a deep inhalation then the sound of air rushing through pinched nostrils. 'Given you appear determined, I'll stay at one of the university apartments when you first get back, then you can be with the dog, see the kids.'

I immediately knee-jerk, assume this will make it more convenient for him to see Midori. Then I marvel at a previously unknown suspiciousness in me. Eventually I rationalise he's being considerate. 'That is a considerate plan, however, I won't feel at home in the house, not anymore.'

'Audrey—'

'Not now, Simon. I'll see you when I'm back.'

Walking across to the hayloft I can't help but think how strange that phone call was. Should I have told my ex-husband about my dalliance? Do you ever need to tell an ex? What do I call Dominic? My fling, blip, moment of madness? No, he's none of those. Despite the kitchen windows being heavy with condensation I can clearly see his outline at the kitchen bench and feel a thrill.

The hayloft is snug. Dominic stops what he's doing and silently turns to check. I smile as an answer, and when he resumes the chopping, I lean against his back, wrap my arms around his chest and feel the movements in his body.

———

Dominic is working on a river cottage renovation. Parisian owners, he says, with no time and lots of money and therefore good for the local economy. At least once a week I walk to meet him. Today he wants to leave his car and walk home.

'We must swim.' His mouth turns up on one side.

'It's nearly Christmas, I think we must get you a psychiatric evaluation.'

I huddle deeper into my clothes, pull at my scarf.

He takes my hand and continues down the towpath in silence until we arrive at what the locals call *the beach*. In the summer this little patch fills with families who splash about and sail miniature boats. Today there's no one. The winter sun imbues the sand a camel-yellow. It is not the bleached white, gritty stretch of home that's for sure.

The look on Dominic's face is a worry.

'I've got a cake in the oven.'

Dominic smiles as he removes his boots and socks. 'Have you?'

'Maybe not.'

Dominic hangs his jumper on a branch.

'The cat is on fire, I must go.'

317

'That is a worse excuse.'

'The water will be freezing.'

He kisses my cheek, skids down the little bank, sheds the rest of his clothes in a flurry of arms and legs, and races in. I watch. Three, four long strides, knees high, then he leaps forward like a salmon and is under the water, breaking the surface a few moments later with a yelp, then laughter.

I undress, slowly, and call out over his splashing. 'I'm not as brave as you.'

He approaches as though to hug me with his icy body.

'Don't you dare.'

Stepping into the river, a little shriek escapes my lips, even though I knew it would be cold. The water laps my ankles. I hop from foot to foot and contemplate how much I have to be grateful for. Contemplate walking back up the bank. But something makes me move in deeper. Calves then knees turn from tingling to chilled. Feet so numb they're no longer able to feel their slimy footing, and the water whirls around my thighs creating a tightness, a dread, a thrill.

As Dominic slices through the surface, his naked body glints gold in the tannin water. Upstream two ducks move into the reeds. My breaths come quickly, little jets of air squeeze past pursed lips. Up to my belly in the water, my lungs spasm, a gasp; I lift both arms high.

It is almost unbearable. There's such a tension in me, it's as though my chest and head are clamped, and all my muscles have turned to iron. Until, at last, I plunge. The river takes away everything that went before in one final contraction, and I wonder why I made such a fuss.

I swim, missing the buoyancy of the ocean, loving the chill.

Then I dive below the icy surface again and come up, gasping, beside Dominic. 'This is fantastic.' I turn onto my stomach and swim out towards the other bank, feeling my arms stretch, legs pump, spine twist. Despite the exertion I'm not getting any warmer and yet it feels incredible. Almost in the middle, I stop to hang vertical in the current, head back, hair wafting, every inch of my skin brushed by the water as it slews around me.

'You know, Dominic,' I shout up towards the sky. 'I have *never* felt more comfortable in my own skin.' The river fills my ears, runs along my cheeks, between my fingers. I am close to myself in this moment.

ACKNOWLEDGEMENTS

In essence, writing these acknowledgements has two components and both are harrowing.

One. Finding the appropriate words which fully express appreciation only to realise most have been hijacked. *Amazing, extraordinary, supreme* – all gone, thrown around and devalued by adverts for lifestyles, moisturisers and savoury biscuits. Yet if I employ mundane language and say, for example, my agent Sarah McKenzie and everyone at Ultimo Press have been *good*, it falls horribly short. These people appeared toward the end of the writing and helped turn a manuscript into a novel. For goodness's sake, *good* is not good enough, they deserve high praise.

As do all those who have been invaluable along the way. Which is a neat segue into the second problem. The paralysing fear of accidently missing someone off the thank you list – hideous.

A solution is to avoid names and instead mention a few of the many precious components held within these pages. Five years in a small Brittany village, my Walyalup home. All the cafés, libraries, airports, parks, sofas, beds, tables I've written at or on. The treasures found in watching the world go by. The umpteen reasons someone clears their throat, the way ice-cream melts, cats' twitch, buttons gape, the see-saw between hope and fear. Bad sign writing, dusty wood, dogs, music. All these things digested with people during shared meals, coffees, conversations, concerns, celebrations. It is all about the people, every friend, writing group meeting and message, colleague, reader, residency, parent, bookshop, mentor, confidant, course taken; all those people who've been there, are there, being brilliant.

To all the above people, places and opportunities – thank you. **I am obscenely grateful.**

READING GROUP QUESTIONS

1. At the start of the novel, Audrey attributes much of her situation to the fact her grown-up children no longer need her in the same way – do you think empty-nest syndrome is real?

2. If you were Audrey's friend, what would you have said to her when she found out her husband was *thinking* about having an affair?

3. *You see, I'm busybodying in other people's lives because I can't stand my own.*

   If, instead of seeing a therapist, Audrey had talked with you about feeling invisible and how meaningless her life had become, what would you have recommended?

4. *If I'd spent my child-rearing years painting, studying, learning the piano, anything – I might have become quite good. But it's as though other people were leading my life during those years.*

   Why do you think Audrey chose to take the backseat during her years as a wife and mother?

5. *It's all the times the word* yes *came out when I would have preferred to decline. My head is still packed tight with the threads of other people's lives, and I need to cut through the Gordian knot I'm living in.*

   Do you think prioritising other people's needs over their own is a universal problem for women?

6. Did you see any aspects of your own life in Audrey's story?

7. *I'm unfamiliar with being nurtured and need all the practice I can get.*

   How would you like to be nurtured?

8. Audrey walks, experiments with tap dancing and jam combinations, making bits of furniture and art, and gardening: what activity would you choose to restore yourself?

9. *Metaphors are a great language tool because they explain the unknown in terms of the known. Like the garden. A garden is one of the great metaphors for humanity. You could also use the river, of course …*

   Do you think the author moved Audrey from Australia to France as a metaphor for change? How did Audrey change or grow?

10. The story spans seven months, do you think this is a realistic time frame to begin to change yourself?

11. Which character or moment prompted the strongest emotional reaction in you and why?

12. What scene do you think was pivotal for Audrey's transformation? Did your opinion of Audrey change over the course of the book?

13. What do you think will happen next for the main characters?

Annie de Monchaux is a West Australian–based writer of fiction and non-fiction. Her non-fiction anthology *Cray Tales* was shortlisted for the WA Premier's Book Awards and was the basis of a CBS/ABC documentary. Prior to this, Annie worked in Hollywood, rewriting scripts for films such as *Superman II, III* and *IV* and *The Shell Game*.